game of two halves

viva city fc
book one

Unoma Nwankwor

KevStel Publications

I'm thankful to God from Whom the gift comes.

To Kevin, Fumnanya & Ugo
To my beloved mother, Amama
I miss you like crazy, and I love you. Always & forever.

Lastly to my readers, thank you for rocking with me!

author's note

Hey there! Welcome to the U. N Universe. If you're new here, welcome. I hope you become a resident. If you are a resident, I hope you're enjoying your stay, welcome back!

So, let's get into it.

Game of Two Halves is a sports romance and the first book in the Viva City Football Club series. Although referred to as soccer in America, it's football all over the world, so that's what we'll use in this book and the whole series.

Game of Two Halves is a football term that alludes to the dynamics of the game change drastically between the first and second halves, often due to tactical adjustments, momentum shifts, or changes in team performance. In this standalone, you meet Nonso and Yinka. Nonso first appeared briefly in Elevate My Soul (The Kalu Wedding Event), while Yinka is totally new to the U.N Universe. Both of them are children of immigrants who grew up in America but were immersed in Nigerian culture at home.

In this story, you'll get everything you normally get from a U.N story. For our new residents that's Black love, faith, family, swoony feels, flights, wrapped in a cozy blanket of African culture and spice.

A few things...

This book primarily takes place in the fictional town of Viva City in North London. A typical English town but with a good size diverse population.

Also, the meaning of all Pidgin/Yoruba/Enuani language is inferred in context. However, if you need translations, there is a glossary at the back of the book to assist you.

Happy Reading!

PS: This is very important. Before you start reading, check out the next page titled "The Basics." Although key elements of the English Football are given in the book, I provide a summary of the workings of English Football and an insight into the Viva City Football Club. I really do suggest you start there before moving on.

Unoma

the basics

The Viva City Football Club series is a sports romance collaboration between me and another African romance author, Kiru Taye. Viva City FC, home of the Panthers is a top fictional club in the 2nd tier of English football (ELF Championship) pyramid. The series will follow the lives of African professional football players that play for Viva City FC.

English football follows a hierarchical structure consisting of multiple divisions. The top-tier league is the ***Premier League***, followed by the ***English Football League*** (EFL) Championship, ***League One***, and ***League Two.*** In this book and series, we'll only primarily be concerned about the ***Premier League*** and the ***EFL*** (the first and second tiers).

Premier League is the highest level of professional soccer in the UK, comprising 20 teams. The EFL has 24 teams. Both tiers operate on a point-based system. The season runs from August to early May for the regular season and any playoffs happen after that.

*Promotion and relegation play a crucial role in the league system, allowing clubs to move up or down the divisions based on their performance each season. The bottom three teams in the Premier League are relegated to the EFL and the top two teams in the EFL are automatically promoted to the Premier League. While the third spot goes to the winner of the playoffs between the teams that finished third to sixth in the EFL.

The theme for the first season is **Rise to Glory**. Follow along as the Viva City Panthers team vies for promotion to the coveted Premiere League (#1 tier in English Football).

You can read details about the club itself here.

offensive foul

actions not allowed in soccer that will result in a foul call and/or ejection from the field.

prologue
Nonso Chijuka

I SHOULD'VE TURNED OFF MY PHONE THE FIRST TIME I sent his call to voicemail.

For the third time in about ten minutes, the ringtone I'd assigned to my father pierced through the quiet of my man cave, distracting me from the next level of the game I was trying to reach. Glancing at the caller ID, I seriously debated whether to let it go to voicemail again. Emmanuel Chijuka was relentless when he wanted something—usually money. Glancing at the clock on the wall, I realized it was late evening in Nigeria where he lived. He should've been getting ready for bed instead of blowing me up.

The ringing stopped and I adjusted myself in the recliner. With a sigh, I set down my controller and leaned back to relish the semi-darkness of the room. The only source of light came from the TV screen, creating the perfect ambiance for relaxation. But with each ring of my phone, the vibe slipped further and further away.

I'd just gotten back from a stint on the road with my team,

Atlanta Allied. After playing three away football games, I looked forward to hitting the club a bit later with Kane. Kane Barnett and I met in middle school, and he had been my boy since then. We rolled for each other deep.

Moments later, the vibe was officially blown when the screen on my phone lit up again. With a resigned feeling, I answered the call.

"*Onowu* Sir," I greeted in our native tongue.

"*Ndo nwa m*, I've been trying to reach you all day." My father's tone held a hint of accusation.

I didn't feel like explaining for the umpteenth time my busy schedule as a professional athlete, so I ignored him and asked about my other family members.

"Nonso, I got the money, but it wasn't complete," my father cut in without any preamble.

My jaw tightened at his words. It had only been two months since I had sent him a large sum of money. Then it was something about one of my uncles needing help. After a quick "Thank you my son," my father went on with his life until last week when he began calling me again. My father rarely called me to check on me. That would be too much to ask. I was a professional athlete so of course I should be able to foot any bill my immediate or extended family could come up with.

"I told the accountant to send it," I replied, trying to keep my tone even.

I was tired of dealing with people who couldn't follow my instructions. This wasn't something I wanted to deal with. That's why I trusted the accountant to handle it.

My father didn't seem to hear me. He continued to talk about how we—meaning he—needed to jump on this prime piece of land he found. My mind drifted as my father rambled on. It would be so much easier if I didn't have to deal with these constant requests for money.

The path that led me to football wasn't one I'd ever regret. However, occasionally, it would be nice for the people that gave me life not to guilt trip me into becoming a living ATM because of the "sacrifices" they made for me. Football may have given me a comfortable life, but it also came with its own set of complications and expectations from those around me.

"Nonso, are you still there?" my father's voice brought me back to the conversation.

"Yes, sir. I'll talk to the accountant again tomorrow. I'll try to get it sorted," I replied.

"Don't try, do it. Time is of the essence."

After placating my father, I ended the call and threw the phone on the couch, frustration taking over my mood. Even though he wasn't thrilled that I played football in the first place, I still let my father's expectations weigh heavily on me.

I got up from the recliner and walked to the window, watching the lights of the city twinkle in the distance. Since I was hitting the club later, I decided to stay in my penthouse apartment in Midtown, Atlanta. My main home was in Alpharetta, north of the city, but I was too tired after getting back from Chicago earlier to drive there. The night was buzzing with activity, a stark contrast to the heaviness that lingered in my chest. The anger simmering within me rose to the surface.

I called my accountant and demanded to know why he hadn't sent the complete amount to my father. When he answered the phone, I listened to him stutter through an explanation of managing the funds going out. But I wasn't having it.

"Phil, that ain't your call to make, man. Do what I tell you next time," I snapped. "My instructions were clear! Do your job properly or I'll find someone else who can."

The accountant tried to justify himself by mentioning that my recent investments were not performing well and how I needed to cut back on spending. He fell short of going into details about the bills I was handling that I needed to put a cap on. Since I had had this conversation with him so many times before, I knew it was on the tip of his tongue. Holding himself back was a good decision on his part because with the way I was feeling right now, crossing that boundary would have me tearing him to shreds, before I fired him.

"I know what I'm doing," I retorted. "Just follow my directions and don't question my decisions. Now send the money immediately."

I hung up before he could say anything else, seething with anger. Taking a deep breath, I tried to calm myself down before returning to the living room where my paused video game awaited. I turned everything off and headed for my room. I sent a text to my siblings telling them I was back in the A. Without waiting for a response, I turned the phone off. With any luck, I could get a few hours of sleep in before I had to head out.

~

"What do you mean you made money off of my game?"

My grip tightened around the glass in my hand as I glared at Kane, boiling with rage. The loud music and flashing lights of the club faded into the background as his words echoed in my head.

He's done some reckless stuff, but I know he didn't just sit up here and say what I think he did.

We were sitting in my private section, surrounded by beautiful, scantily dressed women and expensive alcohol, but all I could feel was the weight of his admission crushing me. I signaled to the bouncer to clear out the women who'd been giving us a show for the past hour. The club's pulsing music suddenly felt like it was taunting me as I waited for them to leave.

Kane shrugged nonchalantly, but I could see the hint of excitement in his eyes. "You've been on fire these past few games. I had to bet on you," he said. "You didn't disappoint." Kane grinned and rubbed his hands together. "A nice chunk of change for both of us."

My mind flashed back to two years ago when we first started betting on sports events. It started off innocently enough with high stake boxing fights in Vegas, but eventually escalated to dangerous territory. I maintained plausible deniability by allowing Kane to handle the details and turning a blind eye to the risks involved. My only rule was we didn't touch football games. That way, I convinced myself betting wasn't that bad.

But now, with one careless move, everything could unravel before my eyes. My carefully constructed world had the potential to collapse around me. If news got out, not only could it end my career, but also tarnish my reputation forever. A wave of panic crashed through me as the gravity of Kane's actions sank in. Not only did he expose me, but he'd subjected my entire team to scrutiny and suspicion. The high and thrill of betting paled in comparison to this descent into uncertainty and fear. The anger within turned to pure rage.

"Are you insane? Do you realize what this could mean for me if anyone found out?"

Kane's expression shifted, understanding the gravity of his admission. But his response was not what I expected.

"Man, relax. This isn't my first time—"

"You've bet on my game before?"

He had the audacity to wave me off. "Don't worry. No one will suspect you."

"That drink must have gotten to your brain. The whole league knows how close we are," I roared.

"Aye! You need to chill out unless you tryin' to let the whole club in your business."

I didn't miss how it was suddenly *my* business. However, he was right because my outburst caught the attention of nearby tables. Done with this night, I slammed my glass down on the table. The weight of betrayal settled in my gut like a heavy stone.

I leaned in close, my voice was low and intense. "You better pray that no one finds out about this."

His expression told me that he finally grasped the severity of the situation, but it was too late. I downed the rest of my drink, feeling the weight of impending consequences crashing down on me. As I stood to leave, I realized I'd have to make some difficult decisions to protect myself. First thing in the morning, I had to call Big Iz, my trusted agent and confidant. He'd kick my behind, but tell me what to do.

~

A week later, I woke up to a barrage of notifications on my phone. My heart dropped into my stomach as I scrolled through them. Hell had opened and I'd been dropped to its pits. Turning on the TV to ESPN, I saw Simone Baxter, a sports reporter from *Atlanta Sports Today* being interviewed. The rolling banner read: **Atlanta Allied Star Midfielder, Nonso Chijuka, Suspended. Faces Possible Ban by FIFA Over Betting Scandal.**

I watched in horror as she read a generic statement from my club's publicist.

How did this crap hit the fan so fast?

I listened as she explained the potential impact of my suspension on our upcoming game in just a few days. But even more worrisome was the possibility of it costing Atlanta Allied thousands in fines. I hadn't even been informed of my suspension. Just then, my phone rang, and my heart skipped a beat. I guess I was about to be informed now.

The caller ID showed it was Big Iz. That night Kane told me about what he had done, I called Big Iz, but then remembered he'd gone to Brazil for an agent conference. I didn't want to discuss it over the phone, so I just carried on as normal.

"You better start talking and fast!" His words were laced with venom and urgency.

Fear clutched at my chest, making it hard to breathe as I admitted, "I messed up...bad."

The football world was unforgiving, and this was only the beginning of the long and treacherous road ahead.

transfer window

designated period during which professional clubs can buy, sell, or loan players to make strategic adjustments, and address any weaknesses in their teams.

one
Nonso

TRAPPED IN THE CHAOTIC GAME OF FATE, MY cherished dreams now clashed against the brutal scrutiny of reality and the harsh judgment of the public. Whether I deserved it or not was up for debate, depending on one's perspective—either black and white or a spectrum of greys and blues. Regardless of public opinion, the past ten months had been pure torment.

The stages of grief were no joke. I'd gone from constantly arguing with fans, fake bloggers, and sports outlets on social media to fighting in nightclubs, drinking excessively to the point of public drunkenness and indecent exposure, to denying that football was no longer a part of my life, to finally accepting my fate and shutting everyone out.

My sports agency, LST, was on the verge of dropping me until Nyce, whose real name was Cheta Kalu, stepped in. The retired NBA player, also represented by the agency, had become a mentor and big brother figure to me over the years. Despite my efforts to dodge his calls for weeks, one day I looked up and he'd managed to bypass my security system and burst into my home like a raging storm. To this day, I still don't know how he managed that, but suddenly my mother and sister arrived cheering him on as he cussed me out in Igbo. He didn't let up until he drove me to a rehab center on the outskirts of Atlanta that he had personally chosen for me.

"I've done everything you've done or at least had my name associated with it," Cheta's voice was stern. "There's no shame in falling down; the shame is in not getting back up." He pointed to the center. Apparently, he had signed me in under an alias. "Nze is getting married in December and you're coming with me and my wife. I don't bring losers around my family, so get yourself together. Now, get out of my car."

I remembered those words as though they were uttered yesterday. Now, I was determined to do whatever it took to reclaim my crown and stand on the business of football. My soul craved the chance for redemption, and not to toot my own horn, but *toot, toot*...I was a beast on the field. I was ready to rise from the ashes and have my rematch with destiny.

"Aye! Black, I'm about to be out." Kane walked from behind the bar in my Alpharetta home.

The day Kane walked into my seventh-grade homeroom, he was assigned to sit next to me. After scanning the class, his attention turned to me, and he greeted me with a head nod. "Wassup, Black," he said, referencing the dark skin I'd inherited from my father. The nickname stuck and followed me into my professional life.

"Dang, I can't believe I ain't gonna be able to fly down with you like back in the day." Kane picked up the keys to his truck.

Next week, I was headed to Viva City, North London to resume my football career as a midfielder for Viva City Football Club. In the past, any time I signed with a club outside the United States, Kane would be with me for the first couple of weeks as I settled down in the new city. This time, I was doing things differently, so I'd told him I was making this trip alone.

Before I could make up another excuse to pacify my friend,

my sister's not so hush whisper permeated the air. *"Chukwu, Daalu."*

I dapped my boy as I cut my eye at my sister, Dumebi. In our native tongue, she thanked God that Kane wasn't coming. She probably thought I didn't hear her, but I did. And so did our younger brother, Jason, who snickered. They were in the living room playing Minecraft.

Dumebi thought Kane was a freeloader and couldn't stand him. Whatever she thought, I'd warned her about her slick mouth. Especially with someone who was sometimes reckless and twice her size. No harm would ever come to her as long as Jason and I were around. Still, she needed to mind her business.

"Don't worry about it. When I settle in, I'll send for you," I said.

"Mba o," Dumebi spoke again.

I was about to caution her when Kane turned to her and chuckled. "Dums, you got something to say to me? You've been speaking under your breath since I got here. Speak ya mind, baby."

"Nah, K, she ain't the one," Jason said.

People often accused me of having a short fuse, but Jason's temper was even more volatile and bordering on unstable. Just moments ago, he and Kane were laughing and bantering like best buddies, but now his voice had turned to ice as he gave Kane a stern warning for addressing our sister. I was sure it was the term "baby" that set him off. Especially with the hint of flirtation in his voice and the look he gave her.

"Jace, I'on want no smoke with you. I'm just playing."

"Find something safer to play with..."

Kane chuckled and raised his hands in surrender. "A'ight, you got it."

I shook my head. "K, I been telling you Dums is off limits. Messing with her can get you hurt."

"She be starting with me..."

"Leave it alone." The sternness of my tone cut through whatever argument he had as I walked him out.

In no reality would I entertain whatever excuse he had for attempting to banter with my sister. I understood Dumebi. Years of Kane's sneakiness fueled her opinion. However, during my middle and high school years when my life was in shambles, Kane was the only one that stood by me.

A few moments later, I walked back into the living room. Before I could say anything, my twenty-seven-year-old sister had her hand on her hip, her stare challenging me to speak. I gently nudged her to the side and sat where she'd been sitting. I picked up the controller she left on the coffee table, ready to play.

"*Bruhda*, I won't apologize. I'm only looking out for you," she argued. "That man is not your friend!"

My face remained trained on the television and Jason laughed when Dumebi did exactly what we knew she would do. Stomp her feet like a child because I didn't give her a response. I often overlooked my sister's overbearing nature because she and I had a relationship no one else could really understand. When our parents only cared about themselves and were blowing up their lives with their toxic relationship, she and I were all we had. We looked out for each other and even though she was three years younger, she acted like my mother figure. She hadn't learned to ease up on that as we got older. Her career as a social worker just made it worse.

"Ain't nobody telling you to apologize. But you need to cut out the slick comments," I finally responded to her.

"Sis, I thought you loved me? Why you actively trying to send me to jail?" Jason asked.

We shared a laugh which caused Dumebi to roll her eyes and head to the kitchen. My brother was the family's jokester and he and I often drove our sister crazy. At twenty-three, he was super smart and already a big-time graphic designer. He had a nerdy look about him, with his light complexion, business formal attire and prescription glasses.

I was six feet, two inches and Jason had me by two inches. Despite our seven-year age difference, Jason had always followed me around. My friends knew about him and looked out for him just as I did. Kane was around a lot, so he and Jason had a closer relationship than most of my other friends, except when it came to our sister. She and Jason were close, and he was overprotective of his big sister, and I wished anyone luck who tried her. Jason was really our step brother, but the fact we didn't share a father had nothing to do with how close we were. He had also been affected by the bad decisions of our parents.

"Bro, you know she ain't wrong tho."

"I know that, but she also gotta trust me and mind her business. I don't need her giving me another reason to be unsettled now that I'm leaving the country."

"First off, K ain't stupid and second, you act like I'm not here."

I chuckled. "Shoot, I'm talking about you too. Dums be slick at the mouth, and you stay ready to fight people without asking questions."

"Agreed, but still Kane might be a lot of things, but he ain't crazy."

I remained silent as my mind traveled through the years of the friendship I had with Kane. Like I said before, we rolled deep. The neighborhood kids tended to disperse when we got to the common play area. Kane and I came from troubled homes, so we'd often hang out in our boy Nate's home since his parents were the only ones who we thought got the parenting game right. Nate, who now lived and worked in DC, rolled with us mostly for the thrill of the messed-up stuff we sometimes got into. We held each other down through bullies, gang members and girl problems.

After our last three-month stint in juvenile detention for spray painting some public statues, Nate had enough of the excitement. He still rolled with us, but whenever Kane suggested something off the wall, Nate would decline and so he grew further and further apart from us. After our stint in juvie, we were court ordered to volunteer in a community center.

It was there my life changed. God sent me an angel in the form of Isaiah Townsend, aka Big Iz. With the fractured paternal relationships I'd had with my father and stepfather, I was initially resistant to the older man's advice and guidance. However, he eventually got the three of us to try out for football camp. In the end, I was the only one who excelled at it and that's how my path to playing in football academies and tournaments throughout the country began.

Nate headed to college in DC, while I tried to juggle my college studies with a professional career on a Division II Detroit football team. Meanwhile, Kane decided to drop out of college during our second year and start his own trucking business.

As soon as I received my first paycheck, I immediately used it to buy Kane two trucks to show him my support. Over the years, I had climbed the ladder to become a professional football player on an international level. However, with my success came an increase in the number of business opportunities Kane pitched to me. Each one of his ventures he believed "would finally turn his life around."

Unfortunately, his latest venture was what caused the current issues I was dealing with. My siblings are understandably worried, but they had to let me handle this on my own. They often referenced how simple it was for Nate to detach himself. However, Nate could easily do that because they didn't share the same level of history as Kane and me. When we were teenagers, Kane had literally rescued me and saved my life.

But now, with what I'd just endured with my career, I could see that he couldn't be bothered about dragging me down. I needed to be strategic and find a way out of this destructive cycle. The first step was heading to London without him. Revisiting my brother's words about Kane not being crazy, I said, "Never underestimate anybody..."

"I won't, I promise. But you need to promise you gonna let go of that shame and guilt you got and get back on the field like the big bro I know," Jason said.

I gave it a few moments before I turned and met his eyes. Nodding, I acquiesced to his command. We gave each other a hug.

"Aww, the two most important men in my life. Not afraid to be vulnerable with each other," Dumebi said in a sing song tone. "I love it for you."

We both chuckled and waved her emotional behind off. She swore she was our psychiatrist, but she had her own problems. Like the fact that she couldn't let any man in because she thought they would disappoint her like our father did. She would never admit it though.

I, on the other hand, admitted that I had a hard time letting go of relationships that didn't serve me because I didn't want to feel like I was giving up on anyone the way my father gave up on me. However, my attempt to be nothing like the man that contributed to my DNA caused me a lot more pain in the long run.

> Lesedi: Hey, my Black Knight. Sorry, I won't be able to make it. Have a safe flight and I know you will do great. Love you, always.

I stared at the text that appeared on my phone screen.

> Thanks Les, talk to u soon.

After typing my reply, I put the device on my lap.

Lesedi Jafta.

Another relationship I hadn't wanted to give up on. My relationship with Les was more complicated, but it didn't negate the fact that somehow the ones I cared about the most had a habit of giving up on me.

The following week, as I relaxed in the plush leather seat, I lifted my Beats headset, replacing the lyrics of Stormzy's latest album with the comforting, gentle purr of the chartered private jet's engines. The journey had been uneventful thus far.

My excitement to land in London was tangible. As I peered out the window, the sun was beginning its descent into the horizon, bathing the clouds in a warm glow. I was about to return my headset over my ears when the intercom crackled on, and the captain's voice filled the cabin.

"Hello, this is your captain speaking. We're currently flying at an altitude of 35,000 feet and we have approximately two and a half hours left until we reach our destination, Heathrow Airport. The weather in London is unusually clear for this January day. Temperatures are four degrees Celsius or thirty-nine degrees Fahrenheit. Thank you for choosing to fly with us and we hope you're enjoying the journey."

Figuring I had two and a half hours before the craziness began, I leaned my head back and shut my eyes. Suddenly, I felt a presence standing over me. I knew who it was. I should, since I'd been dealing with him since I was sixteen.

"Big Iz, I done told you, you need to start announcing yourself when you approach. I ain't gonna be responsible for these reflexes." My eyes remained closed, but a smirk spread across my face.

"Black, I'll have you and your reflexes on the floor before you have time to blink. Don't play with me. Sit your behind up. We need to talk."

The sternness in his voice was laced with some concern. I peeled open my eyes and did as he asked. Taking the seat opposite me in the six-seater, private aircraft we'd boarded from Atlanta this morning, he removed a folder from the portfolio he carried around.

"What's up?" I studied him some more. "Something is telling me I ain't gonna like what you're about to say."

"And you won't because we've talked about it many times. But I need you to listen to me without interrupting."

I nodded. Big Iz was a retired NFL player who got injured in his third year in the league. The injury was to his testicles which affected his ability to be a father. After he left the league, he had a series of run ins with the law that could be chalked up to his dream being taken away prematurely. The night he almost killed himself by driving under the influence was when he cleaned up his act and started to help troubled kids in the community center.

He always went the extra mile for me. He even won the trust of my mother who felt he had enough knowledge to help me navigate my career. He became my agent when I signed my first contract, but refused to take an agent's fee until I became a millionaire. That was three short years later. Since then, he'd been with me every step of the way. Despite his habit of trying to lecture me when, as he put it, I was being childish, and my constant empty threats of firing him when he got me into deals I wasn't really feeling, he had never steered me wrong. I never wanted to imagine what I'd do without him.

"You gonna tell me what it is or we gonna keep beating around the bush?"

"It's about your finances, son."

I turned to look around the cabin. My sister was on this flight, and I hated her to think anything was wrong. Well, according to my accountants and Big Iz, something was wrong. Big Iz was more than an agent to me, so although he wasn't in my pockets, he knew stuff. However, with my new payday, I knew I could turn the situation around.

"Dums is laying down in the back. I know how she is, so I made sure she was a safe distance before speaking," he sighed. "Look, you have a rare second chance here. Not many players can turn their life around after such a public scandal. The pressure and shame alone can push them down the wrong path. However, you got one, but you need to make some changes. First, your spending..."

I opened my mouth to give him the same argument he was used to getting from me, but he cut me off with a head nod.

"I get that it's a cultural thing, but again, I don't understand how you're expected to take care of able-bodied people. From what I know, your stepfather and mother are healthy, Kane is a grown man, your dad and stepmother are fine as well. So why in the world are you taking care of these grown folks? Your dad decided to have two more kids, so why are you responsible for their school tuition?"

In addition to Jason and Dumebi, I also had sixteen-year-old twin sisters, Amara and Anuli. The twins were from my dad's current wife, and they all lived in Asaba, Nigeria.

"I'm not responsible *per se*. I'm helping out..."

"You need to stop helping. You're thirty. True you've had a stellar career, but you'll end up broke if you continue this way. Everyone can't be on your payroll. You said you didn't want to end up like those players who had to keep playing even after their prime, with no other life to live. But with the way you're going, you might have to be, or you'll retire with nothing to show for it."

After a few beats passed between us, I rubbed my hand over my clean-shaven head. I hadn't let my hair grow out in years but with this London weather, I might have to or wear a beanie. I had work to do, and I wasn't trying to fall sick.

"I know your heart, no matter how trauma causes you to want to hide it. But you gotta cut all of them off. Or set a reasonable, and I mean reasonable budget. As much as Dums and Jace look out for you, they should be the only ones you give anything to. And I know how hard they try and fight to return the excess when it hits their account."

Big Iz handed me the brochure he removed from his portfolio. I glanced at it for a few seconds then looked at him. Cocking my brow, I lifted the brochure. He answered my unspoken question by nodding his head.

"Apex Financial Management Consultants. Committed to elevating your financial success. Financial literacy classes? You want me to sit in a class and learn about how to spend my money. Really?"

"Really. It's one of the more prestigious firms in the city you're headed to. Despite your mishap, your five-year contract is sweet. Millions of euros, bonus for goals...a very good deal. This is your chance to shift the scale in another direction."

"I'll cut folks off, but I ain't doing this. I got ball to play, to rise from this dumpster I put myself in." I tossed the brochure on the seat beside me.

"You trust me, right?" he asked.

"Always."

"Then play ball, and let me worry about bringing your image back up. But I still need you to attend these classes so you can become more knowledgeable."

Even though I didn't give him a definite response, he understood me well enough to know I would at least consider his words. I still wasn't doing it, but I always gave Big Iz my attention. I listened as he elaborated on the Viva City FC organization's dedication to the well-being of its players and staff. They set aside a week at the beginning and middle of each season for contracted organizations to send representatives to provide resources in areas such as nutrition, finances, wellness, and mental health.

For the whole week, after practice, these representatives would give presentations. It was up to us as players and staff to sign up for their services if we were interested. The goal of these resources was to support us not just as athletes, but also as individuals, helping us thrive in both our professional and personal lives.

"Are we close?"

I looked up at my sister who was wiping sleep from her eyes. Her brows furrowed as her eyes darted from Big Iz to me. "What's wrong? Why are you guys so serious?"

Big Iz stood and chuckled. He was used to my little big sister by now. He pulled her into a half hug. "Nothing for you to worry about, Baby girl." He glanced toward the cockpit. "Let me go get one of those fine hostesses to give me a drink." He took a few steps then turned. "Baby girl, give our Champ one of your pep talks." He laughed, knowing exactly what he had just set in motion.

"I see you, old man. Don't be mad when I wanna play…"

Dumebi insisted that Jason and I fasted with her for two days before takeoff. Then earlier, she prayed before we got on the plane, then anointed the plane, prayed when we were in midair, and I was sure she wouldn't let us get off when we landed without praying. Dumebi called herself, "Peteress." According to her, she was a prayer warrior who wouldn't hesitate to use her Black belt training to knock someone worthy of a whooping, out.

Dumebi could pass as the actress that played Toni on *Girlfriends*. Lesedi used to love that show. My sister plopped down into the seat next to me and pulled out her phone. I thought she was looking for a Bible verse to start her speech. I sighed and massaged my temple.

"Relax. I've only two things to say. You're *not* your mistake, and you don't owe *anybody* anything. Don't let Mama, Papa, Daddy Carl, Kane or even Lesedi make you think otherwise."

Daddy Carl was what Dumebi called Jason's dad. I just ignored that part because he was never gonna influence anything I had going on.

My sister leaned her head against my shoulder and I placed a kiss in her hair. Coming back from a two-month investigation and trial, a subsequent seven-month football ban, joining a new team, moving to a new country, and being unexpectedly rejected by the person I thought would one day be my wife was enough on my plate. My sister didn't have to worry. Dealing with anyone or anything additional would have to wait until I navigated this whirlwind of adjustments in my life.

My legacy in football wouldn't be defined by my first act. This was my second act in a game of two halves. Failure wasn't an option. I intended to dominate this second chance with all my might.

two

Yinka Martins

"IN 500 METERS, turn right onto Mayfair Avenue. Proceed straight for 200 meters, then the Viva House will be on your left."

I paid close attention to the directions, making sure I didn't miss my turn. Once I was confident I was on the correct street, I returned my focus to my future sister-in-law. It was already ten past eight and I hadn't planned on starting my day so late.

"Okay Bims, where were we? Oh right, I promised I would be there." I glanced at her through my phone mounted on the dashboard of my car. "My boss is being a pain, but I don't care what he says, I'll be there in May for your bridal shower."

"There" was Atlanta, Georgia. It was where my siblings and I grew up, and where our parents still lived. They were both successful professionals — my father a pathologist at Grady Hospital and my mother a professor at Spelman College. As they neared retirement, they were considering traveling the world before settling down in our ancestral home in Ibadan. Out of three children, I was the youngest. My sister, Tolu, was the oldest and an intellectual property attorney, while my brother, Femi, worked as a corporate real estate broker.

"I can't believe you still need a GPS to get to work." Abimbola, or Bims as the family called her, chuckled.

I glanced over at her and rolled my eyes. My brother still lived in Atlanta while my sister had moved to the UK with Oliver, her Kenyan husband, six years ago. I joined her two years later. It would be four years next month and I still struggled with driving on the left side of the road and navigating all the different "avenues" and "squares." In my defense, I had only been living in Viva City – a town in North London – for eighteen months.

"Keep laughing at my expense and I just might lose my ticket," I joked.

"*Maṣe gbiyanju rẹ*. Don't try it. If you do, I'll be one of the worst sisters-in-law you'll ever have," Bims retorted playfully.

"Unless you're planning on divorcing Femi, you're the only sister-in-law I'll have." I laughed as she made a face.

Bims sucked her teeth and gave me a playful glare before we both burst into laughter. I didn't know what it was, but Bims loved my brother down. I mean bad. I knew my brother loved her too, but for some reason he'd been dragging his feet when it came to proposing. A few weeks ago, the whole family had gathered in our family home in Ibadan, Nigeria to celebrate Christmas. Tolu and Oliver with their kids, Femi, Bims, my parents, and I had just been chilling and having a good time on Christmas Eve, when Femi surprised us all by getting down on one knee. After seven years of dating, the couple was now eager to tie the knot.

Cassie: We still on for lunch?

I glanced at the text that came through as I pulled into Viva House and parked in my designated spot. Wrapping up my conversation with Bims, which had gone on longer than I expected, I turned off the engine. Pulling down the visor, I quickly assessed my appearance. I ran my tongue over my teeth, trying to get rid of any coffee residue. After fluffing my golden-brown curls, I unmounted my phone and took a deep breath in preparation for what the day would bring.

"Father, please help me to reflect You no matter what the enemy tries to bring my way. Amen," I muttered.

It was the prayer I recited daily when I parked in front of Apex Financial Management Consultants. Numbers were my passion. I loved my job, clients, and colleagues. But my boss, Mr. Wilson, aka "the enemy" had me almost wanting to forget I was a child of God. I responded to Cassandra, my best friend, before packing up my stuff and getting out of the car. I had a very important meeting that started in less than an hour.

Later that day, I shifted in my chair, trying to get comfortable. I repositioned my laptop and exhaled deeply, trying to calm my nerves. Straightening out the imaginary creases in my crisp, olive-green suit, I could feel sweat forming at the base of my neck. With a few rolls of my shoulders, I tried to relax.

Mr. Chen's face reappeared on the screen, his sharp features accentuated by the bright lights in his luxurious office. We'd been on this Zoom conference call for almost an hour, and it was time for me to wrap it up.

"My apologies, Ms. Martins. I had to take that call."

"No worries, I understand. Are you ready to continue?"

He nodded and I launched into my final pitch, clicking through the remaining slides, and carefully enunciating each point. Mr. Alex Chen was a well-known tech entrepreneur whose recent successes with his IPO launch had been making headlines. This meeting had been several days in the making, and I was determined to make it count. My career kinda depended on it. As our conversation neared its end, I concluded my explanation of the investment strategies I had tailored specifically for him after our initial meeting. He nodded along, occasionally asking questions that I was grateful to have anticipated and prepared for.

Leaning forward in his high-backed leather chair, Mr. Chen interlaced his fingers. I couldn't help but admire his heavy oak desk. Everything around him reflected a minimalistic yet layered traditional look.

"Thank you for this, Ms. Martins," he said. "I'll need to confer with my team on this matter. I'll get back to you soon."

It wasn't the response I was expecting, but I trained my face to camouflage my disappointment. "Of course," I replied, maintaining my professional demeanor.

Thankfully, he told me to reach out to him in a week if I hadn't heard back from him. At least I had a time frame and not an indefinite "soon." As soon as the call ended, I took a deep breath and exhaled slowly, trying to shake off any lingering tension. But before I could fully relax, there was a sharp knock on my office door. Without waiting for a response, my boss, Mr. Wilson, poked his head inside.

"Ms. Martins, a word..."

It took everything in me not to suck my teeth. God did His big thing when He gave me this job within six months of me moving to the UK. I mean, I have two degrees and a certification, but the job market was cut-throat. So, yeah, God did it. The boss I had when I was moved to this office was an angel. She was older, kind, patient and taught me the ropes. However, she moved just a few months later. Mr. Wilson was far younger and had something to prove and the man wanted to prove it on top my head.

"Sure, give me a minute."

Any sane person would leave while I got myself together. Nope. The man leaned against my door frame waiting for me. I gathered my notepad and followed him out of the office. We weaved through the busy corridors of our company's headquarters, heading towards the exclusive area reserved for top-level meetings and strategic discussions – the executive suite located on the top floor. My heart raced with anticipation as we approached the imposing double doors that led into the suite. I glanced at my phone screen. I had an offsite meeting and if I didn't get to it in time, I'd be late for lunch.

It was the second week of January, and we had all submitted our goals for the year, so why I was being singled out for a meeting, I wasn't sure. My mind raced with possibilities as we entered the hushed and elegant atmosphere of the suite. After pointing me towards a chair, he took a seat opposite me. Despite his attempt at a neutral expression, the gravity in his eyes hinted at the impending bad news he was about to reveal.

"Ms. Martins," he began, his tone measured, "We've hit a hiccup. Tom from our financial literacy department is out with a medical emergency, and his backup just handed in her resignation."

I furrowed my brow, feeling a sense of dread creeping in. Financial literacy had been one of my responsibilities when I first started at Apex, and I had despised every minute of it. I knew its importance, but arguing with grown people about the need to be financially responsible was annoying. I couldn't understand why folks were so averse to being knowledgeable about their options and planning. As my girl, Mrs. Monica Coleman-Hunt, would say, "Making a plan without the right tools is trying to build a house without a hammer: you'll be all thumbs and no progress." The multi-million-dollar hospitality mogul was one of my sheroes. Her weekly podcasts were a must for me.

I refocused on the man in front of me. "That's unfortunate, sir. But I'm confused," I replied, trying to keep my tone professional. "I've moved on from that role. My focus has been on developing our client base and working towards a partnership."

Mr. Wilson leaned back in his chair with an unyielding gaze. "I'm aware of your goals, Ms. Martins." His voice was firm. "But right now, we need someone to step in. You have the experience, and let's face it, the pace will be slower. Maybe it'll give you a chance to catch your breath and refocus."

I felt frustration and resistance surging within me. I knew what he was really implying – that I couldn't handle my current role in Client Services and Business Development. I had tirelessly worked to move away from teaching about money, and now it seemed like I was being dragged back into it against my will.

"Sir, with all due respect," I began cautiously, keeping my tone steady, "I believe I'm making a bigger impact in my current role. Can't we explore other options or find a temporary replacement from another department—"

"This isn't a negotiation." Mr. Wilson shook his head, maintaining his unwavering expression. "We need someone to fill in, and you're the most qualified for the job. It's just temporary until we find a suitable replacement." He paused for effect. "You know, being a partner means your responsibilities expand to include strategic decision-making and leadership across multiple departments. Unless, of course, you agree with my assessment that you're not cut out for it."

The insinuation that I wasn't partner material because I hadn't brought in a lot of prominent clients in my current position stung, but I understood that if I wanted to prove myself, I would need to face this challenge head-on. As I exited the room a few minutes later, a feeling of annoyance and resignation engulfed me. It appeared that no matter how much effort I put into progressing, the man always managed to drag me down.

Cassie swirled her piña colada and took a sip, shaking her head in disbelief. "I have no idea how you put up with it. If I were in your shoes, I would've quit and given my boss a piece of my mind."

We were sitting on the patio of our favorite restaurant, enjoying our biweekly lunch date. Fusion Haven was a modern neighborhood restaurant in Viva City. The menu offered a modern interpretation of classical European and African flavors. It was the best and we loved it. I longed for a glass of red wine to relax, but there was too much work left for me to indulge just yet.

Cassie and I had been friends for almost ten years now. We met at a Juneteenth event in Atlanta when she first moved there from Chicago. Back then, she didn't know much about the city, and I was happy to show her around. Now she worked as a Senior Project Manager at Petro Energy's Atlanta office. About seven months ago, she was sent to London to lead a major offshore drilling project in the North Sea.

"I can't just quit. You know how much making partner means to me. I have—"

Cassie raised her hand. "Yeah, yeah, I know all about your timetable. If someone can plan when they do number two it will be you."

I scrunched my nose in disgust. "Eww, not when we're eating."

Cassie waved me off, looking toward the patio door. "Whatever. We're done eating." She inclined her head. "I mean we will be if the waiter comes back with our to-go orders so we can head out."

I smiled at her impatience. It was the second Tuesday of the month, and Cassie had a standing appointment with her loctician. I admired the different styles she had sported since I'd known her, always keeping up with the latest trend. On the other hand, I had been tender headed since I was a kid. Now, as an adult, my hair stayed in simple buns or loose waves.

"All I'm saying is, I know you have a timetable." Cassie began counting on her fingers. "When you'll get married, how long you'll stay in the UK, when you want to have children..."

"Hey now, don't clown my Book of Accountability," I interjected playfully. It was what I called my trusted life planner notebook.

"Don't even get me started on that thing," Cassie groaned. "If I could burn it, I would."

I chuckled at her dramatic response. "Cass, you can't shame me for having a plan for my life."

"You know me well enough to know that's not my intent," Cassie said, her tone softening. "But Yinks, you don't just have a plan for your life. You have a *strict* timetable of events that have you bound."

My phone buzzed on the table, cutting through the tension of the moment. I let out a quiet sigh of relief. I was over defending my need to make plans and stick to them. But as I looked at the caller ID, dread and annoyance washed over me. It was Brandon Enyi, the man who had become a constant source of frustration and disappointment in my life.

Cassie glanced at my phone screen and chuckled, taking a sip of her drink. "How's that plan working out for you?" she teased.

I turned my phone face down on the table, trying to ignore it as it continued to ring. "I hate you," I grumbled.

"No, you don't," Cassie replied with a knowing smile. "You love me, but you hate when I'm right."

And she had been right about Brandon. He was a disaster from the start. But on paper, he seemed perfect – good job, from a God-fearing family, perfect height to snuggle under. But after a year and a half together, the mask fell off and his true colors were anything but perfect.

"You've broken up with him for good, right?" Cassie asked, concern lacing her tone.

I nodded, feeling exhausted just thinking about all the times I had tried to end things with Brandon. "A hundred times. But he always comes up with some excuse. This time it's blaming the London air for clouding my judgement."

"What? You've been here for four years but just broke up with him when you went to Atlanta a few months ago. Right?"

"Yep. After I'd been telling him it was over for months over the phone." My phone started ringing again, and I quickly silenced it. "I'm going to use the restroom. I'll stop by the bar to check on our takeout order."

"Thanks, girl. I need to answer some emails because once this is done, I'm done with work for the day."

"You do realize that guys like Brandon need to see you with someone else before they understand it's really over," Cassie remarked.

"Well, he's going to have to accept it regardless because there is no one else," I replied.

"Oh, believe me, I know..."

Grabbing my phone and purse, I turned towards the double doors leading from the patio into the restaurant, quickly walking away before Cassie could start lecturing me about the men she'd tried to set me up with. A few minutes later, as I exited the restroom, I made a detour to the bar. My phone rang again, and I knew Brandon wouldn't stop calling at this rate. After asking the bartender to check on our orders, I answered the Facetime call.

"Hey, baby, I've been trying to reach you," Brandon said. He was dressed for the gym. He went every evening after work.

"Yeah, sorry about that. What's going on?"

"I don't know. You tell me."

I braced myself for the guilt trip as he went through his usual routine of blaming me for derailing our relationship for continuing to pursue my dreams in another country. I was alone at the bar when we started our Facetime call. Brandon was starting to get loud. As he continued talking aggressively, my eyes wandered around the space. My eyes landed on the most stunning darkskinned man I'd ever seen at the other end of the bar. My heart began to race as our eyes locked, and he winked at me.

Without thinking, I walked towards him, feeling drawn to him like a magnet. I think it was Cassie's words earlier, or the fact that Brandon was more agitated than usual, but what I did next surprised even me.

"Brandon, I didn't want you to find out this way..."

I stood next to the handsome stranger, and he looked back at me with intense eyes. The man was now fully focused on me, and I pleaded with my eyes for him to play along.

"Find out what? Yinks? Find out what?"

"That I'm seeing someone else. Actually, I'm having lunch with him right now." I stared at the stranger, waiting for his response. After what felt like an eternity, he nodded and took the phone from my hand.

"Aye! Brandon...right?" he asked with a distinctive American accent.

So, he isn't a local.

I quickly scanned his appearance. Tall, at least six foot two or more, dressed in a Ziedu yellow and grey sweater over dark jeans, crisp white Jordans and a Cuban link around his neck. His watch looked expensive, and his cologne exuded a scent of wealth. He might be visiting.

"Who are you? Give my girl the phone," Brandon demanded.

"I don't see any girl here..."

The deep tone of the stranger's voice shut Brandon up immediately. He started scanning my body with his eyes, sending a shiver down my spine. I had taken off my jacket earlier, so now I was only wearing a cream camisole over suit pants. I nervously ran my hands over my arms.

"Look, my woman and I have somewhere to be." He glanced at me briefly before turning his attention back to Brandon. "But I'mma need you to make this the last time you call this number. You do not want to see me."

Things were getting out of hand, and I knew I needed to intervene. Taking the phone back from him, I said, "Baby, that's enough. Brandon—"

"Nah, forget it. I'll just call—"

"Didn't I just tell you not to call my woman again?"

I froze as the stranger's hand landed on my hip, giving it a gentle squeeze. He didn't take the phone, he just leaned in over my shoulder, his beard tickling the crook of my neck. My heart pounded erratically, and I was sure I was in the beginning stages of a heart attack.

Brandon was about to say something else, but I had had enough. "Bye Brandon." I ended the call and took a deep breath before turning to face the stranger.

"I'm so so sorry about that...but thank you."

"You're welcome, Specs," he replied with a charming smile.

I furrowed my brows in confusion. "Specs?"

He moved his index finger between his eyes. "Those are so sexy."

I shook my head and scoffed. He was referring to my freckles, something that I was self-conscious about as a kid but now displayed with pride. As a Yoruba girl with caramel skin and freckles, I had often felt like an oddity, but now I embraced my uniqueness. My freckles ran from temple to temple across my eyes and covering most of my cheeks like a big pair of summer sunglasses. Spectacles...specs. I grabbed my bag from the counter and smirked.

"Clever...thanks again."

As I turned to walk away, he chuckled behind me. In just a few minutes of being in his presence, his intense gaze and his touch had me questioning everything in my life. The power of his stare at my back forced me to quicken my pace.

The devil was a lie and I needed to flee.

three
Nonso

"WHO WAS THAT?"

Fusion Haven was one of the restaurants recommended to me by the Viva City FC (or Panthers as the fans called them) team liaison when we touched down in Viva City a week ago. The next day, Dumebi and I dined here, and she'd been semi obsessed with their Safari Delight ever since. The dessert made up of a chocolate syrup thingy, passion fruit and sponge cake were too sweet for me, but my sister loved it.

I shrugged and glanced over my shoulder, watching the sway of Spec's hips while walking out of the restaurant. She was now bundled up in a dark brown trench coat, making it hard to see her figure. But with the temperature at two degrees Celsius outside, I couldn't blame her for wanting to stay warm. Despite the layers, I could still make out her frame. It was a sight I had committed to memory during our brief encounter when I posed as her "man." She and who I assumed to be her friend were now leaving the restaurant.

"Nonso!" Dumebi snapped her fingers in front of my face, and I pushed them away.

"What?" I asked, pushing her to-go dessert bag towards her and narrowing my eyes at her.

"I was calling your name, and you were lost in the gaze of a woman you don't even know."

"I may not know her, but that doesn't mean I can't appreciate God's creation. You need to mind your own business."

"Sorry *o*. I don't know why I keep worrying about you when you clearly don't want me to—"

"There's a difference between worrying about me and constantly being in my business. You always have to insert your-self into everything."

Dumebi sat back in her chair and started scrolling through her phone. I saw her staring at me and Specs at the bar. My sister was worried about me potentially getting into another relationship now, when Lesedi was such a nightmare. Again, I already knew I held onto that relationship for too long, but it irked me how she would slyly point out my shortcomings in the name of worrying about me. She never directly mentioned them because she knew I'd be pissed. But insinuating that I couldn't handle myself was just as frustrating.

I knew that getting back my place in football should be my only focus now. The only reason I cut her some slack was because I knew she wanted what was best for me and I had lied to her in the past about everything that was going on with me – my gambling addiction and failed relationship. She knew something was wrong, kept asking and I kept lying. So, when the news about the scandal broke, and she found out with the whole world, I knew she was heartbroken. I never wanted to see the look on her face or experience the pain of her tears again. My sister was aware that football was my entire life, and she feared what would happen if I never got to play again.

"You gonna act like a brat now?" I asked, frustrated with her behavior.

She rolled her eyes at me. "No, I'm going to mind my business from now on." Her words were curt. "Do what you like," she added, clearly annoyed with me.

I brought out my phone and placed it on the table and hit

the record button. "Repeat that real quick. I need to record it so I can send a copy to Jace." I said, trying to diffuse the tension between us. My sister laughed and pushed the phone away. With that sound, suddenly everything felt right in my world again.

"*Bruhda*, leave me alone. I'm only looking out for you. We don't want another Lesedi..."

I shook my head. Her promise to stay out of my business didn't even last two seconds. I wanted to cuss Jason out for leaving me with her for a whole week. Once the deal with Viva City was finalized, although our relationship was complicated Lesedi was supposed to come with me. But when I received her last text two weeks ago, I knew her family had gotten to her again and I was exhausted from the constant tug of war.

My sister quickly rearranged her schedule and hopped on the jet to be with me. Jason had already planned a trip to Nairobi for a client so couldn't make it.

"What time is your flight again?" I asked, signaling the waiter over.

"In three hours. But you already knew that. And even though you don't want to hear it, here's my advice...again. Focus on yourself."

Before I could respond, the waiter arrived with the bill. After paying, I escorted my sister out of the restaurant to my newly acquired Land Rover Defender.

"Thanks Ray. Let's head to Heathrow," I said to my driver once Dums and I were settled in the back seat.

Since I was still waiting for my work permits, I had some free time to take care of other things. The first thing on my list was getting a four-wheel drive truck. The Viva City FC training facility was only about thirty-five minutes away from the hotel where I was staying, and on the first day, I attempted to drive there myself. I didn't have the time to learn how to drive on the opposite side of the road with everything going on.

When Big Iz returned to the US a few days ago, he connected

me to one of the top female sports agents in the UK, Sharon Ellis. He still oversaw my overall career, with Ms. Ellis reporting to him.

The first thing Ms. Ellis did was hire Ray. He was an American who had been living in the UK for some time. His ability to switch between UK and American slang and terms had been a lifesaver.

A few hours later, my sister had completed the check-in process, and we were sitting in the airport lounge, waiting for her to go through security.

Despite my efforts to conceal my identity with a beanie and sunglasses, I still caught the attention of passersby who asked for an autograph. Some reporters attempted to ask me questions, but I ignored them all. Ever since the scandal, the press had been relentless in their attacks on me before any investigations or hearings could even take place. These were the same reporters I used to give interviews and photoshoots whenever they asked. But not one of them was willing to give me a fair chance. The American media was ruthless, and the British press followed suit after news broke that I would be playing for the Panthers.

"I know you can't make any promises about visiting, but could you please just call Mummy? So she'll stop pestering me?" Dumebi sighed, taking a sip of her water.

For a long time, our mother and I had a strained relationship. We were in a better place now, but not as close as we used to be before she tore our family apart. Unlike my sister, I could only handle talking to our mother once every two weeks. Our experiences with her were different, and I didn't want to interfere with Dumebi's relationship with her.

"I talked to her before we left. She'll be all right."

A text from Ray came in, letting me know where he would be when I was ready. I leaned forward and took off my sunglasses, resting my forearms on my thighs. "You keep giving me advice, but you have your own issues to address. When are you going to talk to someone about them?"

"What issues?" Dumebi asked.

"Emeka, Ismael, Tony, Jide...none of them were ever good enough for you? None of them will ever be in my eyes, but surely there was one who met your standards?"

Our mother left Nigeria to study nursing in America when we were three and one years old respectively. We were raised by our father for three years before our immigration papers were approved. But when we arrived in Atlanta, something happened that I could never forget. Even at thirty years old, the memory of my father's face as my mother took us and the immigration officials escorted him away still haunts me. Our family was torn apart as he was deported back to Nigeria without being able to enter the US with us. Over the years, although our mother allowed us to stay in touch with him, he chose to take his anger out on us. His abandonment deeply affected both my sister and me, and even when our mother remarried and had our younger brother Jason two years later, it did little to heal the rift between us.

"Dums, you—"

"I hear you." She shifted in her seat, showing her annoyance.

"I know you can hear, but are you truly listening? Our family dysfunction has taken so much from us already. I hold on too tight and you let go too easy."

"I know. My therapist tells me the same thing."

"So why haven't you made any changes? Or do you just like paying someone to listen to you talk?"

"What about you?" she challenged.

"Shoot...whatchu think I've been doing the last six months? My therapist has had an earful. Dealing with the root of my gambling addiction, which I'm actively working towards not falling back into that destructive pattern, and discussing my issues with abandonment."

When my job was on the line, I realized the path I was on would only lead to my destruction. While serving out my ban, I sought help from a therapist. It was during this time that I also turned to Jesus for salvation and guidance. While some may view it as cliche, for me, it was necessary as my very soul depended on it.

"I'll work on myself if you let go of Kane and Lesedi once and for all."

"Fine. Are you satisfied now? Don't bring it up again."

Her phone's alarm went off to alert us that it was time for her to head to the gate. We both stood, and I wrapped my arms around her. She pulled away with a mischievous glint in her eye, signaling she was about to say something sassy.

"By the way, that James guy is fionnneee. Personally, I would've gone for Xan, but everyone knows that gospel singer has him wrapped around her finger."

I raised my brow. "You wanna date my teammate?"

James Morrison was our team's captain and Xander Mitchell, a center back, was also a January transfer like me, coming from a club in Brazil.

"*Bruhda*, they're both handsome—"

"No! Get your stuff, let's go."

My sister was my best friend, so she knew how to push my buttons. She giggled as if it was all a joke.

"Dumebi Chijuka, if I find out you've even so much as commented on their social media posts, I'll personally ban you from entering the UK."

She shrugged nonchalantly. "That's fine. I'll just have my boo, James come visit me in the US."

"Ha, very funny. Let me give Jace a call real quick."

Her expression changed quickly, and annoyance crossed her face. Jason was her ace, but he was my right-hand man. If I asked him to keep an eye on her, he would take it seriously. Dumebi knew she wouldn't be able to escape his watchful gaze.

~

TWO DAYS AFTER, I WALKED INTO THE SLEEK, WELL-decked out kitchenette of the hotel suite I was staying in. A rare ray of sunlight cast a glow over the modern set up. The space was nice but after almost two weeks, I was ready to get out and get my own space. The problem was I didn't like any of the apartments the team's liaison recommended. Now, Ms. Elis was hooking me up with a realtor to find something more to my taste. I hoped the listings they were supposed to send over later made sense because I really wanted to be outta here. My work permits came in and I was dressed and ready for my first day of training.

I walked to the coffee maker and I poured a cup and took a moment to turn on the TV. Although I knew I shouldn't, I wanted to catch up on sports news. As I poured cream into my coffee, the screen flickered to life, displaying the faces of the SportsZoneUK Live anchors. They were discussing Viva City FC, and my name was front and center.

"Viva City FC is ahead of their game in transfers this year. The number four EFL team is not leaving any stone unturned in ensuring they get promoted by the end of the season," the male anchor said.

The female anchor stood and walked to the stats board. My and Xander's pictures appeared. She ran down our numbers from previous clubs and what we brought to Viva City. "So far with these two players, they have brought their spending total to one hundred and seventy-five million Euros."

"Let's hope these two can do what they are supposed to do. With Keith Tanner injured and Rio McAllister not meeting expectations, the club did well with these players. But these changes will be an adjustment for the fans. I'm sure the fans will keep the end goal in mind which is the Premier League." The male anchor turned his chair to face another board and my picture appeared. He spoke confidently about my potential impact on the team.

"Nonso Chijuka is going to be a game-changer for Viva City FC," he declared. "His expertise as a midfielder makes him an ideal replacement for Rio McAllister. I have high expectations for his performance this season."

Here they go

I wasn't *replacing* Rio. The veteran midfielder would still play I was told, however because of his several injuries, Coach Sanchez decided I'd have more play time. By my third day at the training facility, I quickly found out Rio wasn't happy. Pacifying folks hurt feelings wasn't in my job description, so I was gonna let him work that out with Coach and the staff. My focus was the field.

Hearing those words of praise from the anchor filled me with determination, but it was short-lived. The female anchor interjected with a more critical perspective, reminding everyone of my past suspension and activities leading to my ban.

"But let's not forget the Nigerian American's troubled history," she pointed out. "Nonso's ban left a mark on his career, and doubts persist about his dedication to the sport. Can he truly overcome his personal struggles and excel on the field again?"

I never considered gambling until Kane introduced it to me. There were many nuances to how even the Vegas boxing betting thing that started it all happened, but at the end of the day, I took on a vice that almost destroyed my life. It was only by the grace of God that when the news broke, Big Iz had already been working on getting me a new contract as a free agent. However, the club that had offered me a spot in the Premier League rescinded their offer once the ban came down.

As I went through therapy and worked to make things right, Big Iz tirelessly searched for other opportunities. Eventually, Viva City FC agreed to take a chance on me, but they were dragging their feet with a solid contract, until Cheta Kalu got involved. That guy had been a godsend to me. Crazy, but godsent.

Cheta knew one of the top Panther alums, Qasim Adesina. The guy had some heavy pull back in the day when he played before an injury took him out. Qasim made a few calls, and I got my contract. But not everyone was happy for me. Lesedi and the public couldn't see why I was willing to relocate for less money instead of waiting for a better offer from another Premier League team. But for me, it wasn't just about the paycheck. I wasn't broke. True, my finances were not where they should be after all my years of hard work and dedication to football. But starting fresh in a new place was more important to me than money at the moment.

I checked my phone and saw it was already 7:15am – time for me to get moving. Turning off the TV, I felt a tinge of frustration as my past mistakes continued to cast shadows over any progress I made in moving on. But I refused to let those setbacks defeat me. Gathering my gear and keys, I headed out for training with a fierce determination to prove all my doubters wrong.

As soon as Ray swung the truck up to the entrance of the club, I hopped out and took a deep breath in anticipation. The day after arriving in London, Dumebi, Big Iz, and I drove to Viva City where we were greeted by a bustling scene at the club head-quarters. We met with the Head of Operations, Head of Medical, Coach Sanchez, and the rest of the training staff. After finalizing my contract and signing on the dotted line, I was proudly handed my #8 jersey. Following a quick press conference and photoshoot, we headed to the state-of-the-art training facility for my medical exams.

The sound of Asake's "Lonely At The Top" blasted through the speakers as I walked into the facility. I exchanged fist bumps with some of the coaching staff and players on my way to the cafeteria. The scent of freshly brewed coffee and clanking of pot and pans filled the air as the kitchen staff made breakfast plates for some of the team members who had placed their orders. Players bustled about, moving between tables and food stations. The hum of conversation filtered through the room, punctuated by bursts of laughter and animated discussions.

My stomach growled as I entered the busy dining area. Wanting to start off on a healthy note, I asked for an omelet with vegetables and a side of fruit. As I scanned the room for an open seat, I spotted Xan. Making my way over to his table, I acknowledged him with a nod.

"Wassup man?" I greeted, taking a seat across from him.

"*How far?*" Xan responded with a warm smile.

My eyes bugged. "*I dey.* What did you do with the real Xan Mitchell?"

"Man, get outta here with that." He waved me off, chuckling.

When I first met him and found out he was Nigerian-American, I assumed he was familiar with the lingo, but I was so wrong. I'd spoken to him in Pidgin English, and he looked so confused.

"You got lessons from your girl?" I snickered.

According to my sister, Xan was dating the Nigerian R&B Afro gospel singer, Yuwa. We laughed again at my jab, before switching gears to discuss the objectives for the upcoming training session and adapting to life as new members of the team. Suddenly, a figure loomed over our table, interrupting our conversation.

I glanced up at Rio, ignoring the disdain on his face, and continued with my breakfast. Xan followed my lead and ignored the unwelcome visitor. Xan didn't get as much attitude as I got from this old dusty and his clique. Xan was replacing someone who was out. I, on the other hand, was regulating Rio to the backburner. But again, that was for him to take up with Coach and management.

Without making eye contact, I took another sip of my coffee and cut straight to the point. "McAllister, either say what you gotta say or keep it moving."

"Yeah, we like to keep it Zen before we go on the field and make magic." Xan held out his fist and I bumped mine against it.

"Don't unpack yet, newbie," Rio muttered under his breath as he walked away from our table.

Xan and I exchanged knowing looks, chuckled and then packed up our trash. He had dealt with this kind of treatment before, having told me about the racism he faced at his previous club that ultimately led him to join Viva City FC.

Leaving the cafeteria, we headed to the team meeting led by Coach Sanchez. The meeting was concise but focused, with Coach outlining the goals for the day's training session and stressing the importance of teamwork and dedication. As the meeting ended, we made our way to the training ground to start our warm-up drills.

The cool morning breeze filled my lungs as I jogged alongside my new teammates, the grass wet beneath my feet. Excitement for the training ahead fueled my energy as we progressed from warm-up exercises to more intense drills on the field. With Coach Sanchez monitoring closely, I focused on perfecting my passing accuracy, ball control, and defensive skills, as well as adapting to the team's playing style, determined to prove myself in this new environment. As the training session continued, a sense of camaraderie developed among us, despite the initial tensions. With each pass, sprint, and goal, I could feel myself getting comfortable in my spot on Viva City FC's roster.

Hours later, showered and dressed, I adjusted my backpack, and made a right turn down the hallway towards the training room. We had been informed earlier that there would only be one training session today because a partner from Viva Wellness Connect was giving a presentation.

As I entered the room through the double doors, I couldn't help but laugh at the idea of Big Iz possessing superhuman abilities, because we were about to meet with the same financial management firm he'd given me the brochure from. He was still bugging me about enrolling in financial literacy classes.

I gave Xan a fist bump as I passed by and took a seat next to Asher, another Nigerian on our team. We chatted for a bit until suddenly, the door flew open, breaking the calm atmosphere of our conversation.

It was *her*.

Specs.

Her golden-brown waves bounced as she rushed into the room, her heels clicking against the polished floor. She rushed through an apology for being three minutes late. To me, it didn't seem like a big deal, but it clearly bothered her. She was so absorbed in her iPad that she didn't even look up until she reached the podium.

"Good afternoon, everyone, my name is Yinka Martins." She smiled wide and her eyes scanned the room. "I am..." Her voice trailed off as her eyes met mine.

From across the room, our intense gaze sent a surge of electricity through my body. Time seemed to stand still as the rest of the world faded away. A small smile crept onto Yinka's lips, and in that moment, I knew that something extraordinary was about to happen.

Unfortunately, the timing couldn't have been worse.

four

Yinka

THE WORLD CANNOT BE *this small.*

With a quick yet graceful motion, I averted my gaze from his piercing eyes, as if breaking a spell that had briefly held me captive. I cleared my throat, exhaled, and tried again. My hands grabbed the clicker and the first slide of my presentation appeared on the projector screen. Luckily, the room was full. Surely one man, as handsome as he may be, wouldn't throw me off my game. I confidently approached the front of the classroom.

"My name is Yinka Martins. I'm a senior certified financial advisor for Apex Financial Management Consultants. As mentioned by Coach Sanchez earlier, I'm here to introduce the Elite Athlete Financial Mastery Program. Our goal is to provide you with the opportunity to develop strong financial literacy skills that'll not only benefit you during your athletic career, but also help you establish a solid foundation for your financial future after football."

"I don't see the point of this. We've got games to win, and we shouldn't be cooped up in a class for an hour learning about money. You do know we have people who handle that for us, right?"

I nodded as the sandy red-haired athlete whined about having to attend a class that would make him more knowledgeable about things "the people that handled his money" told him. I was aware that this program was new. Well, the format. Normally, for their Viva Wellness Connect week, the company that used to handle their financial wellness presentation only gave the basics and the players decided if they wanted to attend the financial classes or not. However, this new season brought about a new requirement for the players – they were now mandated to attend the presentation and classes.

My boss had explained that the players' union had accused Viva City FC of neglecting their players' financial well-being in favor of on-field performance. As they rightfully should, the union pointed out instances where young players, just out of the academy, were given massive amounts of money and then left to their own devices. It could be argued that these players were adults, but being only eighteen or nineteen years old and suddenly having such wealth thrust upon them, it was important to provide some level of support.

That thought process was something I agreed with. However, those with lots of money often resisted being told what to do, and famous athletes were no exception. The new direction was simply an annual box to be checked off for the club, and unfortunately, I was stuck with handling it. As a woman working in finance and now dealing with professional athletes, I knew I had to earn their respect and not back down from their brashness.

My eyes landed on the man from the bar whose name I still didn't know. His eyes were narrowed, arms crossed, and jaw was tightly clenched. He seemed to be challenging me, waiting to see how I would handle the situation. At the restaurant, I'd let him come to my rescue, but that wasn't going to happen again.

Turning towards the athlete who had asked the question, I continued, "Mr...."

I waited for him to introduce himself, but he just stared at me.

"Call me Alpha," he finally said with a wink.

"I won't be calling you that," I replied unamused, refusing to let him assert any dominance over me.

"Stop being a twit," the captain of the team, James Morrison, interrupted. I recognized him from Coach Sanchez's introduction earlier.

"Greer," the man scoffed.

"Well, Mr. Greer," I gave a small smile, trying to remain professional despite the tension in the room. "The statistics show that many professional athletes end their careers broke. Just because someone can handle your money for you doesn't mean you shouldn't at least have a basic understanding of what's going on with your finances. After all, as you said, you work hard to win games."

I could see him preparing his rebuttal, but I needed to move on with the meeting, so I raised my hand to stop him and continued speaking. However, my mistake was glancing at the man from the restaurant and catching his eye – there was a glint of approval in his gaze that caused a warmth to spread through my chest.

Why do I feel pleasure from his approval?

"Continuing on, for the next four weeks we'll cover a range of topics tailored specifically to your needs as professional athletes. This program was designed by Apex Financial in collaboration with Viva City FC organization to be practical and flexible according to your busy schedules. And of course, at the end we can discuss options for continuing to partner with Apex for your financial needs."

Greer scoffed, clearly unimpressed with my explanation. "I don't need some fancy program to tell me how to handle my money," he retorted, leaning back in his chair. "I've been doing just fine on my own."

I raised my eyebrows, maintaining a calm demeanor. "My job isn't to convince you to take this seriously." I stated, failing at camouflaging my annoyance. "My job is to teach a class, and report back on your attendance. I'd like your participation, but you can also come in and pout. But what you won't do is keep disrupting my class."

There was a collective gasp in the room as I made my position clear. Greer's face flushed with anger, and I could see his fists clenching by his sides.

"Listen lady, I—"

"Cut it out, Greer!"

My attention snapped to the man from the bar as he hollered from the back of the room. Greer sneered in his direction.

"It'll be in your best interest to be quiet for the rest of the class," the man growled.

"What you gonna do, Black?"

Black? Is that his name?

"Interrupt her again and find out," came Black's firm response.

Just then, Coach Sanchez entered the room and took a seat in the back. As expected, the energy in the room shifted with his presence. I could finally get back to the business of the day. I cleared my throat, grabbing the attention of the players who had been whispering among themselves. With a nod to Coach, I returned to my notes.

"Now, let's pick up where we left off," I said, scanning the faces of the players. "We were discussing the Elite Athlete Financial Mastery Program and its structure. As mentioned before, this program is designed to teach you important financial skills and will be tailored to your busy schedules, especially during away games." I took a breath, waiting for any questions or comments.

None were forthcoming so I continued, "We'll cover topics like budgeting, investment strategies, and understanding contracts. Each session will be interactive, with flexible timing to accommodate your training and travel commitments. I urge you all to actively participate and ask questions to make the most of this opportunity."

After giving a little more detail, I paused again. This time, some of the players did ask questions, which I did my best to answer while trying to ignore the effect two pairs of eyes had on me. One was from Greer, who probably wanted to put me in my place. The other was from Black. His intense gaze made my skin tingle. For the second time in his presence, I felt a magnetic pull toward him, a sensation that both excited and unnerved me. Throughout the entire class, he didn't participate in any way. He just sat there with his arms crossed over his chest and a stoic expression on his face.

As soon as the session ended, I handed over folders containing class information to the coach and quickly escaped to the bathroom for some privacy. After taking care of my business, I washed my hands and leaned against the sink, pulling out my phone. With a few clicks, I found myself on Viva City FC's website, scrolling through their starting lineup.

"Nonso Chijuka, midfielder, new transfer...hmm. Let me check out his IG..." I mumbled to myself as I found his profile and quickly scrolled through his grid. There wasn't much activity in the last several months, but he seemed to have started posting again around Christmas time. Someone with the username @sedi_j was a top commenter on all his posts. The comments didn't seem like typical fan or groupie comments; they seemed more like they had some sort of situationship going on because they didn't give off girlfriend vibes either.

I went to her page, and she was stunning. Short curly hair, petite...I was five feet six inches, and she looked shorter than me. At first glance, I only saw three pictures of him on her page, but they seemed pretty cozy. I couldn't tell what she did for a living, but she had a fantastic sense of style.

The bathroom door creaked open, and I quickly shoved my phone back into my bag. After washing my hands again, I left. I didn't know this man, yet he already had me playing detective in a public restroom.

As I made my way to the parking lot, my steps slowed when I saw Nonso leaning against my car. His tall, muscular frame was clad in a fitting navy-blue tracksuit. He stood with his legs crossed at the ankles and arms over his chest, exuding an air of cocky confidence. He was so handsome, but had the nerve to look as though I was wasting his time.

"Errr, hi, do you need something? How did you know this was my car?" I asked.

That was a silly question because he could've easily asked the receptionist at the front desk. My nerves were getting the best of me, and it annoyed me. I pulled my coat tighter around me, feeling the chill in the air.

He smirked. "Specs, you did your thing today, and looked good doing it too."

"It's Ms. Martins," I corrected.

"I won't be calling you that," he mimicked my words from earlier. "What I look like addressing my woman by her formal title?"

"Your woman?" I raised my eyebrows.

He placed his hand over his heart. "I'm hurt. You tryin' to dump me, already. It ain't even been a week yet."

A light chuckle escaped my lips. "What do you want from me, Black? Another thank you?"

"Nah, *you* won't be calling *me* that either. The name is Nonso. But as my woman, you can call me babe, bae, or anything sexy that comes to mind."

"Oh, so it's okay for you to call me Specs, but I have to use your name?" I questioned.

He nodded. "You're beginning to understand the dynamics of this relationship."

I giggled. *Gosh, I'm a mess.* I couldn't believe this was happening. "I'll keep that in mind. Can I go now? It's freezing out here."

"Yeah, you right, my bad. I don't want my baby falling sick," he said, stepping aside and opening the car door I'd unlocked. "I mean, who else is going to teach me how to handle my money?"

"How considerate of you." I got into the car and started the engine, anticipating the heat that would soon come. I tried to close the door, but he stepped closer.

"Mr. Considerate, that's me," he joked. "I am a little worried about what kind of woman you gonna be to me, though."

I inclined my head to meet his eyes. "What? I don't meet your standards?" The offense in my tone was undeniable. Why I cared about what he thought was a mystery I'd have to solve later.

"Shoot, I'ono." He shrugged. "You're in the car, enjoying the warmth while your man is freezing out here. I risked my life for you."

"Risked your life?" I quipped. "Don't athletes take ice baths? You should be used to the cold."

"Not when I'm trying to chill with my woman."

"I'm guessing that my rouse is gonna cost me more than just a thank you."

"It's only fair. Your ex...oh if he ain't really your ex yet, he is now. Tell him I say he's done for good. But back to the matter at hand, your ex coulda sent assassins after me."

"Don't tell me you're afraid of some assassins?"

"I'll fight Jackie Chan for you, baby. But I need to know it's worth it."

"What will make it worth it?" I couldn't believe I was playing along with him. My phone buzzed, reminding me that I had fifteen minutes before my meeting with Green Guardians. There was no way I was going to make it now.

"Sharing a meal with me and showing me the city. I'm kinda new here."

"Are you for real?"

"Yep!"

"How do you know I'm not new here too?"

"You have a point. But underneath your American accent, you got some underlying British thing going on, so I'm guessing you've been in the UK for a while."

I didn't want to acknowledge or deny his analysis, so instead I reverted to his initial ask. "So, you're serious?"

"As a heart attack, Specs. I should warn you though...your

man can be very clingy. If you don't answer the phone when I reach out, I might just pop up because I miss my baby."

Father God, one wrong decision and I'm stuck with this man. Why did I let Cassie get in my head? I could have just ignored Brandon as I'd been doing.

"You'll miss me?"

"For sure. No doubt."

"What would Lesedi say?"

I studied his eyes, and they gave nothing away, just like in class. He had a talent for changing moods or shutting down in an instant.

"I see you've been checking up on me," he finally said.

I couldn't admit to stalking his and Lesedi's Instagram pages, so I just shrugged. "People talk..." I let my words trail off, allowing him to interpret them however he wanted.

"You're listening to the wrong people. If you want to know something, just ask me. My woman deserves the truth."

"So, what's the truth?"

He shook his head and rubbed his stomach. "Wrong time. See I'm starving and when I'm hungry, I forget things. I don't wanna mistakenly not give you all the details."

I rolled my eyes, then my phone's reminder buzzed again, bringing me back to reality and reminding me that whatever was going on here was a terrible idea. Nonso took my phone from my hand and dialed his number.

"What are you doing? I'm your teacher. You shouldn't have my personal number. If you need anything, you can send me an email. My address is in the packet."

Nonso stared at me and burst into full laughter. "You were my woman before you became my teacher." He handed the phone back to me and closed my car door. "I'mma let you go handle your business. But remember, you owe me a meal."

"Nonso, I..."

I called after him, but he was already walking towards his truck that had pulled up next to my car.

"Drive safe, Specs. Answer your phone when I call." He winked at me as he climbed into his truck. "Don't make me come look for you."

The driver honked at me, signaling for me to move ahead of them. As I drove away, all I could think about was how to get myself out of this mess.

~

I POURED MY HOMEMADE VINAIGRETTE OVER THE freshly chopped greens while the soft melody of "Prayed For" by Ash B filled the dimly lit living room. My favorite candle, a blend of warm vanilla and calming lavender, flickered on the coffee table. Sitting on my cozy sofa, mindlessly flipping through channels, thoughts of Nonso consumed my mind. Cassie was unavailable when I called earlier, so now I was trying to distract myself with mindless television until she could call me back.

But even watching my go-to comfort program, *Vanishing Shadows,* on KevStel TV wasn't enough to ease my restless thoughts tonight. Suddenly an advertisement for Solaris, the sponsor for Viva City FC, interrupted the broadcast. Though I had seen it countless times before, now that I had met Nonso, it caught my attention. His face floated back into my mind, replaying our earlier interactions.

His easy smile, warm yet intense eyes gave off an energy I couldn't quite shake. The ease with which he switched from being light-hearted to serious seemed so potent. Rugged in his own way, he had a unique charm that was hard to resist. His movements were graceful and smooth, with an underlying strength that was both captivating and alluring. Whether it was the way he leaned in when he wanted to get his point across or the way he'd rub his palms together and lick his lips when he was getting ready to say something outrageous, I was caught in his web.

In our brief time together, I sensed that beneath his confident exterior lay a hint of vulnerability, which intrigued me, igniting a curiosity that had me going along with his plot of an actual relationship between us. I never thought I'd be one of those girlies, but his assertiveness was sexy. It bordered on "telling me what it was gonna be" and "he'd give me whatever I wanted." In the restaurant, he stepped in to help me with no questions asked, but in the Viva City FC parking lot, he was laying down the law for our imaginary relationship.

Brandon was kinda similar in that way, but he would never have praised me after class. He would've given me a list of things I could improve on, as was expected from his girlfriend. I couldn't help but laugh at myself for comparing Nonso to Brandon. It didn't make sense, and yet I couldn't stop myself. But for tonight, I was going to enjoy this fantasy. Tomorrow, my sensible self would return.

My thoughts were interrupted by a notification on my phone, taking my attention away from the TV screen. It was a message from Nonso. I knew because I had programmed his contact as "Danger" in my phone. My heart skipped a beat as I opened the message, unsure of what to expect.

> Danger: Missing me yet?

I chuckled, amazed at how easily this man had taken over my mind. Before I could reply, my phone started ringing, with Cassie's name flashing on the screen. Setting down my empty plate on the side table, I answered the call.

"Hey girl, sorry I missed your call earlier. 911? Wassup?"

Relieved to have someone to talk to about everything swirling in my mind, I blurted out, "You won't believe what happened..."

Over the next several minutes I endured Cassie's "look at God" to her "say you lyin'" to her "well dang" to her "that part" as I ran down the events of earlier. When she laughed at him demanding I answer his call, I was officially done and irritated with her commentary.

"Cass, are you serious right now? I'm laying out my pain for you," I said.

"Girl, bye. Which pain?" she teased. "I can't believe the rando from the bar was Nonso 'Black' Chijuka. Question is how didn't you know that."

I asked myself the same question. I wasn't one of those girls that didn't follow sports. Football was my jam, but I mainly watched the English Premier League and a few teams in La Liga, the Spanish Football League.

"You're not helping here." I sighed.

"I'm not trying to help right now. I seriously want to know how you missed that. You famous for screaming at the television when a football game is on."

"Yeah, real competitive football, not the MLS," I said referring to Major League Soccer in America.

"Oops the shade. You see how God don't like ugly—"

I shrugged. "It's not shade, it's facts. I know you're a season ticket holder for Atlanta Allied, but let's be real."

Another thing Cassie and I bonded over was our love for sports. She was of Nigerian and Zimbabwean descent, but unlike me that frequented the continent, she hadn't been back since she was ten years old. However, with a father and five brothers, she knew football well. We'd even attended some Atlanta Allied games together, and while the MLS wasn't as popular as European football yet, it was gaining momentum. American sports fans were already busy enough with American football, basketball, and baseball; there wasn't much room left for anything else. But in other parts of the world, football was king. In the UK, it was almost like a religion. However, despite all of this, I had never heard of or seen Nonso before Fusion Haven.

"I agree, they aren't English football level, but my boys are trying," she conceded.

"You see, the truth will set you free."

"As it will you. So, are you going to admit you like him?"

"I have to know him to like him. Is he interesting? Yes, but—"

"Don't let your man hear you say that." She laughed at her lame joke.

"He's not my man. I was desperate, but it was all for nothing because Brandon keeps calling me."

"That's a 'he' problem because if you don't know, let me give you a rundown of your new man. Brandon might wanna let this one go."

I listened as Cassie gave me a rundown of Nonso's background. Some of it was from the blogs while some of it was from interviews he had given over the years. I knew about him being Nigerian American, but his family dynamic was interesting. I wasn't so surprised to find out he was in and out of juvie in his teens. It wasn't my aim to stereotype him, but whether we admitted it or not, we all harbor an initial bias towards others. The gag was not to stay in that bias and be open to being educated. The way Nonso spoke and his mannerisms already told me he knew something about the streets or a less-than-straight path.

I was, however, totally blown away when I learned that he was also recently coming off a FIFA ban for betting. I couldn't hide my disapproval at that one. While I understood making mistakes as a youth – in fact, one unfortunate mistake I made as a youth still haunted me – but knowingly, as an adult, engaging in an illegal activity prohibited by your job was insane to me.

People could say whatever, but I knew my limits and what I could and couldn't handle, even in hypothetical situations. Someone with a gambling addiction like Nonso...that was a definite deal-breaker for me.

"He's not that important anyways, so there won't be any problems," I lied to myself, trying to convince myself that the man in question wasn't worth worrying about.

Cassie laughed. "Okay is that what we're doing? If that man made you miss your beloved Green Guardians, he's more important that you realize."

Green Guardians was an environmental conservation volunteer group I was a part of. Conservation and sustainability were things I was passionate about. Cassie was right; since I joined, it was etched into my calendar, and I never missed a meeting.

"He's not..."

"Yeah, I know. He's not even on your man wish list." I could hear the smirk in Cassie's voice.

I glanced over at the coffee table. My book of accountability was open to the "Man Wish" list page. Before Cassie called, I had tried reminding myself of the list and the fact that Nonso checked none of the boxes.

She rattled off entries on my list. "He's an athlete, younger than you, by a few months by the way, he's Nigerian, with a questionable past, makes you feel..." she continued running down my list.

I didn't have anything against Nigerian men. I was a Nigerian and they could love you down, provide and take care of business. But also watching my mom and Bims sometimes play mental warfare games with my dad and brother was exhausting. I could play those games but didn't want to. I wasn't as naïve to think that only Nigerian men were guilty of such behavior because I had dated a Jamaican man also. The fact I still had my mind was the Lord's doing. Be that as it may, I was still going to end up with a Black man.

"I hate when you do that and stop acting like you know me." I sucked my teeth.

"Do what? Say out loud how ridiculous that list is or make you see that someone has come along who doesn't fit it but still makes your heart race and your skin tingle."

"It could just be lust and not lead to anything real. Plus, he has bigger problems to worry about like performing on the field. And let's not forget he already has a girlfriend...or some sort of situation, I don't know. It was just one momentary slip-up and I wanted to share it with you, but it's over now."

"You really were a bathroom detective, huh?" Cassie chuckled. "Well, one thing about your man is that he's not a player. He doesn't sleep around. If he did, the blogs would've reported it. Lesedi has been with him since senior year high school, but they fell out. Girl don't ask me why. But, one day she was flaunting an engagement ring, the next day he deleted all her pictures from his IG, two months later the ring was gone, and the subtweets began."

Cassie laughed. "Girl, she even had Celine Dion's 'Think Twice' playing on her stories for one month straight."

The phone dropped from my hand as I fell over in laughter. I dared not laugh at another woman's pain, but my girl was a whole fool. How she had time to keep up with all the celeb goings on was beyond me.

"There's a special place reserved for you in—"

"Heaven? Yeah, I know," she said.

I had enough of talking about Nonso for the night so I changed the subject to Cassie's upcoming birthday party and the fact that my parents would be visiting London soon. During our conversation, I received another text from Nonso reminding me that he was clingy. After making plans for Cassie's intimate gathering, we ended our call with her advising me to live in the moment.

People always say that. Live in the moment. But moments often became long durations of time filled with distractions, and that was why I needed to stick to my plans.

penalty

High stakes play that represents a major conflict resolution and can shift the balance of the game.

five
Nonso

AS WE FILED into the locker room, the acrid smell of sweat and adrenaline hit me. The tension was thick, our coach's jaw tightly clenched as he addressed us with disappointment in his voice. I sat there, my jersey soaked through with sweat, clinging to my knee. My hands shook as I wiped the sweat off my face with a towel, trying to steady my breathing after the intense match.

My first game of the season was two weeks ago – a home game against Southport FC at our stadium, Northside Park. Thanks to my press runs, interviews, and social media posts hyping up Viva City Panthers, I received a warm welcome on the field. All the anxiety from the last year leading up to that moment melted away as I stepped onto the field in the professional capacity that fueled my soul. We ended up winning that game 2-0, but tension between McAllister and I grew. As Coach said when we went over the play, he increased my playing time and decreased McAllister's, which again, had nothing to do with me. My stats spoke for themselves. But he and his fans weren't happy about it.

As our games continued, McAllister's hostility towards me grew. Though, we managed to win by slim margins, until this moment. We'd just played Duke's Park Rangers here at their home, which was less than four miles from ours, and it ended in a disappointing 2-2 draw. That for me was a loss. On top of that, a horrible tackle by a DPR player resulted in our highest scoring striker Asher being injured. He was looking at weeks of recovery.

The first thing I was told when I joined the Panthers was that Duke's Park Rangers or DPR were the enemy. The rivalry went back decades and was so deep, the supporters called each other names. We were the Pantaloons and they were the Derangers. I was a team player, so I cared about the historic rivalry, but my main issue was that we would suffer in the ratings tables and if we didn't win our upcoming matches, we would be in trouble.

On top of that, Greer was giving me a hard time because I checked him about the way he came at Yinka. Xan joked that I came out swinging, but that wasn't my intention. I simply wanted to win; making friends was not my priority. My problem wasn't with Greer or McAllister; they could stay angry all they wanted. My issue was with ratings. For us to succeed as a team, all these middle school issues needed to be left in the locker room when it was time to play ball.

From the look on Coach's face, it seemed even he had reached his breaking point. "You hear that? The silence? That's the sound of shame that you lot have to carry tonight," his tone was serious and angry. "What happened out there tonight was freaking unacceptable. For goodness' bloody sake! We had a game plan but failed to execute it properly."

He paused, letting his words sink in before continuing. "Our passing was sloppy, our off-ball movement was non-existent, and our decision-making was subpar. We allowed them to dominate the midfield, and that's where we lost control of the game. Chijuka, McAllister, you two need to work together more effectively in the midfield. Chijuka, you need to track back and support defensively. McAllister, you need to provide better offensive support. We can't afford to have a gap in the midfield like we did today."

His gaze swept around the room, making eye contact with each player before landing on me. I would have been offended but I knew part of the reason I was hired was to fill the gaps McAllister left and this rivalry was making that impossible.

"We are a team, and we must play like one! Especially now that we don't have Asher. That means supporting each other, communicating on the field, and working together to execute our game plan. If we had done that today, the outcome would have been different. Chijuka and McAllister, any more problems and I'll freaking bench you myself. Now hit the showers and I'll see you in two days."

The weight of Coach's disappointment hung heavy in the air as he left the locker room. I slammed my locker door and slung my duffle bag over my shoulder.

"Black, you know that wasn't your fault, right?" Xan came up to me.

I nodded since I was in no mood to talk. We fist-bumped and he gave me a pat on the back before rushing off to catch a flight to Wales. His girlfriend was headlining a performance at a church convention concert in Cardiff.

After taking a shower several minutes later, I left the facility and headed towards my car. The feeling of defeat still lingered within me, especially since it was such an unnecessary loss. I had finally gotten used to driving short distances, which meant Ray was off the hook unless I needed to make a longer trip. All I wanted to do now was grab a bite to eat and get in bed.

I was still in that hotel suite, which I had grown to despise after being in it for the last three weeks and some change. I still hadn't found anything I liked. It dawned on me that every house I'd bought in the past, I had input from my sister and Lesedi. Dums was unavailable, and I didn't want to complicate things any further with Lesedi.

I hadn't thought of Les until Yinka brought her up. I used to feel rage when I thought about the way we turned out, but now I felt nothing at all. We had too much history for me to ever wish her bad, but despite what the blogs said about a looming fairy tale between us, my love for her had faded and I was no longer under her spell.

Yinka, on the other hand, was constantly invading my thoughts during my rare moments of free time. After all this time away, I needed to lay eyes on her. Following her first presentation, we had our first real class via Zoom but that wasn't enough. I had the next two days off and I planned to add helping me find an apartment to the list of things she had to do to prove she was worth me laying my life on the line.

I grinned because I enjoyed teasing her. The way she bit her lip and furrowed her brow had a sexy naiveté to it, which fueled my desire for her. She was a Black woman, and a Nigerian at that, so I knew she could see past my jokes and vibes, but I could also tell that I had her rattled.

As I navigated down the busy road, I was about to tell Siri to call *Specs* when Ms. Ellis's name popped up on my phone screen along with "UK Agent." Business came before pleasure, so I answered the call.

"Tell me something good, Sharon," I pleaded. "I need to get out of this hotel," I added with a hint of frustration in my voice.

After having multiple meetings with her where we discussed my vision for my future, we'd developed a friendly relationship. As Big Iz predicted, the Black British woman was all about business and didn't have time for any games. During the first week when I couldn't play due to work permit issues, Sharon had set up an interview with ESPN and other major international media outlets. She had only allowed them to ask one question about my scandal before moving on to the topic at hand.

My return to football.

She chuckled in response. "I've been trying to get you out of there."

"By sending me those mediocre apartments? Come on now, Ms. Ellis, use your magic powers."

"Did you see the email I sent earlier today with new listings?"

"I haven't had a chance to open it yet, but they better be good."

Ignoring my playful threat, she continued, "It's in a prime location with luxury apartments and great amenities. I think it could be the perfect fit for you."

"Bet." I agreed, nodding as I maneuvered through chaotic traffic. "I'll take a look at it once I get settled."

"Now onto potential endorsements," Sharon shifted gears. "There are a few companies interested, a sportswear brand looking for a spokesperson, a fitness app seeking a brand ambassador, an energy drink, and a charity organization focused on addiction rehabilitation that wants your involvement."

"Everything sounds great, except for that last one."

"Nonso, whether you like it or not, you overcame something that many people struggle with – addiction. Whether it's drugs or alcohol or gambling, addiction is very hard to overcome. And you did. You have the opportunity to pay it forward and help others."

She was right and I knew I had a responsibility. It wasn't that I didn't want to help people, but a part of me wanted to forget that dark chapter of my life.

"I got you. Send the information to my email and I'll review them to see which ones align with my values and goals. Then we can discuss my options."

"Good, and I have your updated schedule, so we need to plan your community outreach initiatives," Sharon said, shifting gears again. "Viva City needs to get to know you better. We can choose between hosting youth football clinics or doing meet-and-greets with fans. It's important for the community and at the same time, you get to show your positive impact both on and off the field."

"Sounds good," I replied. This was what I meant when I said she handled business. "Let's make it happen."

"Great," Sharon affirmed. "I'll send you more details about each opportunity so we can start planning. And don't forget to check out those apartment listings and let me know what you think as soon as possible."

"Will do."

I ended the call with my spirits lifted a little. However, that feeling was quickly crushed when I saw my mother's name flashing on my screen. It had been weeks since we last spoke. Dumebi and Jason had been in our group chat trying to give me advice that clearly hadn't worked in years. They insisted that I communicate my feelings and concerns to our mother. The first time I did it and she shut me down, it was a wrap. I let it be. It was funny how just because they didn't experience my pain and disappointment from our mother, whatever my issue was, wasn't that big of a deal.

"*Ogogwu* Ma," I greeted her in our native tongue.

I wondered which version of her I was going to get. The master of guilt tripping and gaslighting, or the one who owned her mistakes. The one I knew before our family was torn apart and Carl Thompson came into it. I'd take a bullet for Jason; I loved him that much. But his father, my stepdad...it was still tricky if I'd give him water if he was in a desert.

"*Ndo nwa m.* Chukwunonso, so I have to beg you to call me? Remember I'm the only mother you have."

I let out a heavy sigh. I couldn't handle tussling with her right now, so I quickly apologized so we could move on.

"Mummy, I've been busy."

"I know. We've been keeping up with your games," she replied. "Your stepfather even watches with me. We're all so proud of you."

I wanted to scoff at her words, but this woman was still the most important person in my life. Despite our strained relationship, I loved her deeply. It pained me that she allowed her new husband to emotionally abuse me while ignoring the pain caused by my father. Pain he inflicted because she took us away from him.

When I got older, I saw the pictures and text messages my mother used to prevent my father from entering the United States. The pictures showed signs of her physical abuse and the texts messages documented his verbal abuse dating back to when she was in Nigeria. I couldn't blame her for wanting a better life with Carl, but she never acknowledged how it affected me and Dumebi. She just moved on with her life.

It wasn't until last year when I was caught up in the betting scandal and the only people I worried about how it would affect were my brother and sister, that I realized how much our relationship needed repairing. My parents may have made a big show of their disappointment and subsequent concern, but I wasn't the least bit bothered about how it looked for them. Only apologizing to Dumebi and Jason for any pain I caused them occupied my mind.

"Thank you, Ma. How is work? Is everything okay? Do you need anything?"

"Don't worry about me, Chukwunonso. I'm fine. I'm more concerned about you. I may have failed you in the past, but I want things to be better now."

It was clear my mum felt guilty about our relationship. Her use of "I may have" was as close to an apology as I would ever get from her. African parents often acknowledged without actually acknowledging their mistakes or your hurt. We both had our truths, and like most Africans, we swept our trauma under the rug and continued on as if nothing happened.

Ignoring that latter part of her statement, I said, "Okay good."

"Your stepfather has his annual check-up tomorrow. It would be nice if you called him and checked on how he's doing."

And just like that, we were back to square one. "Mummy, that's not happening. But I'll reach out to Jace so he can update me since he'll be there."

My stepfather had a cancer scare three years ago, but thankfully it was caught early, and he recovered. However, his annual check-ups still made my mother anxious.

"Nonso, you need to learn to forgive. Your name means 'God is near', but how close can He be if you're still holding a grudge?"

"Mummy, it's been a long day for me. You watch my games, so you know we didn't do good today. This is—"

"There's no excuse for his behavior, but I tried my best to make you two get along. He was trying to discipline you out of love."

"Putting me down every chance he got was not love. Constantly hammering it into my head that I'd become an abuser like my father was not love. How a grown man couldn't understand that a six-year-old boy who had been raised solely by his father for three years since his mother left would be traumatized and would start acting out when suddenly cut off from him was beyond me. He showed me no grace. Instead of helping me, he was angry that I didn't call him daddy. What kind of man measures testosterone levels with a child?

"I complained to you and cried about it, but you always took his side. No, Mummy, I'm not calling him. I've forgiven him, but I can't forget what happened or subject myself to his backhanded compliments. I attend family events and dinners out of respect for you and Jace, but please stop pushing some kind of relationship and let me be!"

I had parked in the underground car park of the hotel in a secluded spot. When I had a bad game, I usually kept to myself and didn't talk much. But this time, I answered my mother's call because of my siblings and her many texts. Looking back, it probably wasn't the best time to have this conversation with her. Now she had me venting about some childhood trauma like a helpless child because she always wanted to defend her loser husband.

There was an awkward silence before my mother sighed. "Okay, my son. Get something to eat and get some rest."

"I already ordered room service. My food should be here soon."

"You need a good girl for a wife, so you don't have to worry about ordering your own food."

I chuckled because my mother couldn't help herself. Now she'd shifted into wanting me to get married. With her track record of partners, she shouldn't be meddling in anyone's relationship, or lack thereof. But that was a conversation for another day.

> Popsie: How are you, my son? I still haven't received the money you promised. Your sisters need to pay for a school trip, and I don't have the funds.

I sighed as I read the text on my phone screen. It seemed like everyone was reaching out to me today. At the news of my ban, my father was livid. I couldn't tell if it was because he was worried about me or his financial supply. We'd talked a few times since I've been in Viva City and the last time, he informed me about the twins' trip.

I wrapped up my call with my mother after she prayed for me and reminded me not to wait for her to reach out before I did. I got out of the car and headed inside without responding to my dad's message. He was a whole other thorn I had to live with.

When I turned fifteen, he got over his hurt feelings and started reaching out more. Silly me, I thought he wanted a real relationship, but he was only trying to convince me to return to Nigeria after high school.

"You are my first and only son. You belong here, with your father," he'd often bellow.

With my mother's permission, Big Iz already had me traveling and playing football with youth academies. When the time came for me to decide about returning to Nigeria, I declined. He stopped talking to me again, but this time I didn't care as much. We maintained our distance until he got injured at work and couldn't afford medical bills or to feed his new family. By then, I had signed my first professional contract, and he reached out for financial assistance. Ever since then, I've been responsible for taking care of his daughter's needs – school fees, clothes, hair, and anything else that involved raising children. They were my sisters, but I didn't bring them into this world.

I had a meeting with my accountant in the morning. I had previously pushed it back, but listening to Yinka's words about smart spending habits and financial stability made me reconsider. I was exhausted from constantly bearing the burden of everyone depending on me. And if they were going to rely on me, I needed to be fully aware of my financial situation. I could no longer mindlessly sign blank checks without consideration of consequences.

~

HOURS LATER, AFTER DINNER AND A SECOND SHOWER, I settled into bed with my laptop. Propped up against the headboard, I scrolled through the listings for potential new apartments in London. There were three I liked, but I was hesitant to trust the fancy descriptions provided by the realtor. I needed a local to tell me the real about these neighborhoods.

I wasn't sure if I would make London my permanent home at the expiration of my contract, but I did know that I was ready to retire from the sport in five years. Unlike other athletes who had to be "carried off the field" due to injuries and could barely function without meds after football, I wanted to leave on my own terms.

Cheta had put me on to a retired footballer called Kamal Danjuma. He was kind of a legend among African sports players and had dominated clubs in Europe before moving to America to play for some years. He'd come back to the UK to play for Turk West when an injury caused him to retire. Despite his reputation as a former bad boy with a sharp tongue, Kamal was doing great things with his Beyond the Sports initiative and Kam Care foundation.

I watched some of his talks on YouTube where he reminded me that there was life beyond football and encouraged athletes not to give up. He was slated to be in London soon and if my schedule allowed, I would be attending his seminar.

During my trying times, everything felt dark and confusing. But Cheta refused to let me wallow in self-pity. He constantly pushed me to get out of the house and out of my own head. He encouraged me with stories from his own life - the challenges and triumphs. He often said when his wife, Reign, came into his life, he hit the jackpot. She was an amazing woman, and I prayed that one day I would find someone I could make that kind of connection with.

My failed relationship with Lesedi didn't make me resentful towards love. If anything, it showed me how much external pressure can harm a relationship. Even though her family had been against us from the start, throughout college we fought for our love and weathered the storm together. But eventually the pressure became too much for us and our relationship turned rocky.

Several months before my scandal broke, we had a conversation. I asked her if with me was where she wanted to be. I told her I loved her, but I wasn't ready to get married. She said she was down, so imagine my surprise when the blogs broke the news that she was engaged. At the time, she'd been in her home country, South Africa, for her sister's wedding. Her fiancé was a South African businessman from her hometown.

Two days later, she showed up at my door, frantic, trying to explain with another man's ring on her finger. She claimed the engagement had been prearranged by her parents without her knowledge. I was livid, but couldn't do nothing but laugh in her face and set her free. Weeks went by, and she broke off her engagement and wanted to rekindle our romance. I couldn't go back after that betrayal and knew it was time to move on.

Yet we remained entangled in a complicated situation, driven by comfort and physical needs. If Les called, I was there and if she sensed I needed her, she would come. My sister, who despised Lesedi for the way she had treated me, hated the cycle. Dums believed Lesedi showed me what she was capable of if her family pushed hard enough. It was tough for me to let go of the solace she provided until I started therapy and realized how toxic our relationship truly was. Choosing to move to London was the final nail in the coffin of our complicated situation.

> Specs: My regular business hours are 8-5, M-F, Sir.

After dealing with the weight of the day's loss, my conversation with my mom, and my dad's message, I texted Yinka once I got back to my room. I wasn't expecting her to respond to my silly question, but I made a mental note to pop up at her office tomorrow if she didn't. Before I left town, I let it slide when she left me on read. I was focused on playing ball and getting my life together. But now that I had some free time, I wanted to see her, and she was going to speed up that process if she didn't respond to my text.

> So, are you saying I can, or I can't buy a different Rolex for each day of the week because "My regular business hours are 8-5, M-F, Sir."

> Specs: I'm sure you already know the answer to that question.

> When are you taking me out to eat?

> Specs: Are we back to this again?

> We never left. Answer the question, baby.

> Specs: I don't know.

> It's like you're not even grateful I put my life on the line.

> Specs: I said thank you.

> Man, pls. A simple thank you ain't worth my life. According to my mom, with me, she was in labor for fourteen hours. Do better, Specs.

Specs: What if I can't?

> You're smart, so you can. You just don't wanna try and it's hurting my feelings.

Yinka responded with a few eye-rolling emojis and one laughing emoji. I couldn't help but smile as I glanced at the clock on my laptop screen. It was already 10:30 PM. Based on her frequent mentions of time and scheduling, the few times I'd heard her speak, she seemed like someone who was bound by it. This must be pretty late for her.

> Why aren't you sleeping?

Specs: I can't.

> Why? You thinking about me? You know all you have to do is say the word and I'll be there.

Specs: You wish, but no. I hv a big client meeting tomorrow that I'm trying to prepare for.

> Tell you what… where are you right now?

Specs: In my house, why?

> Pick up the phone, I'm about to FaceTime you.

She seemed hesitant, probably trying to decide if she should answer or not. I hung up and gave her some time to think it over. I wondered if she would be bold enough. Five minutes later, she answered my Facetime call, and I got my answer. I was momentarily stunned by her beauty.

Yinka's face was void of makeup and her freckles took center stage. Her wild curls were twisted into two braids that fell on each side of her head, framing her face perfectly. She was wearing a grey sweatshirt that hung off one shoulder, revealing blemish free skin, and black leggings that hugged her curves. A comfortable yet alluring outfit.

This was my Specs. She was totally different from Ms. Martins who I had only seen in fitted pant suits. I couldn't help but stare as she stood by the stove, making some kind of warm beverage. From my angle, I could tell that whatever screen I was on was propped against something on her island.

"Hello, Nonso," she said, breaking me out of my trance. "I know you didn't call just to stare at me."

I grinned sheepishly, trying to come up with a clever response. "You take my breath away, baby."

She raised an eyebrow, clearly not impressed. "Does that line work?"

I chuckled. "You tell me. It's been a while."

Her expression softened as she turned off the stove and poured hot water into her mug. "Yeah, the long-time girlfriend. Tell me about that."

I smirked at her trying to throw me off track. "I told you, I can only remember details of that situation when you feed me. So, for now, I want to know why Ms. Martins is so nervous about some client that she's keeping my Specs awake."

Yinka rolled her eyes at me, but I wasn't going to let myself get sucked into talking about Lesedi tonight. I'd had enough emotionally draining conversations for one day.

Yinka's expression shifted, her brows furrowing as she carefully considered her words before finally admitting, "It's this big client I've been working with. They're considering signing on with my agency since they have a major investment in the works and if I can close this deal, it could be a game-changer for my career. There's so much at stake, and I want everything to go perfectly."

I nodded in understanding, knowing the pressure she must be under. "You're worried about making a good impression and securing the deal," I said. "But that's the wrong thing to be focused on. Your focus should be on what you *can* control. You've put in the work and you gotta believe in it. You're more than capable. Just trust yourself and your expertise. I'm sure you've handled tough clients before and came out on top. This is no different. You've got this."

"I know that in my head but still..."

"Okay practice your pitch on me."

"What?"

"I'm assuming this client has a lot of money and they don't like being told they need to manage it—"

"Like you..."

"Exactly, so who better to practice on?"

Yinka smiled and then carried the screen I was on and her mug towards her living room. She propped up the screen and picked up her laptop, placing it on her lap. She gave me a brief overview of her client and spent the next several minutes practicing her pitch on me.

I interrupted her, asked questions, and even argued with her. All things that would likely happen with her real client. She initially seemed irritated by my approach until she realized what I was doing. As she worked through her pitch with me, the tension in her shoulders eased and a grin spread across her face when she realized she had mastered it.

"Thank you very much," she said.

I simply nodded in response.

Yinka's lips lifted at the corners, a sly expression crossing her face. "You must be proud of yourself."

"I'd rather you be proud of me."

"Well, if that's the case, you need to be more proactive in intercepting passes and setting up plays. Your ball control and passing are great, but tonight you missed opportunities where a more precise pass could have led to scoring chances." Yinka paused, her expression softening. "I mean, I saw the tension between you and Rio. But—"

"You watched my game, Specs?" I teased, my heart swelling with pride.

A playful indifference spread across her face. "I watched *a* game. Was that yours?" She lifted her shoulders in a shrug.

"Ah, you trying to be funny." I chuckled. "But you've never looked or sounded sexier to me than you do in this moment."

As the night went on, Yinka and I continued our conversation. We talked a little more about football. Then we shifted gears and she shared about her family, and I did the same. We didn't delve too deeply into details, but it was clear that we came from opposite backgrounds. Being a last-born child in a Nigerian household was vastly different from being a first-born child.

I was also right about the fact that she was an organized planner. I was more spontaneous and adventurous. She preferred predictable and healthy foods, while I enjoyed experimenting with my palette and trying new things, especially during the off-season. I could see where she was coming from when it came to money, but I still believed in treating yourself occasionally. My problem wasn't my own spending habits, it was picking up the tab for everyone else's needs, wants and extravagant purchases.

Eventually, Yinka closed her laptop and settled onto her couch with a blanket. When she yawned, I checked the time and realized it was almost one a.m. Knowing she had to be at work at eight a.m., I gently suggested she get some sleep. The way she whined when I suggested that, was a clear indicator that Ms. Martins was gone, and Specs was in charge. The other one would never admit that they enjoyed my company. We ended our call after I got her to agree to view some apartments with me. I stared at my phone for a few seconds then sent her a text.

> I expect nothing less than a winning goal tomorrow. Sweet dreams.

> Specs: Yes, Coach. Good night.

I couldn't help but grin at her playful nickname for me before heading to the bathroom to brush my teeth and finally call it a night. Despite having a busy day ahead of me in the morning, the company and conversation with Yinka made it all worth it.

six
Yinka

MID MONDAY MORNING, the following day, I quickly made my way back to my office, still feeling energized from the successful meeting. As I turned a corner, a messenger intercepted me in the hallway.

"Ms. Martins, there's a delivery for you. It's waiting on your desk."

I thanked him and hurried into my office, eager to see what awaited me. My eyes widened as I took in the beautiful bouquet of flowers sitting on my desk. Their vibrant colors and sweet scents filled the room. Next to them sat a small package, carefully wrapped with a ribbon. My heart raced with excitement as I untied the ribbon and opened the package, revealing a gorgeous leather-bound journal adorned with intricate designs. As I ran my fingers over the smooth pages and admired the quality of the leather binding and delicate embossing, a slip of paper fell out. Unfolding it, I read a handwritten note:

> Specs, for your thoughts, ideas, and dreams...out-side of the plan.
> Book of Possibilities - Coach

Reading Nonso's words caused a warmth to spread through my chest as a grin stretched across my face. The gift was thoughtful and so unexpected, forcing me to blink away tears that threatened to fall. My siblings always teased me for being too structured and sticking to plans religiously. Even Cassie made fun of my "Book of Accountability."

Somehow, during our conversation last night, it slipped, and I mentioned the book to Nonso. He didn't laugh or dismiss me like others did. He simply said that everyone has their own methods and planning was mine. He insisted that I was entitled to do me. He did suggest that sometimes I should try doing things outside of the plan.

Last night we talked for hours. This journal felt like a tangible symbol of his support, a silent acknowledgment of the unspoken bond forming between us. We were more than strangers, but not quite friends but there was definitely a hypnotic pull between us. I wasn't sure what we were, but after last night, I knew we were something.

Before I could ponder any further, there was a knock on my door. I quickly composed myself as my boss walked in. His gaze flickered towards the gift on my desk, but he didn't comment on it. Instead, he congratulated me again on signing Mr. Chen and in the same breath, delivered a reminder that I needed three more big clients to meet my quota.

"Thank you. I understand," I said calmly.

The slight furrow of his brows showed that he was probably expecting me to react differently. A clear sign that he knew he was wrong for how he was approaching me.

"What about the Viva players? Have any of them taken the bait?" His sharp gaze never left mine as he waited for my answer.

I gave him a brief update on my progress, explaining that we had a one-week delay in starting the classes due to scheduling conflicts with over fifty percent of the players. Because of the weather, the team played a postponed game yesterday, which happened to be Sunday. Their regular play days were Thursdays and Saturdays, so, the classes were moved from Wednesdays to Tuesdays.

"So no one...?"

"I'm not trying to bait them, sir. I want to educate them. As they see my genuine concern for their financial well-being, it'll be easier to bring them on as clients."

Dismissively waving his hand, he said, "I'm sure you've heard of striking while the iron is hot. Remember, if you want to become a partner, you need to be able to wear many hats. Right now, you're only focused on teaching."

"I am fully capable of doing my job, Sir." My phone buzzed with two text messages, but I ignored them.

"And I know how to do mine, which is evaluate all of my senior advisors on their overall performance, not just one aspect of their job." Suddenly, his shoulders relaxed, and his gaze softened. "Your commitment to financial literacy is commendable, but I need to see results across the board. You need to start thinking strategically, not just as a teacher."

I bristled, my muscles tensing, as his words hit me. But with nothing else to say, I nodded. Mr. Wilson turned and left my office. Once again, he left me feeling like he didn't recognize the value and impact of my work. For a split second, I was tempted to let his words linger and darken my mood. But today was a good day, and I refused to let him take that away from me. Signing Mr. Chen as a client was a victory.

I walked around my desk and slumped into my chair. I reached for my phone, remembering I needed to thank Nonso for my gift. His name was already on my screen, and the corners of my mouth lifted into a smile. I felt a familiar tingle spread through my body.

When I woke up earlier, I'd changed his name in my contacts from Danger to Nonso. Although the name was still fitting, because he had the potential to be hella dangerous for my health. A fact that was made clear when I got on Instagram earlier and rolled my eyes at Lesedi's comment under his post about the

Panther's last game. "You always get 'em in the end." With a heart emoji.

My phone buzzed again, bringing me back to Nonso's text messages.

> Nonso: Tell me you scored.

> Nonso: Whether we're celebrating, or I gotta give you more lessons, meet me at this address in an hour.

I plugged the address into my Maps app. It was an apartment complex. Correction – it was one of the most luxurious complexes in Viva City. Nonso had sent the messages ten minutes ago, and the place was about forty minutes away. I had two more meetings, well more like consultations, left for the day, and I also needed to prepare for my class the next day. Logic told me to remain where I was, but *something* about Nonso kept him on my mind and drew me to him in ways I couldn't explain. That same *something* also had me shoving my laptop into its case, grabbing my new journal and purse, and heading to my car.

> On my way. Thank you for the gift.

Not waiting for a response, I mounted my phone onto its stand and backed out of my parking spot.

A while later, I arrived at one of the most luxurious high-rise apartment buildings in Viva City. The views were unlike anything I had ever seen before. I remembered touring these apartments when I first moved to this town. The prestigious Essence Hotel was part of the development, so residents could also take advantage of the hotel-like services that were offered.

I had originally thought I could maybe afford a one-bedroom apartment, but they wanted my entire destiny as payment, so I quickly turned around and walked away. According to the brochure, the place was an eclectic oasis, known for being a vibrant and inclusive community where families and individuals from all backgrounds could find a welcoming and enriching environment to call home. But when I looked at the prices, I couldn't help but wonder which individuals they were referring to because they certainly weren't affordable for someone like me who didn't have football player money.

Once I parked my car, I pulled down the visor to make sure my hair was in place, then refreshed my lipstick before stepping out and into the building. The lobby was elegantly decorated with plush sofas and beautiful artwork hanging on the walls. As I approached the front desk to inquire about the person that brought me here, a familiar cologne wafted up my nostrils. It was Nonso's signature scent with notes of sandalwood, bergamot and cedarwood. It suited him perfectly.

I couldn't resist scanning his form as he sauntered over to me. He was dressed simply in a berry, multicolored, crewneck sweater and matching navy pants with Air Force One sneakers in the same berry color. Jewelry on men was usually a hit or miss for me, but the ring on his right pinky finger, a watch, bracelet, and a Cuban link necklace around his neck, were definitely a hit. He sported a confident smile on his face – something that seemed rare for him in public. He'd perfected the art of remaining expressionless.

"You like what you see, Specs?" he asked playfully.

I rolled my eyes because another thing I noticed about Nonso Chijuka was that he knew exactly how attractive he was. "You look pretty plain to me. I just wanted to make sure your clothes were clean."

He threw his head back and laughed. "Your left eye twitches when you lie, and right now that joker looks like it's having a seizure."

He stopped in front of me and took a deep breath. His eyes roamed my frame before meeting my eyes again.

There goes this erratic heartbeat again.

"You smell good and look good too. So, what's the verdict? You score?"

I smiled. "Yes, yes I did."

Before I knew it, he had enveloped me in a hug and lifted me off the ground. After giving me a spin, he set me down, shifting our energy instantly. The magnetic attraction that I felt without even touching him was now amplified after our brief physical contact. He seemed to feel it too because his eyes were now hooded, and I felt the heat from his intense gaze. We stayed lost in each other's gaze until the flash of a camera brought us back to reality.

Nonso grabbed my hand and led me towards the elevator. When it opened, we entered the see-through cab in complete silence. Nonso positioned himself in front of me, shielding me from any prying eyes. Another camera flashed and I was now sure it was the paparazzi. I furrowed my brows, but he shrugged it off.

"So, that's started already?" I asked, referring to the flashing cameras.

"Don't worry about them. I'd rather talk about you instead. Congratulations," he said.

"Thank you. And thank you for the gift. You really didn't have to."

"I know I didn't, but seeing you happy makes it worth it." He winked at me with a mischievous grin. "So, are you going to tell me about it? I want a play-by-play."

"As soon as you explain why I'm here." The elevator stopped on the eighteenth floor, and we stepped out. Nonso took my hand in his.

"Remember, you're helping me look for a place?" he reminded me. "I've looked at two that were a definite nah, but this one I kinda liked, so..."

As we walked towards the apartment, I soaked up my surroundings. The sound of my heels clicking on the marble floors echoed through the hallway and a faint scent of citrus filled my nostrils from a nearby bouquet of flowers in the central area between two adjacent units. The door to one of the units opened and we were greeted by who I assumed to be the realtor. Stepping inside the apartment, I was immediately struck by its spaciousness and elegance.

The large windows provided natural light and a breathtaking view of the city skyline. The walls were painted in a calming shade of cream, creating a sense of warmth and tranquility. The furniture was modern yet inviting. When I asked Nonso if it came with the place or it was just for staging, he replied that it came with the apartment but there were a few pieces he didn't like. As we followed the realtor further into the apartment, I was in awe. No wonder they wanted my destiny to live here.

"This is the second living room," the realtor announced, gesturing to the open space. "As you can see, it's perfect for hosting guests."

I nodded in agreement, taking in every detail around me. "It's absolutely stunning."

Over the next twenty minutes, the realtor guided us through each area of the apartment, showcasing an impeccable open plan kitchen-dining area equipped with top-of-the-line appliances. The three bedrooms and tiled bathrooms were all spacious, luxurious, and exquisitely designed. With my hand still clasped in Nonso's, despite my attempts to disconnect, he led me through each space, eagerly asking for my opinion. The first time I shrugged, unsure of what to say, he called out to the realtor.

"Aye man, my woman gotta love it. Now, I think she just likes it." He ignored my nudging and continued his spiel. "When she's excited, those beautiful specs on her cheeks stand out." Nonso turned to me. "She's still gorgeous, but they ain't taking center stage. I'd hate to pass on this place too."

My cheeks flushed with embarrassment. "Stop it."

The poor guy came to a halt, confusion etched on his furrowed brows. He already looked nervous enough escorting two Black people through the space alone. Nonso's tall frame towering over the realtor didn't help either. Trying to put the guy at ease, I offered a smile.

Nonso frowned at me. "Nobody told you to smile at him."

Ignoring his playful admonition, I tugged him along. My consultation call was coming up soon and my stomach was growling with hunger. Why wasn't Nonso's sister on FaceTime or something, giving her thoughts? From our conversation, I could tell that he had a complicated relationship with his mother, but he adored his sister.

Nonso's threat of walking away seemed to light a fire under the realtor's feet because he suddenly started rattling off the other amenities that came with the apartment via the hotel. An exclusive lounge and terrace on the roof, taxi, chauffeur, or car-hire options, housekeeping and laundry services, in-house beauty treatments, and even pet care services were part of the package. As an athlete, the cherry on top for Nonso was access to a wellness suite complete with a steam room, sauna, vitality pool, and gym.

"You not done yet?"

I turned to see Nonso peering over my shoulder, his question halting my fingers flying across the keyboard of my laptop. Nonso was as clingy as he said he was. It wasn't in a negative way though, and although I knew he was teasing half of the time, it was still funny to me.

The real estate agent left a few hours ago and Nonso gave his word that this was the place he wanted. No, let me rephrase that – after I agreed that this was what "we" wanted. There was still paperwork to be signed and money to be exchanged, but Nonso managed to convince the realtor to let us stay in the apartment because I had to be on a call soon and he wanted me to have a quiet area to work. I could've taken the meetings in my car, but Nonso insisted I use the kitchen island.

The man was insufferable in a sexy, confident, caring, and funny sorta way. It was endearing no doubt. Yet the bells kept going off in my head warning of how bad an idea getting closer to him would be. Throughout both calls, Nonso stayed in the background like a coach and whispered plays. When he felt I was saying the wrong thing, he blew an imaginary whistle. When he thought I was taking too long to close the deal, he signaled for me to head to an imaginary goal post. The first person was a yes and the second person was a maybe.

Now, I was typing up my notes and Nonso had reentered the kitchen with lunch he'd ordered.

I chuckled. "Stop crying."

"Never that, but as your man, I need you to wrap it up so I can feed you," he said.

"My desperation has gotten me into a situation I can't get out of." I closed my laptop and hopped off the bar stool. I took off my heels and walked over to him, limping slightly. Either these new heels were not as comfortable, or I'd been on my feet more than usual.

He looked at my feet before meeting my gaze. "Baby, whether it was that day or the next week, our paths would've crossed. The only difference is I got to meet Specs, my woman, before Ms. Martins, my teacher, could suffocate her."

"Something is wrong with you. See all the game you're running, just so I'll eat with you." I grabbed the containers of food from the bags.

Nonso walked over and turned me around, leaning me against the kitchen island, his arms caging me in. His intense stare made me shift my weight from one foot to another, while the scent of his cologne threatened to overwhelm me.

"Yinka, listen to me, because I wanna make sure you hear me good. I've been running game since I was fifteen. Everything you can imagine, I probably said it. I don't say this to brag but to be honest. I'm thirty now, baby, and I've been through a lot and worked hard to be better. And on top of it all, I'm a handsome athlete with healthy pockets. I don't have to chase any woman or run game.

"But you...I genuinely like and enjoy your company. Maybe the timing isn't perfect since I'm trying to win a championship, but you and I know that whatever is keeping us together is more potent than the voices in our head and worth exploring. Be rest assured that anything I say, I mean."

We stood there for a moment before he used his thumb to trace my bottom lip.

"I guess you think you read me, huh?"

"I did read your 'not in my plan' behind. Now bring your crippled self on so we can eat. If you're good, maybe I'll even give you a foot massage." He grabbed two containers and headed towards the living room.

I chuckled as I watched him go. "Is that how you talk to your girlfriend?"

"Yeah, when she's talking crazy, accusing me of running game," he replied, glancing back at me with a smile. "But she's still my baby, though."

"And a catch. Don't forget it while you're giving your little speech," I sassed.

He let his gaze roam over my body and smirked. "Trust me I know."

～

WE HAD FINISHED OUR MEAL FROM FUSION HAVEN, AND I was beyond stuffed. Nonso knew it was my favorite place and went all out for lunch. The jollof rice arancini, plantain croquettes with spicy mango salsa, and grilled peri-peri chicken skewers were all so delicious. I knew I had reached my max, but the Safari Delight dessert called my name. Now I was comfortably lounging on the plush sofa, feeling content, but also aware that I should be heading home soon.

"K, ain't nobody switched up on you. I've just been busy trying to be on my game. I got a lotta pressure on me now."

I tilted my head to watch Nonso as he appeared from the kitchen area where he went to put away the leftover food bags. There were creases on his forehead and his shoulders looked tense. Whoever he was talking to, seemed to have made him switch from his usual playful demeanor to this agitated man who appeared weighed down.

"No, right now ain't a good time..." Nonso ran his hand across his head. "I'll send you the stuff later, but I can't fly you out now."

As I continued to observe him, he walked over to the large window and continued talking to the person on the phone. From what I could gather, the person was arguing that Nonso always brought them along whenever he played in a new city. Nonso's explanations kept getting interrupted and he kept rolling his shoulders in frustration until he finally told the person that he wasn't going to keep arguing with them like they were in a relationship. After saying that he would send them the "thing" which I assumed was money, Nonso ended the call. A few moments passed by, and he remained standing by the window.

I sat up on the sofa, debating if I should go over to him. We usually talked about football, pop culture and work with ease, but I realized there were many aspects of his life I didn't know anything about. The air in the room felt tense, and I wanted to make things better. After a few more moments of silence, I decided to approach him in a different way.

With a playful grin, I said. "Three Lies and a Truth."

He turned to me with a confused expression. "Huh?"

I explained further, ignoring his creased handsome face. "You have to figure out which of these statements about me is true."

We remained in silence for a moment before he sauntered over and settled on the floor between my legs, resting his head on my lap. He still hadn't smiled, but let out a deep sigh instead.

"Okay, hit me."

"One, I'm secretly good at impersonating comedians. Two, I've traveled to more than ten countries. Three, I used to sing in my church choir. Four, I only use leaves when cooking moi-moi."

Nonso lifted his head slightly and looked at me directly. "I'm going to guess... that you only use leaves when cooking moi-moi?"

I shook my head with a smile. "Nope, not even close. I don't know how to cook moi-moi at all! The truth is that I'm great at comedic impersonations."

Nonso laughed heartily. "You lyin'? You're always so serious!"

Smiling, I replied, "Well, now you know one of my hidden talents."

He twisted his lips. "Convince me."

For the next few minutes, I recreated popular movie scenes, and then he switched to TikTok and played some viral sounds for me. After watching each one once, I was able to mimic it perfectly. He seemed to enjoy watching me and I was more than willing to keep entertaining him.

"All right, now it's my turn," he announced with a mischievous glint in his eyes. "One, I scored a hat-trick in a championship game. Two, I'm fluent in five languages. Three, I have a fear of heights. And four, I always carry a lucky charm from my childhood."

I took a moment to think before guessing, "You're afraid of heights?"

Nonso chuckled at my guess. "Wrong! The truth is that I have a lucky charm."

I raised an eyebrow in surprise. Nonso didn't strike me as the sentimental type.

"I got it from my grandmother when we were leaving Nigeria as kids," Nonso explained. There was a hint of sadness in his tone. "I've kept it with me since then. Unfortunately, she passed away two years ago."

I expressed my condolences and he fell silent for a moment before continuing.

"We were so excited to finally be reunited with my mom," Nonso revealed. "The path we took led me to where I am today, but I often wonder whether I would change anything."

His voice was filled with regret, and he seemed to retreat into himself again. I placed a comforting hand on his shoulder and squeezed gently.

"I don't know the details, but I do know that playing the 'what if' game won't change anything," I reassured him. "You can only try to do better in the present. Trust me, I know."

"You're right and that's what I've trying to do, but people—"

"Won't let you do right? Is that what was happening with the K person?" I didn't really expect him to answer because another thing Nonso did was laugh off important things.

"Instead of a home as happy as the one I'd known, when we landed in America, I was thrown into a situation that was opposite from what I imagined..."

For the next few minutes, I listened as Nonso narrated his arrival in America, his father's deportation and the later turbulent childhood and teenage years he'd endured because of his home life. He didn't go into a lot of detail, but from what he did say, I now understood the complicated relationship he had with his parents and admired the way he cared for his siblings. Some people would go through all that and not even care about anybody else.

"My siblings are all younger than me and quite frankly, their experience was different from mine. The only person that seemed to understand what I was going through was Kane. We were codependent in rebellion." He chuckled, though there was no humor behind the sound.

"Our actions led to three stints in juvie until Big Iz appeared on the scene. Our last fast grab was at a college basketball game. We ran up on the wrong one and I almost got my head blown off...if not for Kane. I owe that man my life."

"And I'm sure he's not trying to let you forget it..." I said, sensing the underlying tension between Nonso and Kane.

Nonso shrugged, but it was clear he struggled with leaving his friend behind.

After a brief pause, I mustered up the courage to ask him the question that had been on my mind since finding out who he was. "Is he the friend mentioned in your betting scandal? How did that happen?"

"Money, perceived freedom, loneliness, and unresolved trauma are a bad combination. I'm talking disastrous. Like catastrophic." Nonso shook his head grimly. "It's hard to explain how it all happened. It started innocently enough with a trip to Vegas. Kane was into gambling, and I thought, why not try my luck? I won some, lost some, but nothing major. Then things escalated. Kane got more serious, started betting on football games, including mine, without me knowing. I thought it was just a harmless hobby, but it spiraled out of control. I found myself caught up in a world of illegal betting, and by the time I realized how deep I was, it was too late."

It wasn't surprising how friends could lead each other down dark paths; I knew that firsthand. However, I had watched Nonso's hearing on YouTube and his story now seemed different from what he had portrayed there. He had taken sole responsibility for the scandal and even portrayed himself as the mastermind behind the illegal activities. He painted himself as a troubled individual who was driven by greed and recklessness. Nonso wasn't completely innocent in this situation. I knew he had some culpability hence the seven-month ban, but I struggled to understand his loyalty towards someone who knowingly put him in such a dangerous position.

"Look, you don't owe him anything. You—"

He jolted to his feet. "Why can't anyone understand? I can't just leave him out in the cold." His voice was louder and more forceful than I would've liked.

I also stood. "And I'm not saying you should. I'm telling you to set boundaries and not feel guilty about it."

"I've tried that. It still doesn't sit well with me..."

"What feels good versus what's best. You have to decide."

"Not everything is black and white, Specs," he growled. "We can't all plan our way to perfection."

My jaw dropped. Anger surged through my body. "How dare you? You don't know anything about me." I started gathering my things, determined not to be his punching bag because he was in his feelings about someone who didn't even care about him.

"Wait...Specs..."

I could feel him getting closer, but I was quicker. I had my laptop secured and my bag on my shoulder as I headed towards the door.

"Yinka, wait!"

The desperation in his voice stopped me in my tracks, but I didn't turn around. I shouldn't have been there in the first place.

"Wait. I'm really sorry. I didn't mean it," he said, placing his hands on my shoulders and turning me around. "Do you hear me? I'm sorry."

"Yeah, so am I."

Nonso didn't push it and I was grateful. I needed to be alone with my thoughts. This man was taking me on a rollercoaster ride that I wasn't even sure I wanted to be on yet.

seven

Nonso

I CHECKED MY PHONE, but the message wasn't what I was hoping for. My frustration and anger were building up as I grabbed my hotel key to the room I was lodged in and made my way down the hallway. As I rode the elevator, I half-heartedly responded to Lesedi with a quick "Tnxs."

My mind was preoccupied with a certain freckled, feisty woman who had left me feeling wound up and confused. Ms. Martins had taken my girl Specs and buried her, leaving me without any contact with her for two weeks. It wasn't that Yinka was avoiding me; I saw her around and even tried to talk to her. But she shut me out completely.

In class, she gave me short and curt responses. They weren't quite snappy to be unprofessional, but they weren't warm either. In our text conversations, it was only one or two words at a time. I knew I had messed up and hurt her, but no matter how much I apologized or tried to take it back, Yinka wouldn't budge. My mess up reminded her that I wasn't in her plan and that was the end of that. She wanted nothing to do with me anymore.

Or so she thought.

It had been two days since our last class, and all I wanted to do was go see her. I didn't know where she lived, but I was willing to make a surprise visit to her office if needed. However, my own personal battles had me preoccupied. And my team was on the road, playing a pivotal game on the journey to the Championship. I wouldn't be any good to her, and needed to play undistracted, so I was gonna let her rock for now.

The elevator stopped on the next floor and Xander and James joined me. Not feeling very talkative, I gave them a quick fist bump instead.

"You good, Black?" James asked.

"I'm straight."

"No, he ain't. My boy has a thing for Ms. Martins, and she got him twisted," Xan teased.

"You being funny, but you need to focus more on why *Tatafo* thinks your girl has a thing for Niyi Da Silva."

Niyi was a chart-topping, Neo Soul, R&B Gospel singer that was hot right now. The pretty boy was signed to the same label as Yuwa, Xander's girl, whose real name was Abi.

Xander's face contorted, and his fist clenched. "That mess ain't funny. They're releasing a duet together and doing press runs, but leave it to those jobless bloggers to paint another picture."

I agreed with his sentiment about those blogs though. "That's why my guy Nyce almost had them shut down for messing with his wife."

"I wish he succeeded. They're just crazy."

James and I laughed. For two different reasons, I'm sure. James because Xander was normally so cool and all in love, so seeing him rattled was comical. For me, I was so wrong, but I felt a bit better about someone else being in agony because of his woman.

My woman.

What started off as a joke and a way to get under Yinka's skin these last five weeks had turned into something I could see being a reality. Just like me, she played along when I called her my girl-friend or woman. Sometimes using it to get me to do things I normally wouldn't. Like watching a ballet performance online with her, listening to a podcast she recommended about African history or watching her true crime addiction; *Justice: Silent Pursuit.*

"My man wouldn't deprive me of my wishes," she'd say.

"Deal with your women problems on your own time. We're playing Northridge and we need to win," James said, as the elevator came to a stop.

I placed my headset over my head and got into Steven Furtick's "I Will Fight" as we headed towards the bus taking us to the stadium. McAllister and I had gotten into a pretty good rhythm lately. The man still hated my guts, but that was some-thing he had to deal with on his own. On the field, we made magic and won games. That was all I cared about. Even though my personal life was in crumbles, winning on the field was always a win.

"We've got five minutes left, lads. Five minutes to prove that we're not just another team in this league. We're the Panthers... stealth, powerful and swift. Let's close this out and go home."

Coach's voice boomed over the sound of thundering cheers from the opposing team's fans. The pressure was immense, but it only fueled our determination. In unison, we clapped our hands and charged back onto the field. Adrenaline coursed through my veins. The tension was palpable and the atmosphere electric as we battled for every inch of ground. The roars of the crowd were deafening, but I blocked them out. My focus solely on the ball. At one goal each, this game could go either way.

Suddenly, Xander sent a perfectly timed pass my way and I took off like a rocket. Dribbling past defenders with lightning speed, I could feel victory within reach. With a burst of energy, I made it to the penalty area and saw an opening. Without hesita-tion, I unleashed a powerful shot towards the top corner of the net. Time seemed to slow down as I watched the ball sail through the air. The goalkeeper leaped, stretching his body to its limit, but he was no match for my determination. The net rippled as the ball smashed into it, and the stadium erupted in a frenzy of cheers and jeers.

I sprinted towards the corner flag, pulling my shirt over my face in pure ecstasy as my teammates surrounded me in a victorious embrace. With only minutes remaining on the clock, we defended our lead with everything we had left. The Premier League never felt so close.

After our win, Coach was eager to get back to Viva City and avoid another night on the road. So, as soon as the post-game media briefing ended, we checked out of our hotel and made our way back. It was Friday in the wee hours of the morning when we arrived. Once I got to my apartment, I wasted no time taking a shower and crashing.

We'd been away for a week straight, playing a match every other day, and exhaustion wasn't even the word. The job wasn't easy, but I'd been doing this for over ten years and was used to it. The added pressure on my shoulders was there due to the relocation, settling in a new city and getting acclimated to the new team. Also coming off a betting scandal meant that I was held to a different standard. I had to perform at my best always.

Two days later, I maneuvered my truck into the underground parking garage of Dynamo Lounge. It was an exclusive upscale, three-level lounge in the heart of the city. I'd been here once before and enjoyed the sleek, energetic vibe that sorta matched the city's spirit.

The media's opinion of my performance varied, with some praising me while others criticized whether I was truly worth my multi-million Euro price tag. But the tabloids were relentless in their gossip. One day I was supposedly dating Lesedi, the next day Yinka had dumped me because we hadn't been seen together recently. Ever since that photo of us in my apartment was published, she had become a part of my gossip circle.

None of these rumors bothered me as much as Kane's tell-all

interview where he claimed I was a disloyal friend. The last time we talked, he wanted to come to London, and I refused. It wasn't his fault; I always gave him free access to any city I played in. But I was done. I sent him the money he asked for, but he wanted more, and I couldn't do it.

Same went with my father. "Sources close to him" were all over the blogs lamenting on how I cut off my own father financially. If setting strict budgets for those closest to me made me disloyal, then so be it. I had stopped defending myself to the public a long time ago.

I parked the car and hopped out. I was dressed simply in a grey turtleneck and black jeans. Pulling up the collar of my brown trench coat, I locked the car and headed in. I still felt the buzz of our FA game win earlier today and decided to join my teammates at our goalkeeper Andrej's twenty-seventh birthday party. The music was loud, the lights were dim, and the atmosphere was charged with energy.

I made my way to the third level VIP section where my guys were. Xander, Diego, James, and a few others were clustered around a table, their voices raised in laughter as they were having a good time. They cheered and slapped my back as I approached them.

"Black! You killed it out there!" James exclaimed, shaking my shoulder.

"Thanks man," I replied with a grin. "But it was a team effort. We all brought our A-game." The others nodded in agreement as Diego handed me a drink with a deep amber color. I furrowed my brows and lifted it to my nose and took in hints of caramel and oak. "I know y'all ain't drinking, Coach will have all of your behinds."

"We know better," Xan replied before explaining that it was called Zero SpiritBlend 49, a non-alcoholic cognac. "Nah, we're just vibing. Celebrating the youngster."

Andrej shouted, protesting at being called a youngster. He

was the youngest on the team, but hated to be reminded of it. We raised our glasses and toasted.

"To the Panthers and bringing home the victory," James declared, and we all echoed his sentiment.

It was the end of February, and our rankings were strong. If we continued to maintain and improve, we could secure a spot in the Premier League by the end of the season in May. As we celebrated, I couldn't help but feel a sense of pride and camaraderie among us. We'd worked hard and tonight was a well-deserved chance to let loose and enjoy ourselves. Amidst the music and laughter, I felt grateful for the strong bond we shared both on and off the field.

A couple of hours later, I was ready to call it a night. I had fun with the guys just chilling and vibing. A few women came up to our section, but Xander and I quickly directed them to the other guys. The ladies were perfectly crafted by God…at least I knew they originally were, but when they turned around and their backsides looked like they could house a whole kingdom, I knew they had messed with the Master's creation. I had my own thoughts on enhancements, and I mostly kept them to myself.

Besides, there was only one woman on my mind, and I was racking my brain on how I would find out where she lived. Yinka hadn't responded to any of the texts I'd sent her earlier, and I was worried and pissed. I was off tomorrow and wanted to spend the day with her, but more importantly, I didn't want to enter another week without having my Specs back. Standing, I set my glass down and dapped up the guys.

"Yo! Hold up. I'm about to be out too," Xander said.

"Cool, I'mma run to the restroom, then meet you up front," I said.

As I walked, I avoided making eye contact with anyone so I wouldn't be bothered. Luckily, I made it inside without any interruptions and finished quickly before heading back out towards the front of the club. Just as I was about to leave, I heard a familiar voice. At first, joy filled me as I recognized it was Yinka's, but that emotion was quickly replaced by anger when I saw her in one of the VIP sections. She was leaned against the railing and was all cackles in some guy's face.

Yinka was dressed in a mid-thigh, tight black bandage dress that hugged all her curves and accentuated her caramel skin tone. The dress wasn't revealing but still managed to catch attention due to its shape hugging design. What made me even angrier was seeing her not paying attention to the drink in her hand. Her fluid dance movements and the way she tossed her head back told me that she was intoxicated on some level. Anything could happen and the guy with her was clearly taking advantage of the moment. Blinded by my rage, I stormed over to where she was.

Entering the section, I stalked towards Yinka. Her eyes widened in surprise when she saw me approaching.

"Really? So, this is what we on?" I growled, my voice laced with anger.

She stumbled back, caught off guard by my sudden appearance. The man she was with did himself a favor and stepped back. I wasn't sure whether it was because he knew who I was, or he could tell he didn't want these kinds of problems.

Sensing my mood, she cleared her throat. "What are you doing here? The last time I checked, we weren't on anything."

I thumbed my nose. "Oh, is that why you're out here being reckless?"

"I'm here with my friend and I'm fine," she slurred, her speech affected from whatever she'd been drinking.

Her eyes were filled with guilt and regret, but that wasn't enough to quell the fire burning inside me. Looking around for the first time, I noticed the setup of the section was for a birthday party and the theme seemed to be pink and black. I took the drink from her hand.

"Did you notice that your drink is cloudy? How many drinks did you mix in here? Where's your friend anyway?"

She frowned as the gravity of what I said sunk in. "She...she went to see some of our other friends off."

"Get your stuff. We're leaving too."

She opened her mouth to speak, but I didn't give her a chance. I grabbed her arm and pulled her aside.

"I'm not leaving you here alone when you're clearly not your-self," I said firmly, lowering my voice, but not the intensity behind my words. "If you fight me, I'll show my entire Naija behind. I'm used to the attention, you're not."

"Errm, excuse me sir, why are your hands on my friend?" Yinka's friend suddenly appeared next to us. She was pretty with loc'ed hair tied up in a bun on top of her head. A sash across her pink dress read "Birthday Girl."

"It's okay, Cassie," Yinka said. "This is Nonso, Nonso meet—"

"Oh my gosh, I didn't realize it was you!" Cassie exclaimed as she shook my hand.

"Nice to meet you," I replied. "Cassie for...?"

"Cassandra."

"Happy Birthday, Cassandra," I said with a smile. "Your friend was just leaving. I hope you don't mind."

"No! Actually, thank God you're here so she can—"

"Cass!" Yinka interrupted, finding her voice again.

Cassandra grinned and I smirked, satisfied that she'd missed me as much as I missed her.

Cassandra laughed. "It's fine. We're almost done anyway, and my boyfriend went to the bar. He'll be back soon."

I waited while the ladies said their goodbyes and for Cassan-dra's man to return before grabbing Yinka's hand and leading her out of the section. Instead of taking the elevators, I opted for the back stairway used by high profiled people and celebrities to access the parking garage. I knew I had probably already given the paparazzi a photo opportunity, so I wanted to limit any further damage.

"Nonso, I can't do all these stairs," Yinka complained.

The drawl in her voice told me my Specs had made an appear-ance. Even though I was still angry about what could've happened to her if I hadn't shown up, I stayed quiet because I didn't want to say something that would make her even more upset with me.

Plus, I needed Specs around. She was the nicer one. So, I crouched down to take off her heels and gave her a piggyback ride to the parking garage. After making sure she was secure, I rounded the car to get in. Before I could ask her for her address, she had dozed off.

I stared at her, getting lost in the magnificence of God's handiwork. The way she slouched made her curls cascade over her delicate features, masking those freckles that I adored. Without thinking, I tucked the strands behind her ear and felt a strange mix of emotions well up inside me.

The tightness in my chest grew with each passing second until anger, protectiveness, and calm all collided together in a chaotic storm. My heart was at war with itself and some days I wasn't sure if I wanted to lean in or pull away. These past few days without her, I was sure that the connection between us had surpassed undeniable chemistry. We'd transcended the physical and seeing her tonight solidified the fact that I couldn't deny the inexplicable bond that was inevitable and unnerving.

Now that I'd figured out my ish, I needed to know hers. If this was truly one-sided, I was about to hop off this ride. Never again would I try to hold on to what wasn't going anywhere. I played games for a living. My real life was a game-free zone, and I intended to keep it that way.

~

BEFORE I SAW HER, I HEARD THE GENTLE YET purposeful sound of her footsteps. I turned to face Yinka as she entered the kitchen, her hair slightly disheveled from sleep and the morning light casting a soft glow around her. There was an innate elegance to her movements, a quiet confidence that mesmerized me. My eyes traced her form, taking in the way my Panthers hoodie hung over her body.

Last night or rather earlier this morning when we arrived, the toiletries, towels, and wool pajamas I had the concierge get from the attached twenty-four-hour store were waiting at the door. She'd woken up sometime after we got in, but wasn't really in a talking mood. After settling her in one of the guest rooms, I left her to get herself together. After checking in and making sure she'd finally taken a shower and was sleeping, I went back to my room to do the same. However, I couldn't get much sleep in because the interview I had to do the next day was on my mind.

"Good morning," she greeted with a low, melodic voice.

"Morning, Specs." I raised my brow. "So what? You shy now?"

"Nope."

She eased onto the bar stool, and I pushed a cup of coffee her way. I knew she was kinda stuck on the beverage. The night of our first Facetime call, I saw she had a whole bar set up with the girlie stuff she liked to spruce her coffee up with. But I knew nothing about that stuff, so, black with cream and sugar was what she was getting this morning.

"Whatchu wanna eat? I had them bring up a bunch of stuff."

The other side of the island had a variety of English and American breakfast foods. Picking up two plates, I walked over to her and handed her one. After we made our selections, we both took them to the living room.

"Thank you," Yinka said.

We'd been eating in comfortable semi silence for a while, and I could tell that something was on her mind. The way she would sometimes playfully pick sausage off my plate while depositing tomatoes on it told me that it was Specs I was dealing with. However, as I suspected last night, something was bothering her. I'd be talking to her, and she would space out for a few moments.

"What's going on?" I asked.

"What do you mean?"

"Come on, what kind of man would I be if I didn't notice when something was going on with my woman?"

"Which woman? The same one you threatened to show your behind on last night?"

"Yep. Checking you is part of our dynamic, just like you checked me the other day then decided that you didn't need me anymore."

She giggled. "I did not."

"Errm, 'Mr. Chijuka the correct answer to the case study is attached to the previous email.' I mean, what kinda mess is that?"

Yinka laughed harder. She was lucky I had somewhere to be and couldn't call her when that email came in. Granted the attachment to the case study we talked about in class was in the email, but the way she called me Mr. Chijuka just vexed me.

"*See me see wahala*, the last time I checked you were Mr. Chijuka," she said.

"Keep playing with me. Didn't even send me a single congratulatory message while I was away."

"Why? So, your head can expand more? Besides, you got a lot of them from what I could tell," Yinka responded with a hint of sarcasm in her voice.

"You checking up on me, Specs?"

"*Plueeze*, but since the last time you had me here, your fans and the blogs seem to think I need to be informed every time your real girlfriend comments on your posts." She rolled her eyes and stood, grabbing our plates on the way to the kitchen.

I chuckled, knowing she was talking about Lesedi who had been commenting constantly since I started playing for Viva City. My sister even told me that Les walked up to her in Target one day and talked to her as if they were old friends. I hadn't explained the situation to Yinka, so it was understandable that she was feeling salty about it. But at the same time, it was cute to see she was feeling me just as I was her.

"While you over there sulking, grab me a juice from the fridge."

"Come and grab it yourself." She sucked her teeth.

"You gon' do me like that, Specs?"

"Sure am."

"I guess I better go get my real girlfriend to get me juice then since you wanna be like that."

As soon as the words left my mouth, I knew it was the wrong thing to say even though I was teasing. The expression on Yinka's face held annoyance and irritation. I didn't realize that she already had a small bottle of juice in her hand when she sauntered over to me. Suddenly, something dropped into my lap, dangerously close to my groin. In a panic, I jumped up and Yinka burst out in laughter. She covered her mouth with her hand, trying to contain her amusement.

"Oops, sorry."

Feeling a mixture of embarrassment and shock, I stalked towards her, backing her up against the large window in my living room. "You think that's funny?"

"I didn't mean it..." she managed to say between giggles.

"How are we gonna have kids if you injure him?"

Yinka tried to compose herself as she pushed me away. "Nonso, stop...I'm almost at the window."

I stopped when her back was pressed against the glass. "Say you're sorry," I demanded.

She apologized through laughter.

"I don't believe you. Say it like you mean it."

Now we were pressed against each other, and I could feel her breath catching with our proximity. I leaned in, my lips brushing against her ear as I whispered, "Apologize properly, Specs."

Yinka shivered at my touch, her laughter fading into a soft sigh. "I'm sorry," she whispered. Her voice was laced with a mix of playfulness and desire. "I didn't mean to drop the juice on you."

A mischievous grin spread across my face. "You know," I said, trailing a finger along the curve of her face down to her neck. "There are two ways you can make it up to me."

Her breath hitched again, and I could see the fire in her eyes as she met my gaze. "Really now? And they are?"

Without another word, I closed the remaining distance

between us. Our lips collided in a passionate kiss that made time stand still. Her taste hit me like a summer storm, intense and intoxicating. Our bodies fitted together seamlessly. The kiss deepened with every passing moment, the intensity between us growing. Yinka's hands roamed over my back, tracing my muscles with urgency. My hands found their way to her silky hair, tugging her brown curls, unable to get enough of her.

After a few moments, I broke us up. It was my responsibility as the man to ensure we didn't go any further, especially with a lot of things unspoken between us. Our chests heaved with desire as our gazes remained locked with the pure electricity.

"I missed you," I said, my voice catching slightly. My eyes lingered on her, searching for a reaction.

"I missed you too," she breathed, her voice barely above a whisper.

"I need Ms. Martins to remember that feeling next time she tries to freeze my bae, Specs, out."

Yinka shook her head over my antics. "I'm assuming that was the first thing. What's the second? This window is cold." She pulled the sleeves of the hoodie over her manicured hands.

My eyes went to my hoodie she had on. "Don't be stretching out my hoodie, and don't leave with it either."

"Ha! You lost this sucker once I put it on. So, what's the second thing?"

"Oh yeah," I pulled her toward the sitting area. "The second is for you to watch today's sermon with me. The way you were gyrating yesterday can't be of God."

She laughed, smacking me on my back before settling beside me on the couch. Picking up the remote, I turned to the Calvary Is The Way YouTube channel. The live stream was already on. We caught the last few minutes of the worship song, "Great Is Thy Mercy" and soon after, Pastor Mensah walked up to the pulpit. He became one of my go-to spiritual leaders when I stopped going to my church in Atlanta. The ugly stares, gossip, and open judgement when I found myself in trouble became unbearable.

We'd been watching for about half an hour when Pastor Mensah started to narrate a story about his kids. He'd been preaching from Isaiah 43:18-19, reminding us that we had to let go of the past in order to embrace the new. It was a message I'd heard in another form from my old pastor and my therapist.

"Some days ago, I walked up on my kids snickering and giggling in the living room. They were far too relaxed for my liking, especially since they had driven my wife crazy all morning with their antics."

The congregation chuckled at this, and the pastor jokingly apologized to his wife for outing her.

"They were watching a video on social media where a woman filmed herself praying or rather begging God for forgiveness. Now, the reason my kids found it amusing is because I had instilled in them that God was not like man. The good Lord forgives when we ask with a contrite heart. But most of the time we can't forgive ourselves or we can't forgive others who have wronged us, because we attribute our human traits to Him, and think we can have a transactional relationship with Him – if we do this, then God will do that.

"The truth is, no matter what that woman did to drive her to plead like that, God forgave her the first time she asked. God is constantly working in our lives, bringing new opportunities and new beginnings, no matter what mistakes we've made – even during tough times. We must release ourselves from the belief that when facing hardship, God has abandoned us or hasn't forgiven us for something we did in the past."

The sound of sniffling caught my attention, and when I glanced over, I saw Yinka wiping at the corner of her eye. She had been so calm and focused that I didn't want to disturb her. Instead, I pulled her into my lap, wrapped my arms around her and let her cry. I could tell something was troubling her, and it seemed like whatever the pastor said affected her and she needed to let it out.

eight
Yinka

NONSO PARKED his car in front of my apartment complex, which was a little over an hour from his expensive neighborhood. My place wasn't as luxurious or expensive as his, but it was comfortable and in a gated community. When I decided to move from my sister's house to Viva City, my dad, brother, and my sister's husband had to personally see the place I wanted to live in and make sure it was up to their standards. The men in my life tended to be protective and overbearing and now I had another one. I glanced over at Nonso who had his seat slightly reclined with his phone to his ear. This man was everything I didn't want but I desperately needed.

He was currently on an impromptu call from his agent. It was Sunday, but she had to inform him of the change in venue for the big interview he had in the morning. It would be the first live hour long one with British media he would be giving since his ban. He'd shut the press out completely except for pressers he had to do after his games. When he told me why, I saw his point. However, he was in a new city now and I agreed with his agent when she said he had to blend into the community and a part of that was building his personal brand here.

After my breakdown earlier, Nonso didn't bombard me with

questions, but told me he was available when I was ready. Instead, we watched a movie, ate lunch, and played Minecraft. Before I knew it, it was early evening and although I didn't want to end the evening, I had to get home. My Sunday routine had been completely shot. I could still salvage some of it, making sure my calendar was up to date, creating a to-do list for the week and getting some reading done. I'd have to skip out on meal prep because I needed to make it to bed early. I had to travel to Wales in the morning to see a client and use the opportunity to see my sister and her family.

"My bad, I needed to handle that real quick," Nonso said after ending his call. "So, you gonna be back tomorrow, right?"

"Yes, don't act like you'll miss me," I said.

"There you go." He cut his eyes at me. "Anyway, you good tho?"

After leaving his home, I directed him to a place known for serving the best fish and chips in the city. I called in our order and went inside to pick it up. The pub was bustling with a big game on, and I realized if Nonso had gone in, his presence would've caused quite a commotion. Instead, we opted to drive to a nearby park and enjoyed our meal in the car.

There he gave me the full story, or rather his version of his relationship with Lesedi. His version because I was a woman too and I was sure the girl wasn't that crazy to leave her relationship just because. I understood family pressure, but if he was as down for her as he said he was, she would have felt secure enough to not let them sway her.

Then again, maybe he was, but her family was one of those African families that could frustrate someone out of the free air that God gave them to breathe. I wouldn't pretend to understand. All I could worry about was myself and what he showed me. I had no beef with her as long as she didn't come for me.

"You gonna answer me?" he asked again.

He'd shared a lot with me, so it was time for me to do the same. I shifted my body so that I could face him. "When I was fifteen, I was a completely different person. Wild, carefree, always seeking the next thrill." My voice trembled with suppressed emotion. "I would skip school to go to the mall, hang out with older guys, and even tried cigarettes. But that didn't give me enough of a high." The memories still made me cringe. "So, by sixteen, I graduated to weed. One time I was with my friends and we were so high, but I had just gotten my learner's permit, so I got behind the wheel. I ended up wrecking my parent's car. They'd threatened to send me back to Nigeria countless times, but that time, they were really close. So, I straightened up for a while." I glanced at Nonso, but his expression showed no signs of disgust, shock, or disappointment.

"Then months later, one weekend, I told my parents I was staying at my best friend's house. Technically it wasn't a lie; Bisi and I often had sleepovers. Our parents were close. Around midnight, I received a text from one of the popular kids inviting us to a party. I convinced Bisi to come with me by promising we'd be back before her parents woke up. She didn't want to go, but I begged. I should've let her be, but I was always up to some-thing. Eventually she agreed..." I drifted off as that night poured into my memory. Fifteen years later, that day still felt like yesterday.

As we approached the party, I could feel the bass thumping in my chest and see the colorful lights bouncing off the walls. My pulse raced with anticipation of the adventure ahead. Nelly Furtado and Timberland's "Promiscuous" was blasting from the speakers. Bisi, always more cautious than me, lingered on the outskirts of the crowd, her eyes darting nervously. I grabbed her hand and pulled her along, promising her a night we'll never forget. She hesitated but eventually followed me into the crowd of people.

We joined a group of older kids, sipping on drinks that tasted bitter and talking about plans for the summer break. But as the night wore on, things took a darker turn. Suddenly, there was a heated argument between two boys, and Bisi gripped my arm tightly in fear. I tried to steer us away from the commotion, but in all the chaos and noise, we got separated. Panic set in as I frantically searched for her among the sea of dancing bodies.

My heart dropped when I saw her lying motionless on the ground, blood staining her clothes. I rushed to her side, tears welling up in my eyes as I tried to make sense of what happened. An ambulance was called, but despite the best efforts of the paramedics and doctors at the hospital, Bisi didn't make it.

Nonso's thumb brushed away my tears. His comforting touch brought me back to the present.

"She got caught in the middle of a stabbing, trying to run from danger. It was all because I couldn't follow the rules. I just had to go to that party...even though she didn't want to go. I forced her, and now she's gone."

"Baby..."

"No, don't say it. I've heard it all before. Let go of the guilt, it wasn't your fault; anything you can say, I've heard it. But I can't...I don't know how."

The loss of my friend changed me into this cautious and strait-laced person. People couldn't understand why I planned everything out and was so rigid about it. The memory of that horrific night never left me, especially when the anniversary of her death came around which was two days before Cassie's birthday. This year, I was hit with the added emotion of my recent argument with Nonso, making everything even more unbearable for me. It's the reason why I drank too much at Cassie's party.

"People laugh or think I'm crazy for planning everything out so rigidly," I told Nonso through my tears. "If only I had stuck to the plan and actually slept over at her place...she would still be alive."

"Stop," Nonso interjected. "A wise woman once told me that if I go down the rabbit hole of 'what ifs,' I'll get stuck there. Making plans isn't so bad; the reason you think you must and stick to them is."

We sat in silence for a moment before he continued. "My therapist taught me that achieving freedom isn't the same as maintaining it. You must find a way to let go of the guilt and keep it away. If you allow the negative thoughts in your head to control you, you'll lose every time. I know you not trying to keep feeling this way. Just like I can't say I don't sometimes feel the urge to gamble. But the desperation of maintaining my freedom and pleasing God is greater. But none of it is through my own will power...I need help." He wiped away another tear from my cheek.

"Whatever you need, the Holy Spirit gotchu. I got you. You and I are gonna use our weapons of warfare to cast down those thoughts, imaginations, any of those lies that contradict who we know God is. My sister taught me that one. For you, me, and our future kids. What's it gonna look like if they think their mama is crazy because she gotta control everything."

I laughed through my tears. This man was something else. He always had a way of making me feel better.

"Trying to control things obviously isn't working because you're teaching me that I have no control over what's happening between us." I rolled my eyes.

He nodded in approval. "Acceptance. You're making progress."

There was no need denying it; Nonso was a genie I'd taken out the bottle and there was no putting him back.

~

"*Oya, oya*, get up."

My sister's voice woke me from my peaceful nap. I kept my eyes closed and pulled the soft blanket over my head, not wanting to move from the comfortable couch that had enveloped me.

"What for?" I grumbled, knowing exactly why she was waking me up. But that didn't mean I had to be happy about it. I was exhausted after a long day and all I wanted was a little rest before heading back to London.

"*Oya, o ṣe ileri, dide,*" Tolu scolded me, holding a comb and hair products in her hand.

Of course I promised. It was the only way she would make her delicious native jollof rice for me when I arrived earlier.

"*O re mi. O kan nitori iresi kekere?*"

"The rice wasn't small when you begged me to make it and pack some for you to take with you," Tolu retorted, picking up the remote and changing the TV channel to a sports game. "I was going to make amala for lunch, but you put in a special order."

She gave me a sheepish grin, as though turning the TV to sports was supposed to make me feel better about her interrupting my nap so I could cornrow her hair.

"*Oya* now, Yinka, your nieces will soon wake up."

"Fine," I grumbled, sitting up with a frown on my face.

My sister, not one to ever care, placed a cushion on the floor between my legs and settled herself there. As I began to detangle her thick, curly hair, memories of our childhood came flooding back. Tolu had six years on me, so we didn't share the same friends and she treated me like the annoying little sister. I'm sure I was because I couldn't stand the way she would push me to the side when her friends came around. Or the fact that my parents couldn't handle that we were two different people. She was Tolu, and I was Yinka.

"Don't you see what your sister is doing?" Or, "Why can't you learn from Tolu?"

As I told Nonso, I was a wild child until I was humbled by death. One of the few times Tolu and I bonded without resentment or beef was when I was braiding her hair. No matter how many times my mother tried to show us, braiding hair wasn't my sister's ministry. I could do it with ease. She had 4C hair and we both had sensitive scalps.

Growing up, she could come to me to do her hair, but I had to endure the heavy handedness of a professional stylist. She wore a lot of wigs so kept her hair washed and cornrowed. How I didn't remember it was washday when I waltzed my behind in here earlier I wasn't sure. Although I wasn't thrilled about it, braiding my sister's hair was one of the traditions we'd carried into adulthood. The older we got, the more life took us in different directions, so moments like this became rare.

Being the first child and oldest daughter in our traditional African household, she carried a lot of weight on her shoulders – not just for herself, but also for me and our brother. When it was time for college, she chose to go to NYU in New York – as far away from Atlanta as possible. The rigid and strait-laced Tolu Martins found true freedom and eventual rebellion there, but it came with a price.

Her baby girl, my Snuggle Bunny, whose real name was Olivia, was born out of this rebellion and for a few years, she was seen as a disappointment and source of shame by our parents. Having a child out of wedlock added her to a list that was solely occupied by me after the death of my friend, Bisi. Although Oliver was Olivia's dad, their relationship was nowhere near marriage back then.

But now, Tolu was living her best life as a successful, part time IP attorney. I struggled to understand how my sister could find fulfillment in such a simple life. She set her own hours and was more content with her family. She had had so many plans for where she wanted her career to go. Now, none of that seemed to matter.

After they moved to Wales for Oliver's job, my sister became a different person. The shame and opinion of others lifted off her. I couldn't help but feel a tinge of envy at how light and carefree she was now compared to earlier times when she was weighed down with responsibility and expectation. I tried to be like her, but failed. Besides our situations differed vastly. My niece was born out of her rebellion, while I caused someone to lose their life. It wasn't remotely the same. I tried to tell my sister that when she got on me about how I lived my life.

As I braided her hair, we talked about our jobs, friends, our brother's upcoming wedding and all the latest gossip in our family. Our cousins on both sides could have their own reality show with the drama they stayed in. I was only close to two of the bunch and that was more than enough. My siblings kept up with them more. I listened halfheartedly, lost in my own thoughts.

Despite my attempts to distract myself, I couldn't help checking my phone every few minutes for a response from Nonso about his interview. I knew he was nervous, but I also knew he was capable. I idly watched the highlights of the game for the day. Nonso wasn't playing, but the teams on the field would impact the Panther's ranking. Bored with the sports channel, I switched to another and was surprised to see Nonso being interviewed.

It wasn't live now since it had happened earlier in the day. Pride swelled in my chest as he confidently settled into the interview chair, his posture impeccable and composed. Nonso was dressed in a tailored black suit that emphasized his broad shoulders. He paired it with a crisp, mustard yellow shirt that popped against his dark skin, leaving the top button undone for a polished yet casual look. His clean-shaven head emphasized his chiseled features and determined gaze.

Nonso could pull off any look, that much was clear. He'd been dropped by one clothing brand in the US after his trouble, but I knew he was in active talks with another one here in the UK. The interview took place in a sleek, brightly lit modern studio. The backdrop featured a large screen displaying the Viva City Football Club logo.

The interviewer was Brittany Grace. Ugh, I couldn't stand her. Why did his agent not ask for someone else? Ms. Grace had a habit of eating Black players alive. The double standard was glaring any time she did an interview. But connections got you anything you wanted so she was still at *The UK Daily* despite numerous complaints.

She sat facing Nonso. Her legs were crossed at the ankles, and she leaned forward with an eager yet focused expression as she fired off her questions. I watched with a smile on my face as Nonso confidently discussed his goals for the season and upcoming matches. But when asked about his previous betting scandal and suspension, I could see the strain on his face. The question itself wasn't bad. He should have expected anyone to be as inquisitive as I was about that ordeal.

Then her tone shifted. "Nonso, let's be frank, many critics claim that the same recklessness and irresponsibility that got you banned is still present in your game. How do you address those concerns?"

Nonso's jaw clenched. We'd also discussed a recent game where his aggressive style was scrutinized by fans and analysts.

"I understand that everything I do is under scrutiny. In that game, I made a split-second decision that didn't work out as planned. But I stand by my commitment to always give my best for the team and learn from my mistakes," he said.

As the questions continued, I watched with anxiety running amuck in my body. I admired Nonso's composure under pressure, but I could see the effort it took him any time Ms. Grace seemed a little disrespectful. I prayed he kept his temper in check until the end. Then the interviewer told him she wanted to get personal.

"There are rumors about your relationship status. Can you comment on your status with Yinka Martins? Is she your lady or is there still a fairytale ending on the horizon with Lesedi Jafta?"

My heart dropped. How did I get in this? The fear I had was replaced by anger at the mention of Lesedi's name while Nonso took a deep breath to compose himself.

"My personal life is private and not up for discussion here," he said after a few moments with a fake smile on his face.

Tolu was oblivious to anything in the sports world, while Oliver, who was an avid NBA fan, wouldn't give football the time of day. But now, I could see my sister's interest piquing at the mention of my name. She sat up straight.

I resisted the urge to let out a deep sigh and instead focused on the TV screen in front of us. Nonso's decision to remain silent about the relationship status with Lesedi brought some relief, but just hearing her name still being mentioned in conjunction with his stung.

I stole a quick glance at my sister. Tolu's eyebrows raised

slightly, and her head tilted to the side as she focused on the television, her lips forming a subtle frown. Her unrelenting gaze then bore into me. I forced a tight-lipped smile and shifted my position.

Hoping I could avoid her probing questions, I decided to speak. "It's just gossip, nothing to worry about," I said, with a dismissive wave of my hand, trying to quell the suspicious look in her eyes.

But as Ms. Grace continued to probe in another way, I couldn't shake the unease creeping into my stomach. Yeah, he had told me about Lesedi, but I was tired of being mixed up in this imaginary love triangle. Nonso was everything, but I wasn't sure if he was worth all this. The rumors about Nonso and Lesedi had been circulating for weeks now, fueled by her cryptic posts on social media.

"Rumors are swirling about your significant gambling losses, and there's speculation that Ms. Martin's position as a financial advisor could potentially enable your habit, especially if there's a romantic relationship between you two." A faint smirk played on her lips. "Love can make us do reckless things, like seeking her advice for risky investments. The latest pictures show the two of you leaving Jazz It Up together. Therefore, I'm sure your followers are curious: is there a possibility of falling back into old patterns? Should they be worried?"

Past! Past gambling losses!!! These people are so messy.

I shook my head because as soon as Brittany Grace's question left her mouth, I knew Nonso had reached his breaking point. With a screech of his chair against the floor, Nonso was on his feet.

"We done." He yanked his microphone off and walked off the set.

My eyes widened and my heart sank at the sight of Nonso's raw emotions. I knew how much he valued his reputation and how diligently he had worked to restore it. A surge of anger rose within me towards the media's thirst for blood and the interviewer for pushing him over the edge. A news anchor appeared and informed the viewers they'd have a panel to discuss after the break. My sister stood as I reached for my phone. She switched off the TV and I could sense her gaze, but I wasn't in the mood for her judgement that would mirror our mother's.

"I should probably go," I announced, avoiding my sister's probing stare. "I have some work that needs to be done."

"You better get comfortable doing it here," she commented while packing up her hair stuff and heading towards the stairs. "Your old room is still available, and some of your things are still here. Let me check on your nieces and nephew and you can explain why your name is being mentioned in the same sentence as that mess of a man."

My heart rate increased as I tried to come up with a response that would satisfy Tolu without revealing too much. Instead of waiting for her to come back downstairs, I followed her up the stairs. Despite her growth and maturity, there was one trait that Tolu hadn't let go of – judgmentalism, inherited from our mother. For someone who had been the black sheep once, you'd think she'd be more understanding.

While she went to check on her kids, I went to the room I'd occupied before moving to Viva City. The daily, two-hour train ride to my dream job became exhausting, so I made the decision to move. I had been content with my choice until Mrs. Masobe, my former boss, had to relocate to Australia with her family. Then Mr. Wilson, my walking nightmare, took over.

I walked over to the dresser and grabbed a pajama set. Memories rushed back – late-night conversations, sharing secrets, and dreaming about the future.

"*Mo n gbo,* go ahead."

My sister's voice snapped me out of my reverie. I leaned against the dresser, taking a deep breath, and trying to gather my thoughts while bracing myself for what was about to come.

Tolu plopped down on the bed.

"How are they?"

"Still asleep. I spoke to Oli; he's doing well and has settled into his hotel." She leaned against the headboard. "Enough stalling."

"Sis, it's not what you think." I cleared my throat to steady my shaky voice. I was a thirty-one-year-old woman, but memories of our younger years flooded my mind. Years I spent explaining my actions to her so she could butter up our parents.

"Then how is it?"

"How do you even know anything about him?" I really wanted to know how she'd already judged him to be a "mess of a man."

"You're right. I don't know much about him other than what I heard some colleagues say at work a few weeks ago."

"What did they say?"

"That he embarrassed his family by gambling, in America of all places. After everything they had given him – a chance to come to America and better his life. With all the money, fame, talent – he still couldn't keep himself together," she said.

Nonso often complained about being unfairly judged and the media's scrutiny, but watching my sister do it in real time was frustrating and baffling.

"For someone who claims to not know him, you sure have a lot to say."

"Please. When my younger sister starts hanging out with a potential disaster, I can't help but remember what I've been told about him before."

"He was my student, and he's not like—"

"What? He fed you some story about how it wasn't his fault? After checking on the kids, I looked him up online. Yinka, is this really the path you want to go down?"

"*Se diedie o*. He's not my boyfriend. I was assigned to teach his team a mandatory financial planning class." My hands rubbed up and down my arms as if trying to suppress the nausea building in my throat. It felt sickening to have to downplay my connection with Nonso because of my sister's disapproval. "I... I got caught up in all of this because of the nosy media. We happened to be at a few places at the same time." My half-truths tasted like bile.

My sister studied me for a few minutes then her expression softened. She crossed the room and pulled me into a brief embrace then released me. "You know I'm just trying to look out for you. If Mummy and Daddy find out—"

Defiantly, I blurted out, "But I'm an adult. They should trust that I know what's best for me."

"You don't even know what's best for you. One moment, Brandon is your perfect match, the next moment, you can't stand him. One day you want to settle down, the next you want to travel the world. You're naturally carefree and an adventurer, and that innate nature is constantly at odds with your rigid obsession with schedules and plans, something that emerged after Bisi."

She shrugged. "If you ask me, it's a great way to be. But the constant battle against this improved you is unhealthy. You can't keep changing your mind like this. Until you find balance, you'll never be happy. But this guy is *not* who you want to start with."

I rolled my eyes and shifted my weight. "I'm not dating him, but even if I was, it would be my business."

My sister chuckled and got off the bed. "Sure, when you're brave enough to tell that to our parents face-to-face, then I'll know you've grown up."

"Why can't you support me for once?"

"Support what? I thought you said you weren't dating him." She walked towards the door. "But you need to pick a side and stick with it. I'm warning you again, being on that guy's side is not where you want to be."

I rolled my eyes as she turned the doorknob.

"Just think before you do anything that will bring shame to our family... again," she threw over her shoulder.

My jaw dropped at her nerve, and my heart tightened in pain. "Pot calling the kettle black."

My sister sucked her teeth. "The difference is that I understand that we only get one shot at being stupid. You seem to be going for round two."

Tolu left the room, and I was stuck in place for a few minutes before I walked into the bathroom to wash the day off. As I prepared for bed, an inner turmoil consumed me. On the one hand, my spontaneous nature urged me to live in the moment and enjoy the thrill of being in Nonso's orbit. But on the other hand, caution warned me to think about the long-term consequences of a real relationship with Nonso. Before I left him the day before, we talked a little about our feelings for each other, but I convinced him that I didn't want to give us a name yet.

"I'mma let you rock. We don't have to name this, as long as you know *this* is something," he'd warned, forever trying to threaten me.

I crawled into bed, my mind buzzing with thoughts of my career goals. If I wanted to become a partner and have people trust me with their finances, I had to maintain a flawless reputation. Despite the weariness in my bones, my lips curled up in a bitter-sweet smile as I wiped away a stray tear from my cheek. Nonso had ignited a fire within me, pushing me to chase after every opportunity with him.

But now, thanks to my sister's reminder, I couldn't ignore the fact that being in a relationship with him would require a delicate balancing act. Still, all I could think about was Nonso and the potential pain his absence could bring. The lack of response to the text I sent him earlier only amplified those fears.

nine
Nonso

IT HAD BEEN A WEEK, and I was still berating myself for letting that reporter get under my skin. The American press could be harsh, but the UK press was downright ruthless. One day they were singing your praises and the next, you were the garbage they threw away. Luckily, I had managed to dodge most of their attacks by simply ignoring them.

Ms. Ellis, Big Iz, and my publicist, Amara Dike, blew up my phone to give me a piece of their minds. However, at the end of the day, they worked for me, and it was their job to clean up after whatever mess they thought I made. I respected them as individuals and how they handled my business, but they weren't the ones who had to deal with these endless attacks. I'd already served my punishment for my actions, but these people just wouldn't let it go. They could write whatever they wanted about me, but in person, they better tread lightly.

I leaned closer to the mirror to inspect every inch of my face to make sure I was well moisturized. Okay with my reflection, I headed back into my bedroom just as a text from my sister popped up on my phone.

My sister knew that this was a big night for me. As much as I wanted to leave my scandal in the past, in a few hours, I was going to be talking about it again to help an organization that I had become fond of.

Hope's Haven.

With guidance from my agent and input from Yinka, I started working with Hope's Haven over the past month. The non-profit organization was dedicated to helping individuals struggling with addiction through support and rehabilitation services. Their mission was to provide hope, healing, and a safe haven for those seeking to overcome their addictions and rebuild their lives.

The first time I visited their facility, I knew it was the right decision to contribute my time there. After meeting with the leadership team and management, I made myself available whenever my schedule allowed. We filmed a campaign together which I posted on my social media platform to raise awareness about addiction and Hope's Haven. I also attended group therapy sessions and gave a speech at one of their in-house events.

My initial motive for getting involved in the city I now called home was selfish – more centered on ensuring the city accepted me after the initial mixed welcome. But now it had shifted to being a supportive presence for those going through recovery. Having almost lost everything due to my own mistakes, I wanted others to know that there was always hope and a way forward through community and help. I had experienced it firsthand and wanted to share that.

The renewed focus pushed me into accepting the invitation to the Viva Renaissance Annual Gala I was currently heading out for. The prestigious event was aimed at celebrating the city's cultural diversity, promoting community, and raising funds for local charities and initiatives. This year's theme was Sustainability and Community Empowerment. Hope's Haven was one of the organizations chosen to showcase how their initiatives contributed to the goals of the gala.

Tonight, I was not just a footballer, but a spokesperson for Hope's Haven. I'd be sharing my story not only to inspire hope and encourage others to seek help, but to make sure Hope's Haven got the necessary funding they often sought.

This was a night I'd have wanted Yinka on my arm, but things had been awkward between us since that television interview. So, when I got the invitation, I resisted the urge to call her. First, it was short notice; the event was planned before I became affiliated with Hope's Haven, and second, her wishy-washy behavior was starting to wear me down.

I knew I should've answered her call that evening, but with the anger I felt from being bamboozled and everything else going on in my life, dealing with her anger over being mentioned by the interviewer wasn't a top priority. I did send her an apology text later that night, but she never responded, and I let her be.

Despite the constant pressure from others regarding my life choices and boundaries, my brother and sister remained the only constants in my life. I had hoped that Yinka would also be a part of this group, but her attitude towards me seemed to change whenever we were apart or faced any difficulties. When it was just the two of us together, in our own little world that we called "the huddle," Yinka gave me Specs – smart, intelligent, sexy. I was feeling her heavy, but I needed someone who would be solid at all times. Her constant indecisiveness when she got in her head wasn't what I needed right now.

I responded to my sister's text when my phone started ringing, with Jason's name on the screen. Picking up my keys, I swiped to answer the call and headed out the door for the elevator leading to the parking garage.

"What's up, bro?"

"Just checking, making sure you're good?"

I chuckled at my brother. I loved my siblings down. You got

beef with one of us, you got beef with us all. We didn't even need to know what happened or who was at fault. Sometimes the twins in Nigeria took advantage of that by getting themselves in unnecessary trouble. Regardless of the volatility of our parental dynamic, even after all these years, we all rode for each other. What Jason really wanted to know was whether the current story the blogs were on had any effect on me.

Kane's tweet, "First amnesia then faded loyalty. Trust no man," had been retweeted so many times that the blogs took it and made it into a story. Kane had been making sly comments and jabs on social media for some time, but I'd learned to brush them off. I had promised him money, which I sent, but he seemed to be fixated on me flying him out to Viva. Kane used to be my best friend; I didn't take a step without him. But now, I didn't even know what we were. He was careful not to be too direct with his subliminals, but he said just enough so anyone that knew us knew he was talking about me.

"I'm focused, Jace. I came to Viva to do one thing. All the other drama can miss me."

"Okay, that's wassup," he said. The smile in his voice was tangible.

Jason acted like he was my hitta most days. While my sister was overbearing, he stayed on the lookout ready to pounce. The fact that he had boxing experience, having trained in the sport during high school, didn't make it any better. He discovered an interest in boxing at a young age and began training at a local gym. A professional career was never his goal. Which was a good thing because our mother would've been called to glory before her time.

"I'm good. You just take care of home," I said.

"You know I got it. You riding solo tonight or with that Naija babe I see you photographed with?"

I chuckled. "You just as nosy as your sister."

He snickered. "Is that a yes, or no? And best believe I'm gonna tell her you said that."

"Please don't. I ain't trying to hear about how she's concerned about me. Answer to your question though, is no. I'm solo."

"What happened? Last time I called, she was leaving your apartment."

"Long story but the short version is, I ain't got time to be chasing an illusion," I replied, calling the situation with Yinka what it was.

"Well, dang... it's like that? Yeah, you don't need that kind of energy."

"You know it!"

Jason and I talked a little more. I had been doing better at calling my mom, so he didn't need to guilt trip me over the woman that gave us life. His dad was fine; he was given another clean bill of health. I gisted Jason about my pops telling my cousins and some family members that I said I wasn't going to give him money anymore – a total lie, but every other week, the few of them who had my number sent me the "Honor thy father and mother" Bible verse, or my new favorite one, "Do not be weary in doing good." People took God's Word and made it what they wanted it to be.

My brother repeated the same thing my sister said when she found out what our father was up to. After she went on a rant, she ended by advising me to stand my ground. I took her advice. I was no longer moved by unhealthy emotions, something my accountants were happy about. Deep down, though, the backlash I got from every jobless person on social media with a "think piece" any time one of my family members or Kane said something wasn't funny. But I still stayed the course. With a promise to catch up soon, I ended the call and put the phone in its holder.

I instructed Siri to play "Hustle" by Teni as I drove towards the venue where the event was being held. I reflected on my time in the city so far. I was entering into my third month and a lot had happened. Our team had been doing well in the past weeks' games and we were still moving between second and third place on the ratings board. Our chances of being promoted looked good since we didn't fall below third place.

I recently signed with the energy drink, UME and became a brand ambassador for Ziedu Sportswear. Things were going well professionally, but my personal relationships were still struggling. Moving to Viva City may not have seemed like the best decision on paper, but it felt like God had led me here, just like He instructed Abraham to go to a place He would reveal to him, and everything worked out in the end. Now, if only I could get my Sarah to stop running away.

I pulled up to the Viva Grande Hotel and stepped out of my car. Adjusting the sleeves of my sleek black tuxedo, I put my phone in my pocket and checked my Patek Philippe watch. I was ten minutes early. After handing my keys to the valet, I prepared to walk through the flashing lights of photographers. After a few poses on the red carpet, I was approached by Ms. Vicki, the liaison from Hope's Haven, and my guide for the night.

Ms. Vicki greeted me with a warm smile. "Mr. Chijuka, I'm so glad you could make it tonight. Follow me."

We walked through an entrance, then turned towards the ballroom where the event was being held. I felt a surge of nervous energy. After years of doing this, the allure of these kinds of public gatherings had diminished. I knew it was something I had to do, part of my job and brand, but I'd been doing it since I was about twenty years old.

Taking in the ambiance, I had to give the décor team their props. The ballroom was a dazzling display of lights and decorations, with guests mingling and sipping on champagne. The scent of fresh flowers and expensive perfume lingered in the air, mixed with a hint of the rich aroma of hors d'oeuvres being served. Ms. Vicki led me through the crowd, introducing me to sponsors, city officials and a few fans. I shook hands, posed for pictures, and made small talk, all the while scanning the room for any familiar faces. And then, amidst the sea of strangers...I saw her.

From across the crowded ballroom, my eyes remained on her

standing by the bar. Her head was thrown back in laughter and her neck elongated, a spot I loved to nuzzle on. It was almost as if she could feel my gaze because she started looking around until her eyes met mine. She looked stunning in the black sequined, one-shoulder gown that hugged her curves.

As memories flooded back of our time together before she ghosted me...late-night conversations, shared laughter, teasing banter, heated arguments, and shared dreams...my heart skipped a beat. She provided me with a reprieve from being "on" all the time.

But like I said before, her indecisiveness was blowing me. So, I was good on her.

Yinka's eyes held a mixture of surprise and uncertainty, but there was a flicker of something familiar in them. What she refused to say, her eyes conveyed, and that was the reason why I glanced over at Ms. Vicki who was chatting animatedly beside me and excused myself.

"Ms. Martins, it's good to see you," I greeted. "You look very beautiful."

I could tell that she was taken aback with me addressing her by her formal title. I kept my expression unreadable. I wasn't going to pretend like her ghosting me was okay. We were grown. The least she could do was communicate like the grown woman I knew she was. She thanked me and returned the compliment.

"I didn't think I'd see you here," Yinka replied, her voice barely audible above the music. She took a sip of her drink, deliberately avoiding eye contact.

"You would have known if you picked up the phone," I said, trying to keep my tone light, despite the storm of emotions raging inside me.

Yinka narrowed her eyes at me. "Nonso, please. Not here."

"As long as you know you gotta tell me something."

"Yes, look, I'm—"

"Nah, we not doing that here. We're here for a good cause;

let's focus on that. I just came over to speak." I shoved my hands in my pockets.

The fact that she was now trying to explain to me because I walked up to her – something she should've done instead of completely ignoring my texts – rubbed me the wrong way. As she was about to say something else, another woman walked up to her.

Yinka made the introductions. She was the director of the Green Guardians, an organization I knew Yinka belonged to. I hadn't given the theme of sustainability and community much thought, but now it made sense why Yinka was here. Green Guardians was the other organization being featured today.

After making small talk with the women for a few more minutes, I leaned into Yinka's ear and whispered. "Don't leave without seeing me."

Her eyes were defiant, but I wasn't playing with her, and my expression conveyed that. After excusing myself, I walked back to the table Ms. Vicki showed me earlier. Soon after I took my seat, the host began the event. After reiterating the reason we were here, and acknowledging some top members of the community, he invited the Mayor of Viva City to the podium. The man who made his way to the front was of medium height and dressed in a sharp black suit with a bright red tie.

"Good evening, ladies and gentlemen, thank you again for making it tonight," he started. There was applause from the crowd. "Each year, we gather to celebrate the city's cultural diversity, artistic innovation, and commitment to community revitalization. The gala's theme focuses on a different aspect of renaissance, symbolizing a new era of growth, creativity, and positive change for Viva City."

For the next few minutes, he continued to speak with fervor about the importance of the event. After his introductory remarks, guests were treated to a variety of entertainment and interactive exhibits that showcased the city's diversity and sense of unity. The program also included performances by local artists and a panel Q & A on community empowerment.

The spokesperson for Green Guardians was introduced as Mrs. Zaina DuBois-Arazi. The stone-faced, North African guy seated next to her must be her husband with the way he was looking at her. The woman was the CEO of Kutoka Duniani, a sustainable interior design company and one of Green Guardian's governing members. She gave a rousing speech about its mission and significance in the community. According to her, she now lived in Morocco with her family but had previously worked as an environmental consultant in London. Mrs. DuBois-Arazi shared her personal journey towards caring for the Earth, which she viewed as a precious gift from the Almighty.

Soon after, we were served a five-course gourmet dinner. At intervals throughout the evening, my eyes connected to Yinka's and there was an unspoken longing between our gazes. My sound mind instructed me to move on from her. But the feeling I got from being close to her wouldn't allow me to obey that simple command.

Next, there was a lively auction to raise funds for Hope's Haven and Green Guardians.

Ms. Vicki leaned in and whispered, "You're up next."

I nodded, quickly wiping the corners of my mouth, and taking a sip of water to clear my throat. Retrieving my note cards from my suit pocket, I composed my expression for the barrage of camera flashes as the host announced my name. Following the brief introduction, I made my way to the podium. The soft ballroom lights enveloped me in a comfortable warmth, momentarily shielding me from the harsh fluorescent lights shining down on the stage. Taking a deep breath, I scanned the crowd of eager faces staring back at me, ready for my speech.

"Esteemed guests and friends, tonight, we're gathered here for a cause that's very dear to me. As a football player, quite frankly, I'm used to facing challenges on and off the field. But tonight, I want to discuss a different kind of challenge – one that many of us face off the field: addiction.

"I stand before you as a spokesperson for Hope's Haven because I have personally struggled with addiction and found recovery. I know firsthand the difficulties, the pain, and the hopelessness that can come with addiction. But I also know the possibility of healing, strength, and renewal that comes from seeking help and support.

"At first, I refused to acknowledge I had a problem. I wasn't struggling with alcohol or drugs; those are the first vices society points to when addition is mentioned. I'm a rich athlete, having fun with my money. I knew gambling was a dangerous habit. I also knew that what I was gambling on could take my livelihood away, however, I continued to allow myself to believe I was just having fun. Addiction clouds your judgement. Then my life imploded right before my eyes. After being angry at everyone but myself, I reached out to my personal community and received support from organizations like Hope's Haven in the US. With their help, I found the courage and determination to overcome my addiction and rebuild my life." I paused, letting the weight of my words sink in before continuing.

"Tonight, my message is twofold. First, I want to highlight the importance of organizations like Hope's Haven and their importance in the community. Second, I want to provide hope for anyone who may be struggling with addiction. You're not alone. There's help available. And recovery is possible. It may not be easy, but it is worth it. You are worth it."

A thunderous applause halted my next words. After a few moments, I continued. "I also want to thank you for being here tonight and supporting Hope's Haven. Together, we can bring hope and healing to those in need."

As I stepped back from the podium amidst thunderous applause, my eyes met Yinka's – unfortunately for me, the only person who could calm my racing heart. She was on her feet applauding along with everyone else. Despite our situation, the admiration shining in her eyes was the highlight of this evening. As I walked off the stage, a grin stretched across my face. The audience's applause and positive feedback were overwhelming. I spotted Yinka making her way towards me with a proud smile on her face.

"That was incredible," she said, embracing me.

"Thanks. I was going to run my speech by Specs, but it looks like you finally succeeded in suffocating her," I replied, pulling back to look at her.

She waved me off. "Specs is fine."

I raised an eyebrow at Yinka's dismissive tone. "I can't tell. Your rigid self probably felt threatened by her."

She chuckled and shrugged. "So, if she were missing, you're not going to go look for her? You're just going to give up?"

"I wasn't gonna keep chasing whatchu actively trying to hide from me." My gaze roamed over her figure. She looked absolutely stunning in that dress, and it was difficult to focus on our conversation. "I love that dress on you."

Yinka blushed, her caramel skin taking on a faint rosy glow. She lowered her eyes to her feet momentarily with a small smile playing on her lips. "Thank you."

Taking her hand, I led her towards the dance floor where people were starting to gather. As soon as we found a spot, "You're Beautiful" by Kenny G started playing. I wrapped my arm around her waist and pulled her closer, our bodies now moving in sync with the music. As we swayed to the beat, our breaths fell into a rhythm and our gazes remained locked on each other.

"Why you always trying to run away from me?" I asked the question that had been weighing on my mind.

From bits and pieces of our conversations, I knew she had constructed this constrained lifestyle for herself. I also knew that just as she was my calm, I was her escape. She looked up at me, searching my eyes before answering in a soft voice filled with emotion.

"I'm not running from you, Nonso," she said. "I'm running from myself."

A pang of sadness hit me in the chest at her words. I understood all too well what it felt like to be haunted by your own demons and constantly battling against yourself. But I also knew that sometimes, all you needed was someone to stand by your side, to be your rock, and help you find your way back. For me, that was my siblings and Cheta Kalu. I wanted to be that for Yinka, but I also knew she had to want it for herself.

"Well, you don't have to run anymore," I said, tightening my hold around her waist.

She shrugged. "Why? You've already given up on Specs."

"Specs, I promise to chase after you, even if it takes me to the moon and back. Because when I finally make you mine, the reward will be worth it." I leaned in closer, gently nibbling on her earlobe before whispering, "But baby, I gotta know that you wanna be caught. I don't run around the field aimlessly. I play with a goal in mind. To win."

She simpered, understanding my double meaning. Then she leaned her forehead on my chest before returning her gaze to me. "You always say the sweetest things..."

"I say the realest things. But I gotta say tho, your performance as a girlfriend has dropped below a C."

She chuckled and I joined in. In that moment, as we danced, I knew that despite any demons she faced, I wanted to be there by her side, helping her fight them off.

"Huddle?" I asked.

Yinka looked around before returning her gaze to me. "Now? Here?"

"Yes, I might turn around and you'll go Casper."

She giggled at my reference to the disappearing cartoon angel and then shook her head softly. "What are you doing tomorrow?" she asked with a mischievous glint in her eye.

I smiled at her enthusiasm, but knowing Yinka's tendency to rope me into crazy activities, I couldn't give her a definite answer.

Last time I did that, I ended up doing yoga in a park at 6:30am on a Friday morning, wondering how I got there.

"It's Sunday, so I might have some plans," I replied vaguely. "Why do you ask?"

Yinka's smile widened, and she wrapped her arms around my neck, pulling me closer to her lips. In a lower voice, she said, "I was thinking of improving my grade." She brushed a kiss along my jawline.

"Careful now, people might start thinking you're my girl-friend for real."

"Then let them be mad," she retorted.

I raised my brow. "Look at you, all fearless." I chuckled at her sudden boldness.

When the song ended, I took her hand and led her off the dance floor, towards her table. She introduced me to a few people before grabbing her purse and following me to mine. As she leaned lightly into me, my hands naturally found her lower back. I informed Ms. Vicki that we were leaving and hand in hand we walked out of the venue.

I wasn't sure if Yinka realized it, but Specs had taken over. She was more carefree and relaxed. Laughing at my jokes, touching, and leaning into me. I caught the curious looks we received from people as we walked by. Blogs, social media, and some serious media outlets were for sure going to have us as a story by morning. I wasn't going to ink in our appointment until she actually showed up.

Depending on the headline, there was no telling if Yinka would run away or stay by my side.

decisive goal

a goal that firmly affects the result of the game, often being the winning goal or one that secures a crucial victory.

ten
Yinka

I TUCKED my phone in my back pocket and continued to the boutique in Viva Villages. I'd come to know that the ability to take care of others was what made Nonso tick, but then again, I didn't like him spending money on me. He was a gift giver, so I was used to the big and small gifts he sent my way or gave me any time we were together. The tennis bracelet I had on and the one and only Hermes bag I now owned was a testament to that.

But I also felt bad because there was no way I could ever compete at that level in return. I was comfortable but not that comfortable. He always said I was doing enough, but somehow, I doubted it. Although, when I showed up at his apartment Sunday morning and took him to Italy, he was totally blown away. So, maybe I was.

At first, I wasn't sure if he would allow me to take complete control of our trip. He called me a control freak, but I got a peek into his aggravating, well more aggravating than usual, side when I brushed past him and went to pack him an overnight bag. That comment about me having a failing grade as a girlfriend really got under my skin. I had seriously missed him and seeing him at the gala that night knocked the wind out of me.

When I didn't answer his texts and he stopped reaching out to me altogether, I told myself that it was for the best and I was better off focusing on my career. My sister's words stuck with me and try as I did, I couldn't get her voice out of my head.

When he walked into the ballroom looking like God handcrafted him specially, logic ceased to exist. I got lost in the sexy, handsome, and confident man that he was. Not afraid to bare himself to help with a cause that I knew he had a hard time talking about. The way he looked at me, touched me and gave me all his attention in the middle of a room full of people had my head spinning and my body warm.

Of course, the next day as anticipated, the blogs did what they did best, but I didn't let that deter me as it normally would. It had been two weeks since that weekend and I was still reveling in the euphoria of the blissful time we had.

We'd left his apartment and I drove us to the hanger where I had chartered a jet. I had been around Nonso too many times when he had to stop to sign autographs and take pictures. I wanted that weekend to be just for us, so I did what needed to be done. I didn't have "chartered jet money", but it paid to be owed favors from old clients that had connections. After a two-hour flight, we were in Lake Como. The pictures didn't do the place justice. The lake itself, which was in north Italy, was nestled against the Italian Alps and was surrounded by mountains and charming small towns.

"May I help you find something?"

I snapped out of my reverie. Turning to my side, I saw an attendant smiling beside me. I was now in M O Y O's looking for something to use Nonso's money on since we were attending an event later in the evening.

"Hi, I'm looking for something chic but classy, formal but not stiff."

"Any particular color?"

Nonso was wearing dark green, so I wanted to match his swag. After telling the attendant my color, she offered me something to drink and ushered me to a sitting area. M O Y O was a high-end boutique that opened in Viva Villages a few months ago. With this kind of service, I could now see why they were so high. The taste of my cappuccino transported me back to Lake Como.

I'd booked a charming double room in a lakeside hotel, surrounded by lush greenery and sparkling water. Since we'd arrived early and Nonso hadn't had time to eat, I had to hear his mouth about how hungry he was since he didn't want anything the crew had to offer. So, when we settled into our rooms, I had room service get us something which we indulged in on our shared balcony. The balcony overlooked the serene waters of the lake. The sun shone down creating a picturesque scene. The table was elegantly dressed in crisp linens, delicate china, and a vibrant bouquet of flowers. As we ate, the warm sunlight bathed us in a cozy glow. We enjoyed buttery croissants, sausages, eggs, juices, and coffee while taking in the stunning views.

I was comfortable with Nonso. After all we had spent many nights and days over the phone just talking and vibing before our time apart. But something about Italy shifted us. He was more vulnerable and so was I. We confessed our deepest fears and shared our wildest dreams. I had strong feelings for him, but deeper than that, we had developed a good friendship. At some point when he was good and full, he pulled me onto his lap. In between bites, we shared sweet light kisses, lost in our own private sanctuary. It was a moment of pure bliss.

Since we had to be back in London the following night, I didn't want to waste time indoors. After we rested a bit, we strolled along the river walk, explored the quaint shops and some vibrant markets, ending the day with a romantic dinner. The next morning, we indulged in freshly baked pastries and rich coffee, did some more shopping, and took a one-hour cultural excursion. Later that evening, barefoot, we strolled along the beach then came to a stop at a romantic canopy set up with twinkling lights and candles for a private dinner.

"Specs, baby, I have no idea how you put this all together but thank you. Now relax, I got us from here," Nonso had said right before he captured my lips in a soul stirring kiss.

The waves provided a soothing soundtrack as we enjoyed an intimate dinner. Each bite of the delicious meal was complemented by excellent wine. Time seemed to stand still as we relished the moment under the starry sky. In the captivating atmosphere, we danced, talked and laughed some more. After the night we had, I was so tired and full. I thought we would miss our flight back but somehow, a little after midnight, we landed back in London and returned to reality.

Nonso had been gone off and on since then and we'd slipped back into our routine of work, texts, late night Facetimes and something else we just started doing together – praying. One day I had a particularly rough day at work and the Panthers had an away game, so Nonso was out of town. I really craved his arms around me. I knew that if I talked to him, he would worry, so I had dodged his calls. After he sent a few threatening texts, I answered his Facetime. After filling him in, he said he couldn't do anything for me since he was away, but he knew Who could. That was the first time we prayed together. I was no slouch with my faith, but something hit totally different when your man prayed over you.

My man.

Yeah, that weekend in Lake Como, we decided to give our relationship a genuine shot.

I took another look in the dressing room mirror. I liked this dress the best. But to be doubly sure, I called Cassie. She was back in Atlanta for a visit, and I really missed my friend.

"Is that what you're going with?" she asked, her rude behind skipping any type of greeting.

"What? You don't like it?"

"Yinks, all I did was ask a question. Turn and face the camera on the mirror so I can see the back."

I did as she asked. The dress I chose was a green color-block, lantern-sleeve, belted bodycon dress.

"It's nice but too formal. This is like a family casual event, right?"

"Yeah, one hosted by one of his heros. I wanna look good."

"And you will. Go with the jumpsuit."

I had sent her a picture earlier once the attendant gave me some choices. The jumpsuit was a smooth, emerald green fabric that hugged my curves and cinched at my waist. The stand collar added a touch of sophistication, but the open back kept it from being too formal. Even though it was only mid-March in London and not really freezing outside, I still wanted to make sure I stayed warm.

After Cassie gave me a few more suggestions on accessories, we hung up and I went to the register. Nonso had given me way too much to spend so I decided to pick up something for him too. He had an unhealthy obsession with Ziedu Fashions casual footwear line. He wore their clothes sparingly, but he loved their footwear. So, I got him a pair of original Zeidu leather loafers in rich Ankara and chocolate brown.

Just got to the apt, see you in two hours.

Babe: See you soon.

I tossed my phone on the bed and went to take a shower. The hot water cascaded down my body and I breathed a thankful sigh of relief that it was Thursday, and I had the next day off. A three-day weekend was rare for me. The May board meeting was fast approaching, and I was still short "that one big client" according to my boss. I had signed on many others to Apex, however according to him, their portfolio sizes weren't "partner worthy."

"I don't understand you Ms. Martins. You have a big fish within reach, but prefer to play in the pond."

In the past few weeks, whenever I signed on a client that he thought didn't bring in the big bucks, he threw that slick comment at me. I knew he was referring to Nonso and how I had missed the opportunity to bag any of the players during my time as their teacher. I had since moved back to doing my regular job, something I was grateful for, but Mr. Wilson didn't let me forget my failure to snag one of the Viva City players as a client.

Nonso and I talked about money and investments often, but as our dynamic shifted, I didn't think it was ethical to manage his money. Neither did he ask me to. My feelings didn't mean I still wasn't short on my quota. That and the fact that my parents were coming to town gave me anxiety that I hoped to put behind me for the night and the rest of the weekend.

~

"You do know it's rude to stare?" I teased.

"Not when who I'm staring at is mine," Nonso replied, a smirk adorning his face.

He took my hand and twirled me around for the second time since he'd arrived at my apartment. Now we were in the elevator, making our way down and he had me up against the wall, his hands above my head, caging me in. His lips trailed fiery kisses along my neck. My heart raced and the tension between us was palpable, charged with unspoken promises and eager anticipation. My hands went under his black and green blazer and circled his waist. He leaned back a bit, his dark eyes burned with desire and admiration that I was sure mirrored mine.

Planting a brief kiss on my forehead, he caressed my waist, sending shivers down my spine. I could anticipate his next move before it even happened, and when his lips finally met mine in a passionate tango, all else faded away. But too soon, the elevator dinged, and we pulled apart, both of us with racing hearts, gasping for air.

"You drive me crazy," Nonso whispered in my ear.

His words sending a rush of heat through me, making it hard to catch my breath. So, I simply smiled, unable to form any coherent response. He pecked my lips once more before taking my hand and leading me to his car.

Nonso maneuvered the streets of London effortlessly with his hand permanently on my thigh. We were good on time so there was no need for him to rush. He'd gotten better at driving on the left side of the road, and I was seriously impressed.

We were on our way to Kensington for a gathering hosted by Kamal Danjuma and his wife, Ebele. The long-retired football player now ran an organization called Beyond the Sports. According to Nonso, their mission was to prepare athletes for life after professional sports. Kamal was on a mini speaking tour of a few clubs across North London and his last stop was Viva City FC. After his talk, he invited a few of the African players to his home. Nonso was beyond excited although he tried not to show it.

"Should I be worried that all your big homies are reformed, borderline still unhinged, but now have families' bad boys... well now men?"

Nonso cackled at my question, but I was serious.

"Don't forget the love their women part."

"How can I? I researched them. Both Cheta and Kamal are borderline obsessed. They're forever commenting and checking people on their wives' social media pages."

"Shoot, I'm almost obsessed over you, so I get it."

"Almost? Boy, you better be fully obsessed with all this social media hate I'm getting."

"Your man is the ish baby. It's a fact of life you gotta deal with, so people are gonna hate."

I rolled my eyes. This man was annoyingly confident sometimes. "I'm about to push you out of this car."

"You too pretty to be this violent."

I sucked my teeth, and he blew me a kiss.

"Anyway, I'm just playing with you. I'll be fully obsessed when I meet your momsie and get to know what I gotta look forward to." He lightly squeezed my thigh and glanced at me before refocusing on the road. "I'on want me and my kids waking up to a version of you that we can't even recognize in our golden years. Your momsie will be the vision of you in the future."

Nonso was ridiculous and as much as I wanted to scold him, the mere mention of him meeting my parents made me freeze. I had talked to his mom, sister, and brother over the phone. It was nothing I planned. We were out one Saturday cycling and had stopped at a small kiosk to buy a beverage and snack when his phone rang, and his family was on the other end of the line. They were gathered somewhere for someone's baby dedication and decided to give him a call.

I looked a mess, sweaty, hair sticking to my face, but Nonso said I looked beautiful and pulled me in front of him to greet them. I had also talked to Cheta and Kane. Cheta was reckless at the mouth and his wife Reign didn't hesitate to call him to order. I couldn't stand Kane and I knew he probably couldn't stand me either. He talked to my man like he owed him some everlasting homage because he saved him in the past. I hated it, but it was a touchy topic for Nonso, so I left it alone.

I was more involved in Nonso's life than he was in mine, and the upcoming visit from my parents for my nephew's christening had me feeling anxious. Nonso knew a lot about me – he knew Cassie, the ups and downs of my job, my hobbies, things that made me who I was, but he didn't know anything about my family. He knew of them and about them, but hadn't really spoken to any of them.

My sister used to give me a hard time about him, but now she just avoided talking about him altogether. My brother was reserving his opinion until he met Nonso, and my parents had no idea he even existed. Every Sunday, I called my parents and pretended that everything was normal, but I couldn't shake this feeling that they were conspiring against me with my sister. I'd prayed that one of Nonso's games would take him out of town on the day of the christening, but unfortunately, he was going to be there.

"Are you okay?" Nonso asked, noticing my quietness.

"Yeah, why?" I replied quickly.

"You went quiet on me."

"I'm fine, babe," I reassured him with a smile as I squeezed his shoulder.

About two hours later, we had eaten dinner and mingled, then we all gathered by the pool to relax and enjoy each other's company. Kamal and his wife, Ebele, looked even more stunning in person than they did on social media. It was clear that he was an unpredictable character, but seeing them together as a couple was truly beautiful. Ebele looked so portable next to her husband who towered over her. Nonso had told me some stories about them, but it seemed like Kamal had struck a kinda healthy balance between hovering and giving her space.

Their home in Kensington was breathtaking, and I was surprised to learn that this wasn't their main residence; they actually lived in Abuja. I recognized some people from Nonso's team who were also at the gathering. Xander and Jay were the people Nonso hung out with often, so I had met their significant others before. It was great having Abi here. She and Xander were so cute. To be an nward-winning gospel artist, she was more down to earth than I would have imagined. It was like having Cassie there with me because she and I communicated with our eyes most of the night. Nonso joked that he and Xander had to keep us separated because we could sell them, and they wouldn't even know it.

As I made my way back from the washroom, I took a moment

to admire the paintings lining the hallway. One caught my eye in particular. It depicted a woman standing on the edge of a cliff, her hair blowing wildly in the wind as she faced a stormy sea. The painting perfectly captured the raw emotion of facing uncertainty and adversity head-on, yet standing strong and unwavering in the midst of chaos.

"That's one of my favorite paintings."

I turned and Ebele Danjuma was standing close to me.

I smiled. "I can see why. It's like she's speaking to me."

The woman's gaze was fixed on the horizon, portraying determination and resilience in the face of danger. In contrast to the dark blue and grey swirls representing the turbulent sea and sky, the woman herself seemed to radiate with a soft, ethereal light. The rugged cliff she stood upon only added to the sense of risk and danger portrayed in the painting.

"I bought this when my hubby and I – well he was still my fiancé at the time –were set to get married," she said, her eyes remaining on the painting. "I'm sure as you know, professional athletes can be a challenge to be with. It's hard enough to be in any type of relationship, but to be in love with a man whose fans think they have a right to him too is even more difficult. The injuries, the media, the fans, family, I mean, it can be a lot."

I shook my head and she just laughed. She tucked her wild, black curly hair behind her ear. I had firsthand knowledge of what she was talking about. Well, except the in-love part. I didn't think Nonso and I were there yet.

"Kam recovered from an injury some months before our wedding. Things were going great, then the ground just opened, and everything went to hell."

I turned to the painting. "You guys seemed to have recovered well. I mean a blind man can see he's crazy over you."

"That's my baby. And the feeling is mutual. *I carry betta eye go market.*"

I grinned at the Pidgin phrase she used at the end. It meant she made a great choice. I could tell she didn't speak pidgin often.

"Anyway, I saw this painting, and it made me think. Despite everything happening around her, the woman appeared calm and composed, embodying inner strength and peace amidst external turmoil. In the moment I needed Him most, I forgot that Jesus even existed. This painting reminded me that even in the most challenging of circumstances—"

"E, didn't we agree a long time ago that you don't leave my side when there's a crowd?"

Both of us turned and watched Kamal saunter over. His eyes stayed locked on his wife. Apparently, his comment was some kind of inside joke because although she looked at him lovingly, she was also annoyed.

"What? I was about to kick everyone out when I couldn't find you outside," he said, acting completely justified in annoying his wife.

He came to a stop in front of her, cupped her face and kissed her. It wasn't a quick peck either. The man acted like I wasn't standing right there. Ebele was enjoying herself too, but I guess she came to her senses quicker.

"Kam, wait, hold on." Ebele turned to me. "Please excuse us. This is…"

"Yinka Martins, I'm here with Nonso…" I supplied.

Abi and I had chatted with Ebele earlier. I'm sure that was why she felt comfortable talking in depth about the painting. I smiled because that kiss must've been a doozy that she couldn't remember my name.

"Chijuka. Cool dude, nice to meet you." Kamal extended his hand, and I placed mine in it.

After giving me a brief spiel about how the partners of athletes were the real MVPs, he walked his wife and I back outside. Nonso's eyes met mine, and a soft smile tugged at the corners of his lips as he walked over to us. He pulled me to his side and dapped Kamal, then greeted Ebele.

"That's a good look," Kamal said.

Nonso brushed his lips against my forehead. "Trust me, I know."

The Danjumas excused themselves and Nonso wrapped his arms around me from behind. I leaned into him, and he kissed my neck.

"You had fun?" he asked.

"A lot. You?"

"Yeah, it was cool, but I'm ready to get outta here. You game?"

"With you? Of course."

Nonso grabbed my hand, and we headed in the direction of our hosts to tell them that we were headed out. Mrs. Danjuma's words danced around in my mind. Not only about my relationship with Nonso, but also the weight of my shame concerning Bisi. I'd let the guilt of her passing change me from the person I was. I didn't pass through the valley. I remained there and succumbed to it.

True to his word, Nonso had been helping me find peace. Looking at the woman in the painting and Ebele's words about the courage amidst the storm, I realized once again that just as Nonso said, my silent storm had lasted too long because I did not use my tools of warfare to fight. However, over the last several weeks with this man by my side, I had gained a newfound sense of peace and strength. His presence had a way of calming the chaos within me and despite my initial apprehension, Nonso was the beacon of light in my life.

I shuddered to think what would happen if we didn't make it. I drew a quick breath at the realization that maybe I was in love with him after all.

eleven

Nonso

THE AIRPORT WAS BUZZING with activity as people rushed by with their suitcases in tow. I couldn't hide my frustration as I watched the luggage carousel go around for the second time without Yinka's bag in sight. The chaos of voices and movement only added to my impatience. All I wanted was to leave this place, get some food and rest. We'd just landed at Cairo International Airport in Egypt, and instead of being on our way to the hotel, we were stuck here waiting for her suitcase to arrive.

In accordance with FIFA regulations, clubs were required to give their players time off during the third week of March so they could represent their home countries in international friendlies or qualifying matches. I was chosen to represent Nigeria in an inaugural friendly series launched by FIFA. There were no prizes or trophies at stake. The purpose was simply for players from different confederations governed by FIFA to have a chance to play against each other.

I wasn't leaving my woman in Viva City if I didn't have to, so when I was tapped to go, I asked her if she would take some time off and come with me and she agreed. For a minute, I thought I was going to have to kidnap her "it's not in the planner" behind. I mean, she was doing better with the strict planning thing, and I was also to blame for not telling her weeks in advance...but I forgot.

"It's only four days, babe. Tell me again why you had to pack two suitcases?" I asked. I was positive my annoyance was evident.

I should've followed my first mind and just told her to bring her passport, then had her shop when we got here. But I didn't want to hear her mouth about having her own money and my spending habits, so I let her do her thing and pack her own stuff. Normally, I wouldn't pay any attention to her whining about having her own money. I was her man and would always buy her whatever I wanted. But lately I was dealing with some other stuff and the last thing I wanted was to beef with my lady. Even if it wasn't that deep, I might say stuff I shouldn't.

"I like having options," she said, leaning against me and giving me a quick kiss on the lips. Her touch always had a calming effect on me. "What's wrong? You've been moody lately. That's not like you."

I was doing exactly what I promised myself I wouldn't do – let the stress of other things affect our relationship. I pecked her lips and her temple a few more times.

"Nothing, baby. Just tired."

That wasn't entirely untrue. The bad weather a few weeks ago caused some makeup games to be squeezed into our already packed schedule, so it felt like I was playing every day.

I wrapped my arm around Yinka's waist. She was the most beautiful woman I had ever seen, and trust me, I'd seen a lot of women. I had always been a one-woman man. I'd been faithful to Lesedi during our entire relationship. However, after our breakup and during my dark days, I was reckless in these streets. But the reason Yinka had me so gone was because she wasn't only stunning on the outside, but also a brilliant, caring, and independent woman. I couldn't even lie; Lesedi stood on business too...except when it came to her family.

"Thank God. It's here," Yinka's voice broke through my thoughts, and I went to the baggage carousel to load her bags onto a trolley. We were definitely flying private from now on. She could complain about the expense all she wanted, but we weren't doing this again.

Several minutes later, feeling my phone vibrate in my pocket, I glanced up to see Yinka still deep in conversation with the concierge. I furrowed my brows as I read Kane's fifth message of the day. My phone had been turned off during our flight. Ignoring the urgency in his words, I quickly responded with a simple acknowledgement.

> I'm outta town. I'll hit you up when I can.

> K: It's important, Black. Hit me up ASAP.

> I got you.

I finished texting Kane and put my phone away just as Yinka called for me.

"Babe, we're ready."

I rolled my shoulders to shake off the negative headspace Kane had put me in and walked over to the bank of elevators to meet her. When we arrived at the prestigious Hotel Cairo at the Nile Plaza and checked in, I waited while Yinka confirmed with the staff about the excursion opportunities she had found online. The hotel was in the heart of Cairo, located on the banks of the River Nile.

As we rode up to the top floor, I wrapped my arms around my girl and pulled her close. I caught the bellhop sneaking a glance at her. She was wearing a crop top that showed her stomach. Not a lot, but enough to annoy me. I wasn't about to tell her what to wear because I didn't feel like I had to, nor was it my place. But just as I knew it would, this outfit was attracting more attention than I preferred. My woman was fine so I understood it. Besides, this man was no threat, but I still had to mess with him.

"Hey man, I know she fine but don't look too hard. Just a little bit, and we good." I addressed the bellhop.

Yinka playfully nudged me with her elbow, and I nipped at her earlobe with my teeth. "If you wanna wear stuff like this, don't be surprised when I react," I whispered.

She shuddered in my arms, and I couldn't help but smile. The elevator doors opened, and we followed the bellhop to our double royal suite.

"Babe, I can't believe this view. Come look at this," Yinka called out to me from the balcony.

I felt a pang of nerves seeing her out there. I assumed she'd be over the view by now after our lunch and nap, but apparently not. I was in the living room that separated our rooms tying my shoes, while she continued to enjoy the scenery. I lifted my gaze and found myself lost in the sight of her. She was wearing another crop top, this one a stunning deep brown that beautifully complemented her glowing skin. She paired it with shape hugging blue jeans and strappy heels. Her hair was straightened, and her light makeup showcased her beautiful freckles.

When we first arrived, we both retreated to our individual rooms. My stomach was growling, and I needed to eat ASAP. So, we headed downstairs to the restaurant to eat before we made a quick run to where the team was staying. I had early morning team practice, so this evening was all about us... well, mostly about her. She had been under a lot of stress at work, and I just wanted her to unwind and relax.

"Babe, come on. Let's take a picture. This is amazing."

I agreed that the view was breathtaking. From where we stood on the balcony, we had the perfect view of the Nile and distant Pyramids. I got up and adjusted my dark blue jeans and tan Ziedu shirt before wrapping my arms around Yinka and posing for some selfies she took. Then of course, I had to snap some photos of her as well. After making sure I got the perfect shot, she slipped her phone in her purse, and I grabbed her hand so we could leave.

Exiting the hotel, we were greeted by the bustling streets of Cairo. The early evening skies were a mix of pink and purple. The air was comfortably warm, with a slight coolness that foreshadowed the approaching night.

I escorted Yinka to the Porsche 911 ST I'd rented for us to move around in while here. She looked up at me with a smile and I winked. The driver hopped out and handed me the keys. I could feel Yinka's excitement without even looking at her. Once we were both settled in the car, my girl let out a squeal of delight. Yinka usually drove a practical Ford Fiesta, so my SUV always amazed her with its fancy features. One day, a yellow Porsche sped past us, and she mentioned wanting to experience that kind of rush. I made a mental note to fulfill her wish while we were here.

"I can't believe you actually got this, babe," she said, running her hands over the leather seats and dashboard.

"I told you I would."

"But—"

"No buts. You said you wanted to know what it would feel like. Now you will. You ready to ride?"

"With you? Of course."

I punched our destination into the GPS and pulled away from the curb. From the corner of my eye, I watched as Yinka fiddled with the satellite radio until she found a station she liked.

The plan was to get two historic sites in before we had dinner. I'd been to Cairo many times before. Although I never stayed long, my travels offered me some knowledge of the city. However, I wanted Yinka to have the full experience and knowledge of the places we were visiting, so I had arranged for a tour guide to meet us at our first stop – the Coptic Cairo district.

The guide pointed to the tall structures that were the city's signature. "The city is called the—"

"The city of a thousand minarets," Yinka finished.

"Look at you, being all prepared," I teased.

The guide glanced at us and smiled. I guess he approved of her knowledge of the city. He then continued, "The city was given that name because of all the Islamic architecture that make up the city's skyline. But as you can see..." he used his hands to show the expanse of the district. "...old mosques and Pyramids are not the only things the city's history is known for."

While we strolled down the district, the guide told us that the Interfaith Complex was made up of fortress, churches, and synagogues that predated the founding of Cairo by the Muslim Fatimids in 969 AD. Yinka pulled out her camera and took some pictures of the ruins of the Babylon Fortress. It was what remained of an ancient town that was built where a canal connected the Nile to the Red Sea.

"You know you learn about some of these things in history or from the Bible, but to actually see them is chilling," Yinka said.

"I feel you. It's exactly how I felt when I first saw the river Nile."

"I know right? I was thinking about that earlier. The same river or some part of it was where God guided Moses in a basket until he got to his destination. I mean it just blows your mind," she said.

I pulled Yinka closer and kissed her temple. For the next half hour, we visited a few more ancient churches and synagogues. Next, we made our way to the Cairo Citadel, where the Mosque of Muhammad Ali was. The mosque was cool, but what really got us in awe were its ancient walls. Not only could we see the stunning views of the city below, but there were landmarks that could also be seen from that vantage point. We were given the history of the 12th century structure which was built to protect against Crusader attacks.

As night fell, we decided to end the tour and head to dinner. Driving through the streets of the city, we enjoyed the scenic sights on our way to the Giza Pyramid Complex to Khufu's where I had a reservation.

The host greeted us with a warm smile and led us to a

secluded rooftop booth, offering us an incredible view of the Pyramid. Yinka's eyes widened in awe as she took in the breathtaking sight. I grinned, satisfied that I had chosen the perfect spot. As we settled into our seats, the host handed us menus and informed us that our waiter would be with us shortly. Flipping through the menu, Yinka kept turning back to take in the view of the pyramid. I never sat with my back to the exit, but I also wanted her to enjoy the view without the stress.

"Come here." I reached across the table for her hand.

Taking my hand, she walked around and got in next to me. I shifted. We were still a little snug, but I didn't mind her being on me. I would've put her in my lap, but I knew she wouldn't want that. At least not here.

"Better?" I asked.

"Much." She kissed my cheek. "Thank you, babe."

I watched her with contentment, grateful to have her by my side. We scanned through the menu, both of us talking through the items we were familiar with and the items we wanted to try out. My baby could be stuck in her ways and trying out new things was something I was glad I was able to get her to do.

"I can't believe we're dining here." Yinka turned to me with a wide grin. "You really did your thing, babe."

I shrugged modestly, trying to hide my pleased expression. "When you smile, my freckles brighten. Seeing those freckles stand out is the highlight of my every day, so I gotta keep you smiling." My lips lifted in a grin.

"Let the media tell it, you're mean, arrogant and brash, but you're so sweet," she said, taking my hand in hers. "Thank you."

"I am all those things... but not with you," I let her know.

She shook her head, and I nuzzled her neck. She probably thought I was joking, but I wasn't. The only things I cared about in this phase of my life were my family, my game, my walk with Jesus and now her. The public opinion of me was no longer what I lived for. Yinka got the part of me that my family got.

Our waiter arrived to take our orders. We settled on sayadiyah and mu'ammar rice. Yinka ordered a mocktail, but since I had to train in the morning I settled for water. As we waited for our food, we sat in semi-silence and admired the grandeur of the Pyramid.

"You mean this is the actual pyramid of Khufu, the ancient pharaoh?" Yinka asked after a few moments.

I smiled and nodded. "Yep, history says that he built the Great Pyramid of Giza, one of the Seven Wonders of the Ancient World."

My love for history wasn't news to Yinka. She chuckled, noting how much it meant to me.

"I believe it's important to understand our past and how far we've come as a civilization. But more specifically, if you don't know your history, somebody else will tell you their made-up version of it."

She nodded and we both continued to admire the majestic pyramid in front of us. Several minutes later, our waiter brought out our food. Sayadiyah, a steaming plate of rice cooked with singari fish for me and mu'ammar rice, a dish of baked Egyptian rice over beef for Yinka. We said grace and then took a bite of each other's meal. I couldn't get into her rice, but Yinka seemed to enjoy it and my fish. We ate in silence for a few moments before she brought up her earlier conversation about Moses and the River Nile. Sitting so close to such historic landmarks had clearly put her in a contemplative mood.

"I was thinking about Moses," she mused, her gaze fixed ahead. "His true character emerged when he witnessed the mistreatment of the Israelite. He could've ignored it and continued to live as a royal, but he didn't. That decision led him to his true purpose." Turning to me, she smiled. "I'm grateful you came into my life. While everyone else was content to see me defined by my past and one mistake, you helped me see beyond that."

I paused, wanting to respond, but also curious if she had more to say.

"I know I'm responsible for my own healing and I tried. Believe me, I did. I sought therapy, read self-help books..." she continued. "But you helped me see my true worth. The choice between complacency and action. My family...they just..." She trailed off.

"Our families do what they think is best," I interjected, "but ultimately, it's up to us to follow God's direction. Look at Moses, flaws, and all. God still used him without requiring him to change who he was first."

"I know that in my head." Yinka sighed. "But sometimes..."

"The devil is always loud, but we must be louder. Believe me, I know. The level I sunk to, mad at the world for something I did to myself was unbelievable."

Yinka squeezed my shoulder, grounding me in the present moment. My mind had drifted back to a time when I was lost in my destructive tendencies. Multiple women, fights, and excessive drinking consumed me. If anyone told me *then* that there would eventually be a *now*, I would have laughed in their face.

I said, "It just goes to show that God is able. Moses was in that wilderness by himself before he ended up at that well. Those conditions must have been harsh, but he really wasn't by himself because God kept him. For me, the fear of abandonment kept me loyal to the wrong people and not setting up boundaries. My issues had me scared of letting go of dead weight, because I didn't want to walk alone. The boundaries I have set up have truly caused me to soar, even though they have been a huge adjustment for some..." My voice trailed off as I thought about how my extended family led by my dad dragged me through social media mud any chance they got.

"I guess we make each other better," she said.

I leaned in and kissed her lips, still tasting the sweetness of her strawberry mocktail. "It's always you and me, baby." We both laughed. "Okay, enough deep talk. What do you want for dessert?"

As we finished our dinner, we ordered a small box of zalabia, the Egyptian donut, to go. Later we took a leisurely stroll around the Giza Pyramid Complex before heading back to the hotel. As we drove back, Yinka rested her head on my arm and let out a contented sigh. I squeezed her thigh, glad she was happy, and we could have this time. We were entering the crucial stages of the season. Once we got back to Viva City, I wouldn't have as much time, so this was perfect.

twelve
Yinka

THE NEXT MORNING, I was awakened from a delightful dream by the sound of approaching footsteps. I tugged on the luxurious, one thousand thread count sheets that cradled my body before slowly opening my eyes. I saw Nonso standing at the edge of the bed with a warm smile on his face. His figure looked perfect in the green and white tracksuit, representing Nigeria's colors. I was about to compliment him when I noticed my black bonnet dangling from his index finger. Panic rushed through me as I reached for my head and realized my bonnet must have fallen off during the night.

Nonso leaned down and planted a gentle kiss on my forehead, whispering, "Good morning, love."

"Good morning, baby." I reached for my bonnet to cover my messy hair, but he playfully raised his hand.

"How did it end up on the floor? Don't tell me I gotta look forward to you kicking me out of our matrimonial bed. You too pretty to be sleeping this wild."

I ignored his teasing. "My hair is going to be a mess."

"You can be walking around here looking like Edward Scissorhands and I'll still think you're the most beautiful person in the world. It's the freckles for me, baby." He handed me my bonnet.

A smile spread across my face as I sat up. "Tell me anything."

He sat on the edge of the bed. "With you, it's gonna always be the truth."

I checked the time. It was five in the morning. "Why are you up so early?" I asked, stretching.

"I have to go to the training facility. Hit the gym, do some drills, then go over strategy. You, on the other hand, have a full day ahead of you. Breakfast will be brought up in two hours and at ten o'clock, a car will be by to pick you up. You have a spa appointment, and a personal shopper will meet you for some retail therapy."

I was speechless. He knew how much I hated aimlessly wandering around when shopping. I preferred to go in, get what I needed, and leave. But in a foreign country, I wouldn't know where to start. A personal shopper would make the experience more enjoyable for me. My chest felt tight and warm, a sensation that was both comforting and overwhelming. My stomach felt light and tingly, as if butterflies were fluttering wildly within it. Nonso always made me feel so special that it almost overwhelmed me.

"You spoil me, baby," I said as he stood. "Thank you."

"As I should. No thanks necessary." He waggled his brow. "Just keep riding with me."

After reminding me that he would be with the team until game time, he proceeded to warn me about the consequences of not answering his calls when he called me. I rolled my eyes, and he kissed me one more time before he sauntered to the door.

"A car will be here at five to take you to the stadium. I'm serious, Specs. Answer the phone when I call the first ti—"

"See you later, babe," I said, cutting off his rant.

Since we weren't at home, I knew he'd worry if I didn't answer his calls. His continuously repeating it was a waste of time.

He gave me a stern look before leaving the room. I jumped out of bed, put on my robe, and caught him just as he was exiting.

"Be safe."

He kissed my forehead. "I will. Have fun. See you later."

As soon as he left, I took my time in the shower. The hot water was divine. Afterwards, I took care of my skin then dressed for the day ahead. Sure enough, breakfast arrived on time, and I indulged in a delicious spread while still admiring the breathtaking view from our hotel room. I just couldn't get over it. The sun shone brightly, bathing the city below in a warm light.

I responded to my sister's text. Although Tolu wasn't fully sold on Nonso, I was grateful that she was checking up on me. It was nice when she acted like my sister and not my mother. I took more pictures of the stunning view outside.

My social media notifications were blowing up with comments on the photo I posted of Nonso and me on the balcony last night. It was a rule of mine to never post in real-time, so I had just uploaded the picture a few minutes ago. As usual, some comments were positive and congratulatory calling us couple goals, while others predicted that Nonso would eventually dump me like he did Lesedi. At the mention of her name, I clicked over to her profile out of curiosity. As she had been doing lately, she posted an old picture of her and Nonso together.

@sedi_j: Show them how it's done in Cairo, Black Knight. Cheering for you.

My jaw clenched and suddenly the pancakes in my mouth lost their flavor. She used to comment on Nonso's posts until he blocked her. One day, I complained about her constant presence under his posts, and he got frustrated with my insecurities. He picked up his phone, blocked her, and went on to ignore me for the rest of the movie we were watching.

Deep down, I knew I was being childish, but their past made me feel threatened for some reason. Well, not for some reason; I knew exactly what it was. Her family played a role in their breakup, and it made me worry that I could end up like her.

While technically I didn't need my family's approval to be with Nonso, it would make life easier if I had it. Ever since my mistake that brought shame to our family name, I had been on a mission to make them proud and regain their trust.

Some days I thought I had it, but there were some comments they made that had me questioning if I really did. The drive for their approval had led me to change parts of myself, hoping that by conforming to their expectations, I could undo the damage and earn back their respect. But deep down, I yearned to be accepted for who I truly was and my choices.

I let out a sigh and closed Instagram. After Nonso blocked Lesedi, she wrote a cryptic post on Twitter and then switched tactics to trolling me every time I posted a picture of Nonso and me.

The rest of my breakfast went by in a blur. My outfit for the day was simple. I wore a lilac, linen, two-piece outfit, and my hair was wrapped in a bun. I knew I was going to wash it upon my return, so I didn't want to do too much. Nonso had been begging me to wear my hair curly, and for the rest of the trip, his wish would come true.

Right on time, the front desk called to let me know that my car was waiting. A few minutes later, I arrived at the spa, which looked like a luxurious haven for the wealthy. Soothing music played in the background as I entered, complementing the soft lighting, and calming pastel green and blue. The air was infused with a blend of lavender and eucalyptus, with hints of citrus. Walking up to the desk, I gave my name to the receptionist as instructed by Nonso.

"Welcome, Ms. Martins. We've been expecting you. Naria will be your attendant for the day."

I nodded and she signaled for another woman to join us. After we exchanged greetings, she informed me that I would be receiving their premium deluxe package: massage, facial, manicure, and pedicure. She led me to a private room and returned shortly with refreshing cucumber water and a tray of fresh fruit.

About fifteen minutes later, I undressed and settled onto the massage table in a dimly lit inner room. The warm scent of essential oils wafted up my nostrils. My masseuse, a petite woman with long dark hair and a serene smile, greeted me with a gentle bow before beginning her skilled work on my muscles. The soft music playing in the background transported me into deeper relaxation, and for once in a long time, my mind felt calm instead of chaotic.

Later that evening, my phone buzzed in my hand, and I smiled as I read Nonso's message. I had sent him a picture of my outfit. It was nothing spectacular. I had on the Nigerian jersey he got for me and some black jeans. I accessorized the outfit with a pair of green and white Addidas and a black leather crossbody. But to him, I could be wearing a trash bag and look good.

> Babe: You look beautiful. I can't wait to wrap my arms around you.

> I'll be there soon. I missed you today.

> Babe: I missed you more. Hurry. But tell that driver to be safe.

I sent him a couple of laughing emojis. That man always wanted to eat his cake and have it. I sank into the back seat of the SUV and enjoyed the scenery as the driver took me to Cairo International Stadium.

I'd had a masterclass in self-care, and I couldn't keep from smiling even if I wanted to. After the full works at the spa, the personal shopper met me there as planned. The stylish woman with a warm smile introduced herself as Sophia and at once put me at ease with her friendly demeanor. We discussed my preferences and style before setting off for a day of retail therapy in the bustling city.

Sophia led me through chic boutiques and designer stores, selecting pieces I would never have considered on my own. I knew what personal shoppers did, but my money conscious mind made me wonder if the expense was necessary. Hanging out with Sophia, I concluded that it certainly was. With her expert guidance, I tried on outfits that made me not only look beautiful, but feel more confident. I insisted she had lunch with me before we went our separate ways. When I got back, I took a shower to wash off the day then set my alarm to get up an hour and a half before I was supposed to leave. Then I slipped into the freshly made bed and crashed.

Soon enough, I arrived at the stadium, and someone was waiting to escort me to where Nonso was. I was only able to share a brief hug before he told someone to usher me to the VIP skybox. I wasn't expecting to get a lot of words from him because that wasn't his style when he was focused on the task ahead.

In the skybox, there were who I guessed to be top officials and their families. It wasn't crowded though. The suite exuded luxury, with leather seats and a great view of the stadium. Sports memorabilia adorned the walls, showcasing the Egyptian national team's history. Waiters offered drinks and a variety of traditional finger food and snacks. It was exciting to watch my man play from this exclusive vantage point.

"This referee better not call that play. Fair is fair and Black is blazing with that ball."

I looked to my left and a man that seemed to watch this whole match on his feet groused. I was now on my feet too. Hours had gone by, and we were now at a crucial place in the match. Everyone around me cheered as Nonso made his way towards the goal post. I felt a surge of excitement within me. My heart thudded against my rib cage as he effortlessly dribbled past defenders, showcasing his talent and determination with every step. I could see the entire stadium also erupt into cheers as he finally took the shot. The ball soared through the air towards the net. Hushed silence enveloped the place. The Nigerian team playing against Croatia was down by one and there were only two minutes left in the game.

I held my breath as the ball hit the back of the net with a

resounding thud. And then, all at once, the entire stadium erupted into a deafening roar of cheers and applause. You could hear the Nigerian fan club delegation the loudest. They were playing tunes that brought back a sense of nostalgia. My heart sometime hurt at how Nigerians were so dedicated to a country that often failed them at every turn. I read someone's caption on IG some time ago that said one day they hoped Nigeria loved her people half as much as they loved her. I felt that.

I sighed and refocused on the celebration. I watched as Nonso celebrated in the corner of the field and his teammates piled on top of him in sheer joy. When my schedule permitted, I went to Panther games, although in London, I preferred to watch football from my living room. I was not at all for the recklessness that often occurred in the stadiums with overzealous fans.

For this tournament, I feared Nonso getting hurt for a friendly and jeopardizing his full-time job with Viva. I had advised him to take it easy on the field. With the ease with which he had said, "Okay," I should've known he wasn't paying me any attention. He was going to always bring one hundred percent to his game no matter the circumstances. That was why I'd learned to be present, but give him space whenever his team lost.

The noise in the room slowly quieted down, and I returned to my seat in the comfortable leather chair. I placed my phone on my knee, ready to answer if Nonso called now that the game was over. While waiting, I pulled out my compact from my purse to touch up my makeup when suddenly, I heard my name being called.

"Ms. Martins."

"Yes?" I responded, looking at the man standing next to me who was wearing a shirt labeled "Stadium Security."

"Mr. Chijuka has requested that I escort you to him."

Smiling, I nodded and packed up my trash to discard and followed the man out. I was escorted to a door marked "Players Only." I waited outside as instructed and a few minutes later, Nonso emerged. I smiled as he strolled toward me. The familiar scent of his shower gel and perfume wafted up my nostrils. He was now dressed in another style of tracksuit with the Nigerian colors. He grinned and opened his arms for a hug.

"You were incredible out there," I gushed as we pulled away.

Nonso's face lit up even more, and he kissed me on the forehead. "I'm glad you could be here. Don't tell nobody, but I had an extra battery in my back knowing you were somewhere up there watching me play."

"It'll be our little secret," I squeezed his waist.

"You see, you all right with me, Specs. Come on, let's go get some food. I wanna cuddle, watch movies and chill. With any luck, I can dodge these reporters."

With our hands intertwined, we walked out of the stadium, to cheers and high-fives from fans. Nonso ended up having to stop and answer some questions from one reporter, but he managed to dodge the rest. I couldn't help but feel proud to be standing by his side. His teammates and coaches all congratulated him on his performance. It was evident that he was respected and loved.

Nonso led us to his car, opened the passenger door for me, then got into the driver's seat. We drove through the city, the cool night air whipping through the open windows. Nonso's hand rested on my knee as he navigated the streets, his eyes occasionally darting to meet mine, a playful smile tugging at the corner of his lips. I wished in some reality, we could stay here away from the world.

～

WHAT'S THAT THING ABOUT IF WISHES WERE HORSES? Anyway, horses hadn't flown and Nonso had just turned the corner down the road leading to my apartment. We landed back in the UK about an hour ago.

The four days in Cairo were absolute bliss. The morning after the team's victory, Nonso and I ventured out of the hotel for another day of exploration. We spent a few hours in the Egyptian Museum, marveling at the extensive collection of artifacts from ancient Egypt. Then we went to Bab Zuweila. I was dressed comfortably, but when I saw those one hundred and fifty steps of the spiral staircase, I told Nonso we needed to go somewhere else. Being one of the three remaining medieval gates in the old city walls of Cairo, I really wanted to experience it, but I wasn't exerting all that energy for it. After much persuasion, we settled on going up only two out of the three levels. I still was able to get some good pictures.

As the evening approached, we took a leisurely walk through the bustling Khan el-Khalili market. We were told it was one of the oldest bazaars in the Middle East. There were countless varieties of colorful displays of textiles, spices, and trinkets. We indulged in local delicacies, some Egyptian street food and admired the vibrant displays of goods. Nonso even surprised me with a beautiful handmade necklace as a souvenir.

Later that night, we went on a romantic dinner cruise along the Nile. Over traditional Egyptian cuisine, we were serenaded with live music and the gentle lapping of water against the boat. Nonso and I danced under the stars, lost in the enchantment of our surroundings.

"Specs, you good?"

"What? Huh...Oh yeah, I'm fine."

It hadn't occurred to me that we were now parked in front of my building. Nonso was looking at me with concerned confusion. I shook my head, trying to clear the fog of memories that enveloped me from our time away.

"I promise, I'm fine."

He snaked his hand around the back of my neck and drew me in for a quick kiss. His fingers massaged my nape, and I was in heaven. A moan escaped my lips and he chuckled.

"Stop doing that. I'm trying as it is."

He was talking about our near accident on our last night in Cairo. Dancing under the stars while on the river Nile almost had us about to consummate the fire that had long since burned within us. Luckily the Holy Spirit's conviction and our desire to remain right with the Lord took over the moment.

But then he made another bold declaration. "We gotta slow down. I intend to be your next and forever because one day you're gonna be my wife."

I chuckled as he let my neck go. "Then stop touching me."

"See, that's a problem because I can't do that." He opened his door and stepped out of the car, then rounded the car and opened mine. I glanced up at the familiar facade of my apartment building, its red bricks glowing in the warm evening light. Nonso got out my luggage and we made our way up the elevator and empty hallway to my flat.

Once inside, I kicked off my shoes and sank onto the couch, feeling a mix of exhaustion and contentment wash over me. Nonso appeared from my room where he had taken my bags. He leaned over me.

"I gotta go babe, come lock up."

I pouted. "You can't stay just a little bit. I'll whip us up something to eat."

He brushed his lips against my forehead and lifted himself up. "Nah, I gotta get some sleep and be at the training facility early."

He yawned and I let it rest. It was Sunday evening and although I had the next day off, I knew he had a game on Tuesday and needed his rest. If I pushed, he would stay, but that would be selfish. He pulled me up and draped his arm around my neck as I walked him to the door. Giving him a final hug, I locked the door after him and made my way to my room.

The following morning, I trudged to the kitchen to brew a cup of coffee. I could've stopped at my favorite coffee shop to get one, but I was pressed for time. I needed this cup to keep me awake while I drove to Wales. What I thought would be a restful evening with me meal prepping, listening to my favorite podcast and resetting for the week, turned out to be a chaotic evening once I got my sister's text to be at her place in the afternoon.

She knew I was back because I texted her the minute Nonso

left. But some hours later, right when I was about to start cooking, her text came through.

> Sis T: Our parents are in town.

They were a week early and I wasn't prepared. It would be too much to ask my sister to be my ally, so I knew I was on my own. Once I had this coffee I'd hit the road. Hopefully by the time I arrived, I would've sorted out everything I wanted to say.

> I'm leaving, now, babe.

> Babe: Be safe and let me know when you get there.

Immediately I got the text from my sister, I told Nonso. He was befuddled about why I had to be summoned on such short notice. So was I, but I knew better than to not show up. It was better to deal with them on my sister's turf than have them show up at my flat because they would.

The drive to Wales felt longer than usual as I tried to mentally prepare myself for whatever awaited me. Memories of my childhood flooded back, both pleasant and painful. Our family was like any other immigrant family – my parents came to America as students, then stayed and raised us there.

Despite being raised in Atlanta, we frequently visited Nigeria and spent our summers in Ibadan, where we learned most of our language and culture from my grandparents. After graduation, my parents chose to stay in America instead of returning to Nigeria like some of their college friends did. Thanks to their careers, we lived a comfortable life and were able to travel and see the world. My childhood wasn't laden with trauma – that wasn't my story, but everything changed during my teenage years.

Tolu and I made our mistakes and although my brother got into some trouble, nothing ever reached my parents' ears. Overnight, our once close-knit family began to unravel. My sister's actions brought shame and judgement from our relatives, tarnishing our previously pristine reputation. But that was nothing compared to what happened when my best friend died. My parents were being blamed for raising a rebellious daughter (me) who ultimately caused the death of a shining star.

Bisi was more than just my best friend – she was everything to me. Her passing left a permanent dark cloud over our family. After a few months, my parents sold our home and moved us to a new neighborhood. The new home marked not only a fresh start, but also marked the beginning of a new me. The structured Yinka who didn't oppose her parents anymore. If they said jump, I asked how high. But each time I went against my true self, I felt lost. And I felt disconnected from this fractured version of my family.

Slowly but surely, we began to heal – or rather, they began to heal. No one seemed to notice that I hadn't fully recovered. My sister knew, but she feared knocking her now sturdy boat. Instead, she joked about the "strange new me" and we all just swept it under the rug. To my parents, I was now "the daughter they raised" – their words, not mine. The funny thing was "the daughter they raised" was foreign to me. Until I met Nonso.

My Nonso.

Brandon was more their type. My parents adored him and were oblivious to our breakup. They were in for a double surprise, and I wasn't sure if I was ready for what would come after.

When I finally arrived at my sister's house, I took a deep breath before getting out of the car. She greeted me at the door with a smug look on her face. "Looks like you had a good time. At least he treated you well."

"His name is Nonso," I reminded her.

"Hmm, whatever. Come on, mom is in the kitchen."

I dropped my bag on the sofa and followed her into the kitchen. "Kitchen? I see you're using her already."

"Don't be jealous."

I replied with an eyeroll before entering the kitchen. My mother's attention was focused on the stove as she stirred a pot, her back facing me. The comforting scent of yam and beans wafted through the air, immediately taking me back to my childhood. I stood there for a moment, observing her in silence. My sister shuffled past me, causing my mother to turn.

"Ah Olayinka, *omo mi*." My mother walked toward me, and I met her halfway, kneeling before her.

"*Ẹ káàsán*, ma."

"*Káàsán*, my dear. *Kú àbọ̀*"

"Come and sit down, I know you're hungry," she said.

"Mummy, stop babying her, she's a grown woman," Tolu said.

"I don't care how grown all of you are. You will always be my babies," my mother responded.

I playfully stuck my tongue out at my sister as she went to the fridge to get the cold Zobo drink our mother had requested. We gathered around the island in the kitchen, chatting and catching up. My dad and brother-in-law had taken the kids out to run some errands for the upcoming christening this weekend. My mother asked about my job and promised to pray about my boss.

"I did not give birth to a child so that he can make it his mission to harass her. Don't worry, I will carry him to the Almighty in prayer." She picked her teeth with a toothpick while speaking a few choice words in Yoruba.

My grandmother was known for being able to seamlessly pray and curse in one sitting, and my mother definitely inherited that skill from her.

"After my darling grandson's christening, we will start planning Femi's wedding in full force," my mother announced. I looked over at my sister, who seemed to conveniently avoid eye contact with me. "Tell your Brandon that he should wait a little bit before proposing. Let us catch our breath first."

There it was. The opening to the conversation that I knew my sister had talked to our mother about beforehand. This way, I couldn't directly blame her. Instead, she shot me a knowing look and began clearing the dishes and loading them into the dishwasher. After an awkward silence, I cleared my throat to break the tension.

"*Mami*, Brandon is no longer in the picture." I looked up from the glass in my hand and met her gaze directly.

"*Kilode?* Why? Don't tell me that the rumors are true. You've been gallivanting about with one nonsense boy that kicks a football around for a living. Isn't he a Nigerian? He didn't see any school to attend. It's ball he saw to kick around?" My mother sucked her teeth loudly, the sound echoing through the room.

"Mummy, he's not useless. I met him as a client. He—"

"Oh, so you're teaching him how to manage his finances?"

I started to reply, but my mother didn't let me.

"Ah, *adupe lowo Olorun*," she said as she rubbed her hands together in gratitude to God. "You know I'm not into this social media thing you kids are obsessed with. But imagine my surprise when one of my students started talking about my daughter...*omo mi*..." she placed a hand on her chest. "My child is all over social media with this football player. So, I did some research on him...I couldn't believe that the daughter I raised, Olayinka Elizabeth Martins, would attach herself to a gambler. Is she out of her mind? But now that you say he's a client—"

"Mummy, he's not my—"

"Your boyfriend... I knew it couldn't be true. I asked your sister and for a moment I wasn't sure because she said to wait until you got here. A gambler? With an arrest record? A disgrace to his family," my mother continued. She didn't even pause for a breath.

"Mummy, he's turned his life around. People go through rough patches."

"I understand that, but I hope you have enough common sense not to be used on his road to recovery."

"Mummy, you—"

"Have you thought about how being with him will affect your career? No wonder your boss is giving you a hard time. I saw a picture where he was looking at you like a piece of meat. Do you want to be another one of his conquests? If you've chosen to be someone's mistress, your father can arrange a respectable Alhaji for you." My mother clicked her tongue. "Olayinka, God gave you common sense, use it." Shaking her head, she turned and left the kitchen.

My mouth hung open in shock as I struggled to find the right words. My palms were sweating, and my heart raced. I knew this conversation would be difficult, but nothing could have prepared me for this. I felt a lump form in my throat as guilt weighed me down. I'd let her totally crush Nonso's character. I looked at my sister, who was now folding a dish towel.

"You couldn't even defend me?" I asked, drained by what had just happened.

"Why? You claim to be grown and know what you're doing. Ask yourself how 'grown' you really are if you can't even defend the man you're head over heels for, against your mother." My sister's tone wasn't accusatory, but I still wanted to strangle her. "If you can't stand up for the man when he's not here, then I feel sorry for him – and for you – come Sunday." She walked out of the kitchen.

My shoulders slumped and my gaze fell to the ground. My eyes filled with tears, blurring my vision. I tried to steady my shaking hands by squeezing them into tight fists. The disappointment weighed heavily on me, a deep ache settling in my chest. In that moment, I felt like a complete failure. With a heavy sigh I accepted that tonight was a dud. I'd try again when things calmed down, but definitely before the weekend. After being off for almost a week, I had to be in the office in the morning, so yeah, I'd have to give it a rest tonight.

thirteen

Nonso

"WAIT, roll that back for me. *Isi ki*? What did you say? Why were you in a boy's house for a sleepover?" I asked Anuli, my baby sister.

"No, *bruhda*, Oluchi is our friend. It was her house we went for a sleepover and her senior brother was there. His university is UNN, so he just came back from Nsukka earlier that day," her twin, Amara tried to explain.

With a scowl on my face, I glanced at the phone mounted on its stand before returning my eyes to the road. I was on my way to Wales and decided to check up on my girls. Since the twins would soon be going to bed, I decided to call them first. I had talked to their mother and my father before they ran up the stairs with the phone.

My father still had an attitude with me, but he seemed to be doing okay. There were no more "sources close to him" and he was speaking to me again. I guess he figured some money was better than no money. The girls had bounced on their beds and began telling me stories left over since the last time I'd talked to them. I was fine with what they'd been telling me so far. I even acquiesced when they thought they were finessing money out of me, but hearing about them sleeping under a stranger's roof with a college guy in the same house was where I drew the line. My sisters were sixteen and just like every teenager their age, they thought they were smarter than they actually are. They were book smart, I gave them that, but like I'd told them before, whatever they're thinking of doing now or in the future, I'd already done and would catch it every time.

"Nah, I'm not feeling that."

"*Bruhda* Nonso, it was not that—"

"*Asim mba*! No. I ain't feeling it. Anything can happen."

They both frowned and mumbled their understanding of my directive. There wasn't any other option and to make sure they didn't try to be sneaky, I was going to call one of my guys to check in on who they were hanging out with. After promising to send money to their accounts, I told them I loved them, we said our goodbyes and I disconnected the call. Then I asked Siri to call Dumebi. After the second ring, she picked up.

"*Ezi okwu*," she exclaimed in disbelief.

"Don't start." I chuckled at her dramatics.

The last time we talked was three weeks ago. She'd called me, but I was with Specs and promised to call her back, but never got around to it.

"I was telling Jace that you've found a wife and abandoned us."

"I ain't in it, sis," Jason hollered from the back. "Bro is in love. Let him breathe."

I knew they would be together. After Sunday brunch at our childhood home, it was tradition that we went to one of our houses to chill for a bit. When I lived in Atlanta, it was always mine. Now it was Dumebi's. She made it known that she wasn't going to Jason's house unless she absolutely had to. According to her, she'd mess around and slap one of his little "friends" for not knowing how to respect their elders.

"Ha! Both my brothers, traitors."

"How about I trait on off this phone," I teased.

"No, why. That you're a traitor doesn't mean I don't love you. It's just a fact of life I have to deal with."

My sister's mouth was too reckless for her own good. No one was safe. I cackled at her using one of my favorite phrases against me. Indeed, when they or Specs complained about something I did, that was often my response.

"Where are you off to? Sundays you are normally cooped up with our wife."

Dumebi liked Yinka so she resorted to, according to her, "speaking those things that are not as though they were." My mom, on the other hand, was respectful and cordial to Yinka. She said she didn't want to get too close until I put a ring on her finger. My mother kept talking about how she now had to hide her face whenever she saw Lesedi or her parents around town. Claimed I made her treat Les like a daughter only for us to break up. If my mom knew the real reason we broke up she'd hold her head high, but that was in the past for me. I was okay with both my sister and mom's approach as long as Yinka was comfortable. She was important to me and anyone who couldn't get with it could step to the side.

That was where Kane was now...the side. After we got back from Egypt, I called him, and he went off. He blamed Yinka for plotting against him. Saying that the first day he talked to her, he knew she had an attitude with him and was envious of our bond. A bond he reiterated predated her. Dude acted like he and I were married. Talking about how he needed me, and I wasn't there. Come to find out it was about money.

"I'm on my way to Yinka's people's place. Her sister's son was christened today and they're having a little reception."

"Why didn't you go to the christening?" Dumebi asked.

I hadn't seen my woman in a week. I missed her and couldn't wait to see her, but even the thought of that couldn't get me out of bed in time this morning to make the drive to church. The team had been on a roll, and everyone was focused on promotion to the Premier League. We were a strong number three and unless something happened in the weeks to come, we'd advance to number two. With Yinka's schedule and mine, all we had time for was a brief call at night before one of us dozed off.

"Couldn't get up in time," I said.

"You scared of meeting the family, bro?" Jason teased.

"Imagine me being scared."

"I know that's right. My brother is a catch. They better recognize," Dumebi hyped me up.

I laughed and talked a bit more, then we updated each other on our week ahead. After telling them I loved them, we disconnected the call.

I continued to drive for another thirty minutes, enjoying the music playing in the car. According to the GPS, I was almost at my destination. Following Yinka's instructions, I parked the car and stepped out into the bright afternoon sun. My fit was formal for the occasion. Catching a glimpse of myself in the car window, I straightened my jacket. I was wearing a crisp sky blue shirt, a navy blazer, and tailored trousers. I adjusted my sunglasses and ran my hand over my clean-shaven head.

Yinka had told me she would meet me outside and walk me in, but knowing Nigerian gatherings, she was probably busy somewhere hosting. She knew I'd be arriving soon, so I decided not to bother her. As I walked towards the house, I felt a flutter of nervous anticipation in my stomach. Contrary to what Jason believed, I wasn't afraid to meet her family; I just wanted everything to go smoothly for Yinka's sake. However, if any of her elders showed disrespect, I wouldn't hesitate to put them in their place. I checked my own parents when they crossed the line, so anyone could get the same treatment.

Taking a deep breath as I approached the entrance, I was amazed by the magnificence of Yinka's sister's house. The English style home was surrounded by lush vegetation. The sounds of joy and conversation filled the air. As I ascended the steps to the front door, a sense of familiarity washed over me. This scene felt familiar, yet so unlike my family gatherings back in Atlanta. Just as my hand reached out to ring the doorbell, the door swung open, revealing a beaming Yinka standing there. She looked stunning in a vibrant Ankara dress that hugged her curves. Her eyes gleamed with excitement.

"Hey, you made it!" she exclaimed, embracing me tightly. "I'm so glad you're here."

Returning her hug, I couldn't help but notice her stiffness and fake smile.

"You good?" I asked cupping her face.

She gave me a forced smile. "Yeah, I'm fine, just tired. It's like they invited the whole community."

Yinka grabbed my hand and led me inside. As we entered the bustling household, the aroma of mouth-watering Nigerian dishes greeted us, making my stomach growl with hunger. She introduced me to some people, but I noticed the trend in her not mentioning our relation to each other. As we journeyed on, I tried not to let it bother me too much since these folks weren't her immediate family.

As we rounded the corner to where she said her sister was, we heard her name being called. We turned around and immediately, I knew the older woman approaching was her mother. She was darker in complexion, but they looked alike. Yinka must have gotten her fair skin from her father. As I was about to greet the older woman, I felt Yinka drop my hand like a bad habit. I trained my expression to remain neutral as her mother approached. Mrs. Martins glanced at me for a nano second and then completely ignored my presence and focused on her daughter. I had to be trippin.'

"Olayinka, I wondered where you went. The Adeyemis are leaving, and they wanted to say goodbye," her mother said.

"Okay Mummy, t—"

"And who's this handsome young man?" she asked, finally acknowledging I was standing there.

From the snark in her tone, I could tell she was being funny. I waited for Yinka to introduce me, but she didn't. My brows furrowed watching my sassy, confident woman wring her hands.

"This is Nonso, he's—"

"Oh, that your client! The one you're helping with his money, *abi*?" her mother asked and had the nerve to whisper like we were sharing a dirty secret.

I turned to Yinka, expecting her to correct her mother, but again, she was mute. Instead, she just shrank further. That quick I saw red. Anger traveled up my spine, my chest tightened, brows furrowed, and truth be told, I was low key hurt. Before I could say anything, a man walked up to us. He was flanked by who I figured to be the Adeyemis.

"Ah, darling, come and met one of Olayinka's client, Nonso," her mother introduced me to Yinka's dad.

"Good day, Sir," I greeted. It was like I was watching myself in a horror movie.

"Good day. Welcome." He shook my hand. "I'm sure Yinka will show you around, there's plenty to eat and drink."

The couple that was with them knew who I was. The man asked me a couple of questions about Viva City FC before they turned to Yinka to tell her how good it was to see her after a long time. Mrs. Adeyemi grabbed Yinka's hand so she could walk them out. It was only then that Yinka looked at me. The look in her eyes pleaded for my understanding, but I had none.

I searched for the nearest exit but ran into who I knew to be her brother. We shook hands and exchanged greetings.

"Aye man, glad you made it. Now, maybe baby sis can calm down," he joked.

"I doubt it," I replied. My tone was flat. "I was just leaving."

"So soon?" he asked in surprise.

"Yeah, something came up just now." My response was hurried, but I needed to get out of here and he was wasting my time.

Yinka's brother arched a brow at someone behind me. I turned to see Yinka's desperate gaze flicking back and forth between us. I was sure he could sense the tension between us, but I had no cares to give.

I nodded, trying to sound composed. "It was nice meeting you."

Yinka's brother studied me for a moment before nodding in understanding. "All right, man. Take care then."

I turned to Yinka. Her distress was visible on her face.

"I'll see myself out," I whispered before making my exit.

After a few steps, I pushed open the door and a flood of conflicting emotions hit me. Anger, betrayal, and hurt. The evening that I had been looking forward to quickly turned into a nightmare.

"Nonso, wait...please," Yinka called out as I stormed past her.

I ignored her and kept it pushing until I got to my car. I pressed the button on my key fob to unlock the doors when I heard her running towards me.

"Wait, please," she begged, panting for breath.

I opened the driver's door, but she caught hold of the handle. I had no empathy or compassion left in me as I waited for her to say what she had to say so I could leave.

"Yinka, what do you want? I gotta hit the road," I said sharply, one foot already inside the car.

I didn't have the luxury of telling her what I really wanted to say now that my emotions were on ten. If I said anything to her now, my words would be scathing and too heavy for her to bear. To be responsible, I had to remove myself from the situation since I didn't trust myself in this heightened state. This wasn't like our normal arguments or quarrels. She basically "Petered" my behind in front of her folks. Too bad the cock didn't crow.

"Please...I'm sorry. It's just that—"

Her attempt to justify her actions only fueled my anger. I turned away from her, but she grabbed my arm.

"I didn't tell my mother you were my client. She just assumed it."

"And you didn't correct her?"

"I tried, but she started going on and on about your past and my poor decisions—"

For the first time since I laid eyes on her, I looked at her with disgust. "Yinka, go inside. I need to hit the road. See you around."

Without waiting for a response, I got into my car and drove away, ignoring her pleas and apologies. The roar of the engine filled my ears as I sped down the unfamiliar street, trying to outrun the turmoil swirling inside me.

Yinka's words echoed in my mind, her apology falling on deaf ears. How could she have let her mother believe such a thing? The betrayal cut deep, leaving a bitter taste in my mouth. As the city lights blurred past my window, I realized that this wasn't just about her family or their assumptions. It was about trust, about respect.

Yinka had revealed a side of her that I never knew existed. The realization made my chest tighten with a mix of sorrow and anger. She knew what happened between Lesedi and I. I wasn't about to be with another woman who knew what she wanted but lacked the courage to get and keep it. Up until the moment she denied me, I had questioned if what I felt for her was love. My brother teased me about it, but I brushed it off.

But now, in this moment, I knew that I was indeed in love with Yinka. If not, her actions would only have angered me, but instead, they caused a sharp pain in my chest. And now, I had to let her go. Love was supposed to feel like God, but what I was feeling right now was straight from the devil.

I drove aimlessly, lost in my thoughts and the dark night that enveloped me like a shroud. Eventually, the roads led me to a quiet spot overlooking the city skyline. I parked the car and got out, needing the cool night air to clear my mind. Leaning against the hood of the car, I gazed out at the sparkling lights in the sky. My phone kept buzzing with calls from Yinka as it had been doing for the past hour, but I ignored them and sent each one to voicemail.

Just as I was about to block her number, I realized this was a text from Kane. Opening it, I saw a picture of his battered and bloody face with a plea for help.

> K: Man, I'm in trouble. You gotta come please. They won't let me go unless you show your face.

I got back in the car and had my foot on the pedal until I made it back to Viva City. As I entered my apartment, I made two calls before I went to pack a bag. One to Coach Sanchez and the other to Jason. I needed my brother on standby. I had two days to do what needed to be done and get back to minding my business.

"Bro, you're messing up. First you get on a flight to come see about that no-good Kane. That man knew what he was doing getting you involved in his mess. Then to make it worse, you letting Les sniff behind you again. I can tell you and your girl are beefing, but this ain't it, bro."

I headed to the kitchen to grab some water, half-listening as my brother gave a different variation of the same lecture he gave when I arrived in Atlanta last night. If we wanted to keep it a buck, it was partly his fault. If he'd been at the airport on time, I wouldn't have run into Lesedi's sister. So, it wasn't a surprise when Lesedi showed up at my door this morning with breakfast.

"Whatchu complaining for? You let her in," I countered.

"I wasn't about to just shut the door in her face. But then again, nobody told you to scarf down her food and let her rub your shoulder like she's your girl. And then she had the nerve to sing while she was cleaning up the kitchen, talking about she'll be back later to take care of dinner."

I chuckled at my brother's annoyance. We were currently in my house waiting for Phil, my accountant, to arrive with the money I needed to get Kane from where his creditors had him held up. As soon as I landed, I called the number Kane sent over and I got somewhat of a summary of what he had going on. It wasn't surprising that money was involved. I wouldn't dare go to this place if his captors hadn't made threats to his life.

"You worry too much, bro," I said.

"And you're being reckless. But it's on you when sis kicks your behind."

"As long as it ain't yours, we're good, right?"

Jason ignored my comment and continued playing his video game. He'd been with me since last night, and I hoped we would finish our business before Dumebi noticed that both her brothers were missing in action. Neither she nor my mother knew I was in town.

When Lesedi came over earlier, I told her to keep my arrival quiet. She probably thought she was part of some exclusive club, but that wasn't the case at all. Even if I never spoke to Yinka again, Lesedi wouldn't be taking her place. As for Yinka, I ended up blocking her number. I knew I'd eventually answer if she kept calling, and I wasn't ready to hear what she had to say. Jason was only speculating because I hadn't told him anything, but when he asked how she was and my tone was flat, he could tell something was off.

The doorbell rang, interrupting our conversation. Strolling over, I opened the door to find Phil with a worried look on his face. I didn't have time to assuage any concerns he had. We greeted and my gaze went to the duffle bag he was carrying as I let him in.

"Phil, my man. What's good?" Jason hailed him.

"Hello Jason, working that's all."

Jason patted him on the back before turning to me. "Let me go get a shirt," he said, heading for the stairs.

"It's all here. Three hundred and fifty thousand dollars." Phil placed the bag on the coffee table.

I nodded, unzipped the bag and looked at my hard-earned money I had to use to get this man out of a bind...again. I thanked Phil and he left soon after. I picked up the duffle bag and called out to Jason.

"Jace, let's go."

About forty minutes later, as we stepped out of the car, I was reminded of why I disliked Atlanta in April. The humidity and pollen were taking a toll on me, a stark contrast to the cooler climate in the UK.

Jason carried the duffle bag while I trailed behind them. If everything went according to plan, I'd be catching a flight out of here the following morning. I'd told Coach that there was a family emergency, and he didn't ask any questions before giving me permission to leave. He knew there wasn't an actual death or anything, so he gave me two days, but said to contact him if I needed more time. But there wouldn't be any need for that. My goal was to be back on the field playing when the Panthers were promoted.

The neighborhood we were in was eerie and unfamiliar, a stark reminder of the enormity of the trouble Kane had gotten himself into. We finally arrived at a rundown building that looked like it had seen better days. The stench of decay lingered in the air, mixing with the sounds of the city in the background. As we entered the building, our footsteps echoed off the walls, creating an unsettling atmosphere. The dimly lit corridor led us to a small room where three large, intimidating figures with rough, scarred skin and sneering expressions were seated. The tension in the air was thick, but I kept my cool, knowing that any wrong move could escalate things.

One of them stepped forward. "Kane, my man. Looks like you'll be going home today."

I looked over at my friend. He didn't look any worse than in the picture, but I could tell he was in bad shape. Anger and disappointment rippled through me.

"I got your money. Can we get this over with?" I didn't want to be here a second longer than necessary.

"You must be the famous Black," the man said calmly. "My nephew Nino is a huge fan. Eddie, call Nino, tell him to get down here."

I couldn't believe it. The person I was summoned all the way from the UK to meet was just the low-level goon's nephew. It felt like I was living in an alternate universe. *This can't be real life.* I exchanged an annoyed glance with Kane, who quickly looked away.

Jason placed the duffle bag on the table and another man began counting the money. Soon after, Nino showed up, clearly excited. He was a true fan, but I couldn't bring myself to be happy or grateful. He had a bunch of stuff for me to sign and even asked for a photo. I scanned the room for a less sketchy background before reluctantly taking some pictures with him. It all felt surreal, posing for photos while my insides churned with anger. After the money was counted and everyone seemed satisfied, I tapped my brother on the shoulder to signal that we should leave. One of the men went to untie Kane but I wasn't waiting around. If he wanted a ride back with me, he had better hurry up.

Jason had been driving for a few minutes when Kane who was in the back seat spoke.

"Thank you, Black. I really appreciate this," he said.

I had no response for him, so I just nodded. Seconds later, I asked. "So, K, explain this thing to me again. It's done, but I wanna be clear."

Kane leaned forward and let out a deep sigh. "Man, one of my guys told me about this stock. It was supposed to be doing good. He got a really good payout from it. So, I decided to invest, but didn't have enough money, so I borrowed from some guys and bought the stock on a margin. It seemed like a good deal. Come to find out, just a week later, the stocks started to tank and so the margin was called. I didn't have the money. My business is making do, but not enough to pay back almost one hundred and fifty thousand dollars," Kane explained, his voice strained, as he ran a shaky hand over his hair.

I remained silent, my heart sinking at the gravity of his situation as I waited for him to explain how I got involved in this mess.

"For their money, folks were showing up at my house, one of

my buses was vandalized...it was bad. So, I went to a loan shark, to settle that debt...man. Worst mistake of my life..." He shook his head.

I highly doubted that was the worst mistake he had made, but I kept my mouth shut and let him rock, knowing that whatever was coming next wouldn't be good.

"I made a couple of payments but defaulted on some, and with the interest they gave me...I turned around and suddenly, I owed three hundred and fifty thousand dollars. I've been paying them a little bit, but coming up short," he continued.

Pausing, he sighed. "Then get this, one day I get there and see one of the guys was rocking your merch and watching one of your games. I asked him if he was a fan, he started going on and on about all your stats." He clenched his fist and thumped it into his open hand. "I knew I shouldn't have...but I thought if I could somehow use our connection to my advantage, maybe I could negotiate a better deal or get some leeway with the payments. So, I showed him pictures of us together and offered him new auto-graphed merch. I was desperate."

I turned and glanced at him briefly. Kane's eyes pleaded for understanding.

I felt a fire ignite inside of me. I looked at Jason. His knuckles were almost white with how hard he was clutching the steering wheel. I was sure he felt my eyes on him because he glanced at me. I saw pure disgust in his eyes before he returned his focus to the road. I knew he was about to go off.

"Yo! K, you mean you put my brother's name in some stupidity to get yourself out of a jam. You foul man, on so many levels. That's really mes—"

"Jace, chill. Let him finish," I cut him off.

Jason looked like he wanted to take *me* out for being so calm. But I knew he heard what I said and would govern himself accordingly.

"J, man, I didn't know. It wasn't done out of malice. You know your brother is my day one," Kane said.

"Day one? The same one you got in your feelings and decided to do an exposé interview on? Yeah, right." Jason waved him off.

My brother was done talking. I could see his chest heaving so it was best he just concentrated on the road. I turned to Kane, and it almost looked like he cared. But I knew that was only because I bailed him out. Once he didn't get what he wanted from me the next time, it would be back to tweeting about me.

"I promise, when they said they didn't want merch, but they wanted to see you in person, I started to dodge them. But then they caught me one night when I was with my old lady. Man, they roughed me up bad."

That part of his story was clear because his lips were still a little swollen and I could still see the bruise under his left eye. I lowered my head for a moment, trying to reel in my frustration.

"At the end of the day, not only did I jeopardize all I'm trying to rebuild, but I covered the debt because they still wanted their money even after meeting me?"

Kane didn't respond, but I didn't need him to. At this point I wasn't even angry, just numb, and disappointed.

Sometime later, we arrived back at my house. I headed to my room and took a refreshing shower. The hot water washed away the tension from earlier and allowed me to gather my thoughts. Dressed in comfortable clothes, I descended the carpeted stairs, my bare feet sinking into the plush fibers. The smell of lemon pepper wings wafted through the air as I entered the kitchen. Kane sat at the island, his fingers covered in spice with a paper towel next to him. Our eyes met as I reached for a juice from the fridge then leaned against the cool brushed nickel sink.

He wiped his mouth and fingers before speaking. "I really appreciate you coming over on such short notice. Next time I—"

"Nah K, there won't be a next time. I'm trying to do things different, rise above my past, but you keep dragging me back at every turn."

"What? Dragging you back? I knew it. You went over there and...it's that new chick you with...ain't it? She got you—"

"I'mma stop you right there before this gets real ugly. How you opening your mouth to speak on her like you and I were in a relationship and you scorned or something?" Now I was heated. "Man, get outta here. You giving all these exclusive interviews and making cryptic statements about me on Twitter, but still...when you called, I came."

"My bad, Black, it's just that—"

"K, man I love you like a brother. We've been through some tough stuff together. But if there was a price tag on what you did for me, I've paid it a hundred times over."

"So, what you trying to say? That's it?" His eyebrows arched, creating a deep furrow in his forehead.

"Love is unconditional, but I'm revoking your access to me. If you have any regard for me, or where I'm trying to go after almost losing my livelihood, you won't put me in situations that could jeopardize what I got going on."

Kane abruptly stood up from his chair, causing it to fall to the floor with a loud thud. His chest heaved in anger as he glared at me. I remained calm and watched him, ready to move if he jumped funny. The noise must have gotten to Jason because he appeared in the kitchen. His eyes roamed the space accessing the situation. Kane didn't bother picking up the chair, so Jason did it before coming over to stand by my side.

"So that's it then. You just gonna shove me to the side over a mistake?" Kane growled.

"A mistake is a one-time thing, maybe two. When we get into three, four, ten, it's a pattern and I can't rock with it anymore," I explained.

Despite my demeanor, separating myself from him hurt. Indeed, he was my day one, but as Yinka would say, what feels good and what is best can be two different things. Now, this was what was best, but it didn't feel good.

Kane's fists clenched at his sides as he struggled to contain his emotions. I could see the turmoil in his eyes, regret mingled with frustration. He opened his mouth to speak, but then closed it again, unable to find the right words to say, he turned and left my house.

"Wow. That was interesting."

I ignored Jason and left the kitchen. I never would have foreseen what Kane and I had become. The wounds he'd inflicted on our friendship were still fresh, but a part of me wanted to believe that people could change. If he did, then I'd be always down to ride, but right now, I had to protect me.

I left the kitchen and headed towards the stairs to go to my room. Before I could even take a step, the doorbell rang. I let out a sigh, completely drained and wanting nothing more than to sleep the rest of the day away. My thoughts turned to Yinka. I really missed her and right now, she would have the perfect words to say to ease the chaos in my mind. But I was still so angry at her for our current situation, that I was punishing myself.

I made my way to the front door and opened it. Lesedi stood there with a big smile on her face. With everything going on, I forgot she was supposed to be coming over. I tried to keep my expression neutral, not wanting to give her the impression that she was welcome, or there was the potential for some kind of reunion.

"Hey," she said softly.

"Hi." I stepped to the side, motioning for her to come in.

"I know I'm late, but I had to make a stop at the grocery store. When I was here in the morning, I noticed you didn't have the noodles for the lasagna you like."

As she walked past me, I couldn't help but notice that she was still as beautiful as ever. Her short, curly, haircut was styled perfectly. She had on a bright colored, wraparound short skirt and a matching blouse. Her petite frame still showed signs that she took good care of herself in the gym. But unlike before, I felt nothing. I still cared for her well-being, but my heart didn't race, nor did my stomach do flip flops when she was in my presence. In fact, I needed to have a conversation with her as well. Again, Yinka was still on my block list, but I wasn't about to let anyone disrespect or troll her if I had anything to do with it.

I walked into the kitchen and Jason glared at me before shaking his head and leaving. Lesedi opened the cupboard and started pulling out pots and pans.

"Hey, Les, let's rap real quick," I said.

"Okay, Baby, let me just get the food started."

I placed my hand over the tap she was about to turn on. "Nah, come on."

Lesedi peered up at me, sighed and set the pots on the island, her expression a mix of curiosity and apprehension. I led her to the living room, gesturing for her to take a seat on the couch. She hesitated for a moment before complying, perching on the edge as if ready to bolt at any moment.

"What's wrong, Baby?" she asked.

I took a deep breath, trying to choose my words carefully. "Let's start there. You gotta stop all the 'My Black Knight' and the 'Baby' stuff. Chill. I'm in a committed relationship that means a lot to me. I need you to respect it and her."

Lesedi's expression turned defiant. "So that's why you bl—"

"I'm not going back and forth on this," I interrupted her. "We had our time, but your actions led us down this path. I'm not gonna say it wasn't for the best. But you know me well. I'm not gonna let anyone play games in my woman's face. Yinka is my woman."

I expected Lesedi to put up a fight or justify her stance, but instead she just gave me a reassuring smile. "I guess you're right. Just know that I'm here for you if you ever need to talk or if there's anything I can do to help."

"Thanks, but that won't be necessary." I got up from the couch and she did the same. I watched her gather her purse and stuff then I walked her to the door. After a quick hug, I watched her leave before heading back inside, feeling a mix of emotions. My mind went back to Yinka. I had to face her at some point and that had me wondering what came next.

As I made my way up the stairs, here comes my knucklehead brother clapping like this was some kind of show.

"Look at my big bro, having adult conversations and growing up."

"Shut up," I retorted playfully. "Be ready to take me to the airport in the morning, then lock up my house and go home."

"I feel used."

"You'll live." Climbing two steps at a time, I made my way to bed, turning on ESPN so I could catch the highlights before crashing for the night. Once I landed in Viva City, I'd go see about my girl.

final whistle

signals the end of the match, after the allotted time for the game has elapsed.

fourteen
Yinka

FOR ONCE, I wish my sister would be on time. I wiped down the countertops in the kitchen as I listened to my mother, who was in my living room, tell my father that he should make sure they were checked in online. After three weeks in the UK, they were finally heading back to Atlanta tomorrow evening. Tolu was on her way over to take my mom back to Wales. I enjoyed having my mother stay with me for a few days, but I was ready to resume my normal routine. So, I really needed Tolu to be on time.

"I just saw that your non-client friend made the news again," my mother said with a mix of accusation and amusement in her tone. She entered the kitchen and walked over to the meat she'd fried earlier.

"Mummy, his name is Nonso, and don't believe everything you see on the news." I rinsed off the kitchen cloth in the sink. "You should know better," I murmured under my breath.

"Olayinka, don't make me slap you. I listened to you express your opinions about what happened at your nephew's christening." She sucked her teeth. "Your daddy always takes your side, so like he asked, I tried to see things from your perspective. But don't get beside yourself."

"I'm sorry, but Mummy please, if you can't call him Nonso,

let's not talk about him at all." I was done with her snark regarding him.

"My concerns are still valid. Why is he constantly making headlines? Negative headlines."

I offered her a strained smile; it was the only way to stop myself from crying. I hadn't seen my man in two weeks. I didn't even know if I still had a man. I stopped calling after realizing he blocked me. My heart was hurting and at first, I was sad. Now, I was downright angry.

That man left for Atlanta and didn't even say anything. Only for the news to break later that he was seen in an alleyway with a known criminal ring. Imagine my surprise when the headline flashed on the television while I was watching a movie some days ago.

Nonso Chijuka's Controversial Night Out Raises Eyebrows in the Sports Community!

The blogs, however, had their own spin on it. A more salacious one. I wouldn't have believed it until I saw the grainy picture of him and Kane. I told Nonso that man was no good. I hadn't bothered calling because I was afraid of his reaction with so much between us. Calling wouldn't do any good anyway since he had blocked me.

Besides, I put us in the position we were in and until my mom and I came to an understanding, what was the point? Surprisingly, my dad and brother were on my side, while Tolu stayed neutral. My mother's opinion always changed depending on the day.

"I don't know, Mummy. I haven't talked to him since then..."

"Why? Don't tell me he broke up with you already?"

"No... I don't know, Mummy."

"I'm hearing a lot of 'I don't knows.' What happened? Don't tell me it's because of me."

"Well...actually, it's because of what I didn't do."

"Stand up for him?"

I furrowed my eyebrows, wondering how she knew. "Yes..."

She shrugged. "Why didn't you?"

"What?" I couldn't believe she was the one saying this. *Now?*

"Why didn't you stand up for him?" She snapped her fingers a few times, her expression turning serious. "If anyone dares treat or talk to your father like they have no sense in my presence..." She shook her head. "I will wash them from head to toe." She sucked her teeth. The thought alone seeming to appall her. "The person will be thinking about their life for months to come."

My eyes widened in surprise. "Are you serious? Then why did you do it to Nonso?"

"I didn't do anything to him. I wanted to see if you were truly committed and understood the challenges that come with fame, even if it's just through association. It isn't easy."

"Wow..."

"You keep blaming us for decisions you make influenced by your past mistake. First, you moved to the UK and cut off Brandon, then I hear about this guy, Nonso. Olayinka, we have forgiven you. It was fifteen years ago. You... haven't forgiven yourself, which is why you're always on edge and so rigid, until you're not.

"I may not approve of Nonso's past or current situation, but if he loves you, I'm willing to give him a chance. However, I agree with him; if you can't defend him in front of others, including your parents, then it's you who doesn't deserve him. At least demand he is respected. My liking and trusting him with you will take time."

I took a deep breath as the weight of my mother's words sank in. She was right, as always. I had been so caught up in my own guilt and insecurities that I had failed to stand up for the man I loved when he needed me the most. Not because he couldn't defend himself, but because I knew the only reason he didn't lose it was that the person disrespecting him was my mother. And he knew how that would affect me.

Nonso deserved someone who would fight for, with and beside him against anything and anyone. I stared at my mother.

Her eyes held a glint of sympathy, as if she understood the turmoil inside me. I felt a renewed sense of determination. I couldn't change the past, but I could do better.

"*Mo ti gbo*. I hear you, Mummy," I said, my voice steady. "I need to talk to Nonso. I need to make things right."

My mother nodded. "Good. Love is not only about the glitz and good times. It's about standing by each other through the storms too."

The following morning, I walked back into my office with the signed papers from another client. I still wasn't where I wanted to be in quality, but my quantity had gone up. I plopped down in my chair and leaned back. I shook my mouse to wake my computer and glanced at my calendar which was up. I was meeting Cassie for lunch at Fusion Haven, and I couldn't wait. My girl was back, but we hadn't seen each other yet.

She had already told me about myself over the whole Nonso thing. I almost hung up on her because the truth she was giving was kicking my behind. I had so many regrets. While we were on the phone, the memory of that day replayed in my mind over and over. I was full of regret for not handling things differently.

The sports headline this morning stated that the Viva City FC leadership was concluding their investigation into the Atlanta trip Nonso made and the alleged alliance with the criminal ring. According to their spokesperson, the announcement would come soon because they wanted to put the matter behind them and get back to the focus of the season.

As soon as I read that, I called him. Surprisingly, he had unblocked my number, but he didn't answer either. Instead, I received a text saying he would see me later. I knew I made a mistake, but his prolonged reaction seemed extreme.

A sudden knock on my door broke my concentration, and I looked up to see my boss standing in the doorway. I stood from my desk and motioned for him to enter.

"Ms. Martins, can I have a moment of your time?"

"Of course, what can I do for you?"

"We have the shareholder and board meeting coming up soon, and I'll need to give an update on this branch."

"All right, is there anything I can help prepare?"

"I appreciate the offer, but no thank you." A brief moment passed before he spoke again. "Have you been able to sign the footballer?"

I couldn't stop the deep crease that formed on my forehead. "Who? Mr. Chijuka?"

"Yes, you were supposed to convince him to sign with our agency."

"I wasn't—"

"As the head of this office, part of my charge is to show exemplary conduct of all staff under my supervision. Your association with the footballer who has ties to a criminal gang reflects poorly on our office," he stated. "At least if he was a client..." He allowed his words to trail off.

"I'm sorry, what exactly are you saying?"

This man's nerve continues to amaze me.

"We were hoping your proximity to the team would bring in some clients for us. However, instead of signing him as a client like we expected, you've been seen socializing with this individual."

"With all due respect, sir, it's no one's business who I associate with outside of work. But I'm confused. First, you wanted me to sign him, now my association with him is harmful to the company's image?"

"Let me clarify," he started. "Our concern is not with your personal life, but with the potential impact it may have on the reputation of our agency. We cannot afford to be associated with any negative publicity, especially when it involves criminal elements."

I nodded, biting back a retort, and started gathering my things. I needed to get out of here. As a Black woman in a predominantly white work environment, I constantly adjusted myself to make others comfortable while still doing my job. But right now, I didn't trust myself to make him feel comfortable.

My name wasn't even mentioned in the news. His latest issue with me seemed warped. I wanted to give him a piece of my mind, but I wouldn't give him the satisfaction of me becoming a stereotype or him seeing me quit. I'd report him to higher authorities before that happened. But for now, I needed a break.

"I'm trying to help you become partner, but if that is no longer your goal, then so be it."

"I don't need your help, sir. I will meet my quota. As for Mr. Chijuka, he is my business and has nothing to do with this office."

Mr. Wilson gave me a disapproving look, but left without saying anything else. I couldn't help but think that maybe I hadn't been praying hard enough. This man should have transferred out of here by now.

Or God is he the thorn that has been put in my side like brother Paul? Abeg o.

As I was about to exit the building, I heard someone call my name. I halted and noticed the receptionist approaching me.

"Ms. Martins, did you happen to see your visitor? I sent him to your office before taking my break."

Confusion washed over my features as I responded, "Visitor? No, I didn't see anyone."

"Hmm, that's odd," she said.

"Can you describe the person? Male or female?" I asked.

"It was a man, tall, but he may have changed his mind. He seemed hesitant," she replied.

"I see. Well, I'll see you tomorrow," I said, and continued on my way. I was almost certain it could be Nonso. He did say he would see me later. Whatever the case, after the talk with my mom the day before, I'd made up my mind to head to him after lunch with Cassie. Whether he liked it or not, he was going to talk to me.

Hours later, I was sitting across from Cassie, finishing up lunch at Fusion Haven. We caught up on everything that had happened since we last saw each other. Even though we'd kept in touch while she was away, it was always better to talk face to face. As I recounted the latest drama with my boss, Cassie's eyes widened and her brown locs bounced with her movements.

"Girl, you need to get out of there," she said emphatically. "That man is toxic. Consider your mental health. And you deserve better."

I let out a sigh. She was right, but the thought of leaving my job and all the uncertainties that came with it made my heart race. Plus, I had other pressing matters to attend to.

I sucked my teeth. "It's so frustrating and he's even hassling me over someone who isn't even talking to me."

"You guys still haven't made up?" Cassie asked.

I rolled my eyes. "At this point, I'm really aggravated. Ha! I know what I did was wrong, but two weeks of silent treatment? That's going too far."

Cassie chuckled. "You're such a last born. Only a last born thinks the world revolves around them and expects others to be ready to make nice because they are." She took a sip of her soda. "Take your punishment like a grown woman. And if you're tired of waiting, then pop up on him. He's your man after all."

"Low key, I'm scared of what I might find if I do that," I admitted, picking at a loose thread on the tablecloth.

"I've told you before, I highly doubt Nonso is a cheater."

"I know he isn't. But what happened between us is like what happened between him and that girl." I shrugged.

"Lesedi?" Cassie sighed. "You have two options. Go claim your man before someone else does. You did deny him, so he's free game. Or sit here and wait until he's ready to talk to you."

We sat in silence for a few moments as I contemplated her words. It was nothing that I hadn't already thought about. Nonso had a lot going on – the media was tearing him up because of the Atlanta thing, which resulted in him having to sit out two games while an investigation took place. I didn't have all the details, but I knew for a fact that Nonso was innocent. He needed me just as much as I needed him, and him not allowing me to be there for him was breaking my heart.

"Well, hate to be the bearer of bad news, but you might want to go check on your man...right now. Like now!"

My eyebrows furrowed as I struggled to make sense of her words. She was fixated on her phone screen.

"What's going on? What's the matter?" I reached out and took her phone.

A metallic taste filled my mouth as my teeth clenched in fear and anger. My heart thudded loudly in my chest. "What the—"

"It's just *Tatafo Tales* being messy. You know how they are."

"How are they messy? All they did was this caption. The pictures were reposted directly from her page."

#BaeReunionAlert: True Love Always Finds A Way

That was the caption on *Tatafo Tales'* latest post. As I read the article on Cassie's phone, my stomach dropped. I went over to Lesedi's Instagram page where she shared a few photos. She made sure not to show Nonso's face, but I could recognize him anywhere, and so could the media. It was obvious that she had taken these pictures herself. One showed a table set for two at breakfast, with half of her profile visible while Nonso's appeared blurry in the background as he ate with a fork in hand. The next photo showed his kitchen and ingredients for his favorite meal, lasagna, spread out on the island. The third was a selfie of her lounging on Nonso's couch, and the last one captured her leaving his house with a faint silhouette of Nonso in the background. I hadn't been to Nonso's home in Atlanta, but he had shown me pictures, and I had spoken to his sister a few times while she was there.

Lesedi's caption read:

@sedi_j: This just how we roll.

My hands trembled as I handed Cassie her phone back. I quickly gathered my things to head out. Taking a deep breath, I looked up at Cassie with determination in my eyes.

"You got this, right?" I gestured to the empty dishes. My voice was firm and unwavering.

"Of course. You're sure you don't want me to drive you?"

"I'm good. Besides you can't be subpoenaed if you don't know anything."

The drive to Nonso's house felt like an eternity, each passing minute fueling the fire of indignation burning within me. The cool evening air did little to calm the storm brewing within.

When I reached Nonso's apartment, I knocked on the door several times, but there was no answer. Growing impatient, I started to bang on it. Finally, I heard the locks turn and the door opened to reveal Nonso standing before me. My focus momentarily shifted as my eyes took in his shirtless ripped torso. The black sweatpants he had on hung low on his waist.

"Yinka? Why are you banging on my door like the opps? What are you doing here, anyway?" he asked.

His groggy voice was a clear indication that I'd woken him up from sleep. Instead of answering his questions, I pushed past him and entered his condo. Dropping my bag on the table, I demanded, "Where is she? Did you bring her back here?"

I headed towards the back of the apartment, searching every bedroom, bathroom, closet and even cupboards for any sign of Lesedi. A few minutes later, satisfied that he was alone in the apartment, I returned to the living room.

Nonso was stretched out on the couch with his arm over his forehead and his eyes closed. I approached him, but he didn't move. After a few moments of stillness, with his eyes still closed, he spoke.

"You done acting crazy?" he asked coolly.

"Crazy?" I repeated in disbelief. "You're parading your supposed ex on social media and I'm the crazy one?"

"I never said you were crazy, just acting crazy." Nonso stood and walked past me towards the kitchen. "And where was all this energy you got for an imaginary situation that you didn't have when your people were disrespecting me? You just went mute." He retrieved a plate of food from the warmer and placed it in the microwave.

His calm demeanor was aggravating as I watched him grab a bottle of water from the fridge.

"Why are you being so mean?" I asked.

"Why are you being so spoiled?" he mimicked me.

He took a sip of the water and said stiffly. "Ms. Martins, if you're here to try again at using your proximity to the team to sign me as a client, I hate to break it to you, but I already got financial people. So, there isn't even the potential of me being your client."

The sting of his words lingered in the air, and I could feel the heat rising to my cheeks. I was right. He'd overheard Mr. Wilson berating me in my office earlier and then left. Nonso raised an eyebrow, daring me to deny it.

The microwave beeped, and he set down his plate of food before saying grace and starting to eat. He handed me a fork and I swallowed hard, feeling a lump form in my throat. Despite his anger, he still cared enough to offer me something to eat. Our interactions when we were angry with each other were always like this – he remained calm while I struggled to keep my emotions in check.

As Nonso settled back on the couch with half of his food left, I remembered the words of advice my mother often gave when I was growing up. "Do you want to win the battle or the war?" I knew that our argument over Lesedi was just one small battle in the grand scheme of things. So, without another word, I took off my shoes and made my way over to Nonso, who watched me closely, but didn't say anything. I climbed onto his lap, almost losing my balance in the process. He steadied me and I buried my face in his chest.

"Yinka, I got a busy day tomorrow. What do you want?" He sounded irritated, but I paid him no mind.

"I'm sorry for what happened. There's no excuse for my behavior and I regret hurting both you and I in the process. I'm truly sorry. I should have said something. I should have stood up to my mother and shut her down, but...I didn't. I didn't and I regret it with all my heart. I sincerely apologize. I let my past affect my present and I hurt you. I've been trying to get better, to be better, but..." I let out a deep breath. "My family still had a stronghold on me. Had...but no more. I don't want to lose you."

I took the fact that he let one of his arms snake around my waist while the other rubbed my back as encouragement to keep going.

"And everything you heard at the office was my boss's idea. I never intended to use you like that. If you had waited, you would've heard me tell him so."

I pulled back to look at his face. To see his eyes so I could gauge his reaction.

He stared at me. His eyes were no longer cold, but he remained silent, and it made me nervous.

"Yinka—"

"Stop calling me that!"

He chuckled. "I've created a monster."

"That sounds like a you problem," I shrugged.

"So you dealt with your parents? I ain't trying to be part of a tussle you gonna be involved in because of me."

"Get this – my mom thinks I don't deserve you because I didn't stand up to her for her behavior towards you," I confessed.

"For real?" He nodded and thought for a minute. Then he chuckled. "Well, she's okay in my book. I'll have to get her a gift."

"But she's not fully on board with us."

"And? I don't need her to be. I need you to be okay with us. In private and in public. Can you handle that? Because if not—"

"I can! I love you, Nonso, so much," I pleaded.

A smile spread across his face like a Cheshire cat. "Are you sure? Because there are women waiting to make me breakfast and lasagna. I mean, I—"

I swatted his shoulder and tried to get off his lap, but he chuckled and held onto my wrists. "Relax, I'm just messing with you." He kissed my lips. "I love your spoiled behind too much to let you go. If you can't handle it, I was just gonna get an outside chick who could handle her parents and the media."

I sucked my teeth. "You know what, let me up. I can't stand you. Move."

He held onto me tightly, laughing. "Where are you going to go? You're stuck with me."

He tried to kiss me, but I rolled my eyes and turned my head away. I did this a couple of times before he apparently got tired of my stubbornness. Nonso stood and lifted me up with him. He sat me on the tall stool he had nearby and cupped my face in his hands.

"Specs, stop playing with me."

I had a snappy comeback ready, but it died on my lips when he called me by his special nickname for me. He leaned in and gave me a passionate kiss. I breathed him in. I had missed him so much. I didn't realize how much the thought of losing him had me gasping for air. Now I could relax. Breathe. Exhale.

I laid my head against his chest, feeling the rise and fall of it. He rubbed my back. I was grateful for this moment and would try my best never to jeopardize what we had built and what we were building.

"Woman, get off me. I'm hungry. Let me eat this food."

I giggled and lifted my head off his chest before letting go of his waist.

He reheated his food and we remained in the kitchen and began to chat. He told me everything that happened in Atlanta, including the Lesedi stuff. Then he gave me the good news that right before I arrived, he received a call from the club saying they found no wrongdoing and he was off suspension.

"But Coach was not happy with me. At all." Nonso chuckled. "That man went off."

"As he should. Sorry babe, but that was risky. I understand *sha,* that it was a life or death situation."

Nonso grunted. By the time we finished talking, it was late. We cleaned up the kitchen and Nonso headed down the hall.

"Wait, where are you going?" I asked.

His eyebrows knit together. "To bed. I gotta be at the facility at six a.m."

My hands went to my hips. "So, you're just going to leave me here?"

Nonso glanced at the huge wooden wall clock. "You know better than to leave at this time of night. Besides, you're not a stranger."

He was right, but still... "Wow."

"Wow, nothing. And make sure you stay in the guest room too. Don't sneak into my bed later in the night talking about you heard a noise."

This man was so ridiculous. I laughed because that happened only once before, and he always teased me about it. He moved the side table to its rightful place and adjusted one of his standing plants.

"I can't believe you. Where did my Nonso go?" I whined.

"Shoot. The rooster don' crowed, so he's probably crying by the well somewhere. You should know the way." He carried on like what he just said was normal.

I chuckled at his reference to Peter denying Jesus and playfully threw a pillow at his back. "I really can't stand you."

"Yes, you can. I love you, Specs. But you gotta take this punishment like a pro." He winked at me and disappeared down the hall.

I knew the stuff I needed to take a shower and relax would be in the guest room. So, in the morning, I'd make a quick run to my apartment for a change of clothes before heading to work. Nonso had a magnetic pull that I found irresistible, and even during our toughest moments, I knew deep down that we were destined to be together.

fifteen

Nonso

THE ATMOSPHERE in the locker room was charged with tension as we prepared for the upcoming match against Northshire United FC. Coach Sanchez's authoritative voice echoed off the walls as he gave one of his impassioned motivational speeches before a crucial game. I remained pensive, but caught sight of Xander and Jay exchanging knowing glances. Their focus reflected the gravity of our current situation. We were all aware of what was at stake – a victory would secure us second place in the EFL Championship and automatic promotion to the Premier League.

"Listen up, lads," Coach Sanchez commanded, his words cutting through the buzz of nerves and excitement. "This is our moment. We've put in the work all season for this opportunity. Show the world what we're capable of. Give it your all, leave everything on the field, and we'll emerge victorious!"

Xander nodded. "We've got this, guys." His eyes held a spark of determination as we exchanged a silent vow.

"We will make it happen out there," Jay affirmed.

I tried to focus on the game ahead, but my mind kept drifting back to that whole messed up Atlanta fiasco that caused me to be benched for two games. Coach was cool now but the speech he gave when I got back was scathing.

"Your irresponsible and foolish actions have resulted in a two-game suspension, and I am incredibly disappointed. You're a valuable member of this team, but that does not give you the right to ignore the rules. You told me it was a freaking family emergency. Not the same stupidity that brought you here in the first place.

"It seems you're bent on repeating the same mistakes and I will not have it on my watch. Did you consider how your actions will affect the team? You're a valuable member of this team, but no one is above the rules. Shape up or I'll make sure you're out...for good."

My publicist, agent and Big Iz went to work immediately clearing my name, which was the main reason why the investigation went by so quickly. However, I couldn't shake off the feeling of disappointment and regret at where we were as a team because of those missed games. I wasn't God, but that didn't stop me from wondering if I had played, could I have made a difference and helped our team secure a more solid second place? Right now, point wise, we were at the mercy of Westfield Wanderers FC 's performance in a different game across town.

I looked at the timer, and they were about to start their game as well. A win was a must for us. We couldn't afford to draw or lose. The thought weighed heavily on my mind, threatening to overshadow my determination. If either of those things happened, we would drop to third place and face the dreaded playoffs. The pressure was almost suffocating.

A few minutes later, we walked onto the field, the roaring crowd filled always filled us with a sense of purpose. Our pregame routines were completed, and I made the sign of the Cross before sending a silent plea to the Almighty.

Next, my gaze turned towards the VIP box where Yinka was watching. Even though I couldn't see her, I knew she was there. It had been two weeks since we reconciled, and our bond was stronger than ever. Despite my tight schedule, we were intentional about making time for each other, making us practically inseparable. We were seen around town, at the theater, picnics, and volunteer events, as well as dining at top notch restaurants. However, our favorite day was Sunday when we just lounged around, either in my apartment or hers.

Sweat dripped down the team members' faces as we huddled together, strategizing for the last quarter of the game. The score was two-one in our favor, but we couldn't let up now. Every pass and tackle felt like a matter of life or death. Our coach's words echoed in my mind as the team jogged back on the field. The goal was to defend our lead and secure the win. The referee blew the whistle and the game resumed.

A few minutes of play went by and the cheers from the crowd sounded distant as I concentrated on the game. The ball was coming towards me, and I stopped it with a swift movement. My eyes quickly scanned the field, searching for my teammate on the left wing or my striker making a break for the goal. Spotting Harper, I swiftly passed the ball to him. But as soon as the ball left, I was tackled from behind and a sharp sensation shot through me. The smell of freshly cut grass overwhelmed my senses as I tumbled, temporarily blinded by the sharp pain.

Though I could hear shouts from both my teammates and opponents, their voices seemed distant as I struggled to regain my balance. I fought to push through the agony, but my leg refused to cooperate, causing me to stumble with each step. The taste of sweat on my tongue served as a reminder of just how intense this game was and how much was at stake. I knew I had to stay strong for myself and my team. But fate had a different plan for me in that moment.

As I collapsed onto the grass again, my heart sank. Gritting my teeth, I tried to ignore the pain, but it was unbearable, shooting through my body with every heartbeat. Coach rushed over; his face contorted with concern as he assessed my condition.

"We need medical attention over here!" he yelled, his voice cutting through the chaos of the game.

Jay and Xander hovered nearby, their expressions riddled with worry. The fear in their eyes reflected my own. The crowd buzzed as the medical team hurried onto the field. Their footsteps seemed loud in my ears. They lifted me onto a stretcher, the world spinning around me as they carried me off the field. The noise of the crowd became a distant hum as we moved towards the tunnel, leaving behind the game that would determine the team's fate.

Back in the sterile environment of the medical area, while I was awaiting evaluation, my mind raced with a whirlwind of emotions. The excitement and anticipation of the match were replaced by disappointment and frustration. The harsh white light above seemed to pierce through me as the staff rushed around me, their voices blending in a blur as they assessed my injury. Coach Sanchez stood beside me; his usual no nonsense authority was replaced with concern.

"It's going to be okay," he said reassuringly. "You gave it your all out there. Now it's time to focus on getting you back on your feet. We'll finish the game."

With those words, he left, returning to the field. The thought of letting my team down weighed heavily on me, knowing our fate rested on this game. But Coach's words gave me a little hope. The guys got this. Time seemed to blur together as I underwent a series of tests and examinations. The machines around me beeped steadily, providing a constant background noise. X-rays were taken and a huge ice pack placed on my leg.

"What's wrong with you people? Why are you acting like you don't know who I am? Let me back there."

I heard Yinka's voice echo through the hall. I knew it would only be a matter of time before she came down here showing out. We were playing a home game, so the staff knew her. After all the sports clinics and charity events she'd been a part of because she was my woman, they had better.

"I don't care if he hasn't been seen by a doctor, yet. I want to see him now. You, Eric, I know you. Why are—"

Tired of hearing the distress in her voice, I removed the

oxygen mask I had on. "Aye! Let her back. What's wrong with y'all?" I hollered.

In a matter of seconds, the medical team parted ways like the Red Sea as she scurried through, her gaze locked on mine. Concern etched her features as she reached for my hand. Her touch ignited a flame within me, pushing away the pain as I focused solely on her. I admired the jersey she wore over her black jeans. She'd sent me a picture before now, but actually seeing my number, 8, and the words, 'His Specs' on the back of her gold and black jersey filled me with pride.

She brushed her lips against mine and whispered, "Are you okay?" Her voice shook. Her eyes were laden with worry. Before I could even respond, she stopped herself and shook her head. "Don't answer that. I know you're not okay. I saw everything. I've never been so scared in my life. Is the pain—"

I interrupted her, managing a weak smile and squeezing her hand gently. "Specs, relax, baby. Take a breath." Despite the throbbing ache in my leg, I tried to reassure her. "They've done X-rays, and we'll know more soon. It's just a little bump in the road. I'll be back in no time."

Her eyes searched mine for any hint of deception. She mustn't have found any because she nodded firmly. "You better be. You're not allowed to get hurt," she declared, tightening her grip on my hand.

A serious-looking doctor approached us. He introduced himself and after a few minutes examining my leg, he looked at the X-ray again. "The X-rays don't show any fractures and based on my exam, there don't appear to be any torn tendons or ligaments. We would have to confirm with an MRI but based on my initial exam, I'm pretty confident that you don't have any tears. Seems like you've got a serious strain of your quadriceps." He paused. "If that's the case, then you just need some rest and physical therapy. But I can't stress enough how important it is for you to avoid overexertion."

I nodded, fully aware of the challenge ahead. The reality of being benched for the remainder of the season hit me hard. Hopefully, our season would end tonight.

~

I settled onto the couch in my living room, trying to relax. The sunlight streamed through the sheer curtains creating a soft glow. It annoyed me, but was another one of Yinka's "brighten the mood" ideas. I preferred to be in the dark, but her hovering behind wouldn't let me sulk in peace.

A mindless sitcom played on the TV screen, its flickering images failing to distract me from the reality that my thigh was wrapped in bandages, and I couldn't walk properly. The crutches leaning against the other end of the couch were a constant reminder of this limitation.

"I'm fine, Yinka," I snapped, feeling annoyed by her constant attention.

She sighed and shook her head. "Can you stop being so annoying. You're not fine and I'm trying to help you." She cut her eyes at me, then rolled them and walked away.

A grin flashed across my face. She had to really love me because I'd been giving her a hard time. "I love you," I hollered.

"Yeah, whatever," she yelled back.

I couldn't help the small smile that formed on my lips. I knew she only wanted what was best for me, even though I really wanted space to process the last few days. Soon after, she returned, squeezed my shoulder, and threw a shirt at me. Before she could walk away, I caught her wrist. She resisted a bit, but I was stronger and managed to pull her down on me. I wrapped my arms around her and kissed her forehead a few times, apologizing. She relaxed and brushed her lips against mine

"Don't forget you have an interview via Zoom in thirty minutes," she reminded me. "I brought that shirt for you to change."

I groaned inwardly, but forced myself to get up and follow her instructions. The last thing I needed was to look unkempt on a live YouTube broadcast.

"I appreciate you, baby, for real."

She winked at me and disappeared to my home office. It was Saturday and she had a meeting with a client she'd been courting on Monday. She was busy and I understood her not being able to come over every day. She wasn't here yesterday and as I knew she would, she showed up a few hours ago with breakfast and her laptop.

I dressed and adjusted myself on the couch so I could be comfortable. I couldn't help feeling nervous about the upcoming interview. *Game Changers: The Inside Scoop on Sports* was one of the top sports podcasts in the country. I was cool with their hosts Dele and Chris, but I knew they still wouldn't take it easy on me.

Before I knew it, it was time for the interview. I joined the call after taking a deep breath and plastered a smile on my face as the host greeted me.

"Hello, Nonso! How are you?" Dele, the more outspoken of the duo asked enthusiastically.

"Hey, man. I don't know how to answer that, considering," I gave a polite smile and gestured to my leg. "So, I'mma just say I'm making it."

We engaged in some small talk, jokes, then they wished me a speedy recovery. Chris nodded before diving into business. "Let's talk about your journey this season. Your stats were remarkable, twenty-eight goals, twelve assists. Pass accuracy was at roughly eighty-five percent, and fifty... fifty successful dribbles and thirty-six hundred hours of play."

I nodded because just like I set out to do, I was on beast mode when I joined the Panthers, but still fell short. "I can't take all the credit. To God be the glory and I have a great support system."

"With all that though, it must be disappointing to end up injured and not secure automatic promotion. Tell us how you're feeling. I'm sure the fans want to know."

Fans...I never relied on what they were giving. Right now,

they were giving concerned and supportive. But fans were fanatical and very fickle when it came to the players. Especially the Black ones. I'd learned a long time ago not to live by their praise because you'd end up dead by their boos. Of course, I got an influx of messages on social media wishing me well. Yinka read most of them and helped me construct a generic message of thanks.

"You hit it on the head. Ain't much I can add to that. It sucks, but there's no use worrying about something I can't change," I said.

"A win would've secured the second place for the Panthers. Do you think there's anything the team could've done differently in your absence?" Dele asked.

"I alone don't make up the Panthers. We're a team and there's no doubt in my mind that the team gave it their all." I'd anticipated the question, but my heart still skipped a beat remembering our loss.

"I can imagine. But there has been some controversy surrounding the Panthers not being promoted to the Premier League and having to play in the playoffs. There are rumors suggesting that there was an intentional error in the tabulation of points, favoring Westfield over the Panthers. How do you respond to these allegations?"

My smile faltered slightly. I leaned forward, making sure that Chris saw the seriousness of my expression. "I'm not even gonna touch that. The competition was close, but I have faith in the integrity of the league and its officials. We're here to play football, and that's what we'll focus on."

Chris nodded in understanding then looked at his cue card. "There have also been rumors that you may be scouted by some top teams in the Premier League after your impressive performance this season. Is there any truth to that?"

I chuckled. I felt a sense of pride at being recognized by top teams. These media outlets though, they worked fast. My agent mentioned something along those lines, but I wasn't in the right frame of mind to fully explore the possibility. Being on the team that got the Panthers promoted was still my driving force. Despite my playful irritation with my over caring woman, she knew what my goals were and was making sure I strictly followed the doctor's orders. With any luck, I'd be playing in the playoffs. It was only after that I would think about any offers.

"I can't comment on any potential offers or transfer rumors at this time."

Dele laughed then tried to ask the same question in another way. I gave him the same answer before he moved on to other topics – my childhood dreams of becoming a professional foot-baller, my role models in the sport, and predictions for the play-offs which were going to start soon and my thoughts on how far the team could go in the playoffs.

"Okay, let's get personal for a minute," Chris said.

"Uh oh, here you go…" I relaxed my body into the couch.

"After your long-term relationship ended, you were a free agent for a while. But now it seems like you've found love here in the UK."

I smiled. On the screen, they displayed a picture that had been circulating in the blogs of Yinka and I. She'd come to pick me up from physical therapy. My girl was stunning in her white and pink dress, with her hair up in a bun and oversized sunglasses covering her eyes. My arm was around her neck, and I'd given her a brief kiss when the photo was taken.

"I got nothing to say, but that's my wife. I—"

"Oh, are we getting an exclusive?" Chris asked, eagerly.

"Don't get ahead of yourself, no." I laughed. "But she will be someday, so I'm letting folks know…I got hands. When you see her, just walk on by." I finished before remembering something else. "Oh, wait, my girl is a guru at financial planning, so if anyone needs advice on that, you can contact her. That's the only reason I'm giving for y'all out there to contact her. If you ain't trying to let her be your financial advisor, keep it moving." I gave a mock salute.

Dele laughed and Chris shook his head.

"Well, you heard him folks. Thank you so much for joining us today, Nonso," Dele said with a smile as they wrapped up. "We wish you and your team all the best in the upcoming playoff matches."

"Thank you. It was a pleasure being on the show," I replied sincerely because I really did have fun.

As soon as the call ended, Yinka burst into the room with a huge grin on her face, playfully swaying her hips as she approached me. I smiled, thanking God for bringing me to Viva City and my sister forcing me to have lunch at Fusion Haven.

"You gonna marry me, Mr. Chijuka?" She waggled her brows and stood in front of me.

"Whatchu think we doing?" I smirked. "I'm not letting you get on my nerves just because."

"You get on my nerves too, buddy," she shot back.

"I know. I'm trying to love you and get on your nerves... forever. Whatchu tryin' to do?"

She scrunched her nose. "This better not be my proposal."

"When I propose, there'll be no doubt in your mind that I'm trying to change your last name." I chuckled before pulling her to me and kissing her stomach.

"Okay, then I wanna love and get on your nerves forever, too." Her smile was bright and satisfying. "I love you, Babe," she said, softly while cupping my face in her hands.

"And I love you too." I wrapped her in a warm embrace.

Even though the season didn't end with the result I'd had hoped for, I knew the real victory was having Yinka by my side. Both of us cheering each other on through every twist and turn of our own Game of Two Halves.

epilogue
Nonso

"**WHAT GOD CANNOT** do does not exist o!" Yinka yelled with a flute of champagne in her hand.

I picked up my glass, shook my head and leaned back in the lounge chair on our cabin's porch. "You right. But don't make that face, sticking your tongue out like that." I leaned back in the chair on our cabin's porch.

I was talking to Cheta one day and told him I wanted to take my girl on a quick getaway, and he suggested I use the cabin he owned in Blue Ridge Mountains in north Georgia. When he said cabin, I thought it was going to be a little quaint house. I forgot Nyce never does anything small. This place was massive and quiet.

Quiet.

That was exactly what Specs and I needed. After that inter-view, you would think I had announced that we were getting married. The blogs and media in general went crazy. At one point, I had to play the interview back myself to make sure I didn't say anything about Yinka and I being engaged.

My phone buzzed and I looked at the screen. I sighed when I saw it was one of those Apple news alerts. The only reason I had the device on was because I was waiting for a call from my boy, Xander. Everyone should've been up his behind, not mine. He was currently in Luxe Noir with his girl, Abi. The small beach town on the outskirts of South Carolina was where I initially wanted to take Yinka. After Xander told me about the history of the town and the house he owned over there, it was a no-brainer. The way he described the place and the stuff they had on their website had me immediately wanting to buy property out there. Xander teased that he wasn't sure I'd like the small-town feel. Since I was looking for where to duck off to, he suggested I stayed at his house and use the opportunity to check the town out firsthand.

But then two of the venues Abi was supposed to perform at in Denver had some issues so the promoter cancelled the event. She now had some free time and was trying to see him. The next stop of her tour was in Alabama, so it made sense for him to hop on a plane to the US. I'd never seen my boy so happy. I mean, I would have been too if I hadn't seen my girl in three months due to impromptu changes in her tour schedule. Xander had no choice but to be understanding, even though he was clearly upset. Jay and I got an earful as he vented.

It was two weeks after that interview and the playoffs would start in a few days. According to the doctor, I might not be able to start the first game with my team, but he was hopeful that I would be good enough to join a few games in. I still blamed myself for letting the team down, but not so much that when my girl made partner last week, I didn't hop my behind up and get us tickets to get away to celebrate. After the doctor gave the okay, of course. There was a stark difference between walking around and being able to kick the ball around in precise movements. Since I could now walk fine, nothing was stopping me from celebrating the love of my life.

Yinka giggled. "Babe, everyone does it." She sashayed over to me.

"Everyone but my girl. It's so—"

"Don't even open your mouth and say it cos I know exactly what you want to say."

I hooked my finger in the belt hoop of her shorts and drew her down to me. After pecking her lips a few times, I let her go. She was dancing to "That's My King" by CeCe Winans and I loved to watch the fluid movements of her body.

Mr. Wilson should be the one thanking God, because with all the frustration in me from being in the playoffs and all, I was 2.1 seconds off his behind if my girl left work one more day complaining about how he might be trying to block her promotion. She was able to sign that big client she was preparing for that day I'd done the interview. Her promotion should have been sure, but still that old man was trying to get in the way of what was rightfully hers.

A few minutes later, Yinka had tired herself out with all that praise gyration. She stumbled over to me and plopped down between my legs then leaned back on me. She was panting so hard that I had to mess with her.

"Dang, baby. You lazy, lazy." I nuzzled her neck. "You supposed to be dancing like David danced. Ain't nowhere in the Bible it says he was outta breath and gave up."

She nudged me off her, or at least she tried to. "Nonso move, I'm not lazy. You're so annoying."

I chuckled. "How you leaning on me but telling me to move? Make it make sense. Where am I supposed to go?"

"Leave me *jor*." She grunted, knowing her request made no sense.

"You're so spoiled, man."

"Like I said, that's a you problem," she whined, snuggling into me. "Besides, you love it."

I wrapped my arms around her. "I sure do."

I loved the heck out of this woman. Especially now that Ms. Martins and Specs knew how to balance themselves and showed up when needed. Yinka shivered and I leaned over to grab the blanket to cover her. I ran my hand up and down her arms to warm her up. Although it was summer, we were in the mountains and the evenings were chilly.

My baby was worn out. We'd arrived three days ago and after a full day of just lounging about resting, we were energized enough to see what the town had to offer. Over the last two days, our routine was pretty much the same. We'd start our day with breakfast at this diner Cheta recommended, then embark on the activity for the day. I no longer needed crutches and was stable on my feet, but we still took it easy.

The first day, Yinka took the wheel of our rental car, and we went on a scenic drive along the winding roads of the Blue Ridge Parkway. We marveled at God's creation – stunning mountain views, lush forests, and majestic peaks. After we had lunch, we visited local famous waterfalls and enjoyed the cool mist and rushing water. I held on to my lady tight, not trusting the tour guide or other tourists when they swore the water was calm. I'd never taken chances with Mother Nature, and I wasn't about to start now.

The day after, we went to a local winery for a tour and tasting, learning about different grape varieties, and enjoying panoramic countryside views. We ended our day with a romantic dinner at a restaurant with a view of the mountains. As the sun set, we shared stories and laughter, feeling content and just vibing, enjoying each other's company.

Yinka was not only my woman, but she was also my best friend. We loved just as much as we argued. But it was just couple stuff – nothing that got us to the point of disrespecting each other or playing silly mind games. Since we'd be heading back to Viva City in the morning, all we did earlier was shop and visit one of the museums the town was known for. We'd just had dinner when we decided to head out here on the deck.

The sun was setting, painting the sky in hues of orange and pink. In its stillness, the last five months played like a reel in my head. The beauty of the moment was almost overwhelming – a stark contrast to the turmoil and challenges we had faced in recent months.

Light snores escaped Yinka's lips as she drifted off to sleep. I placed a light kiss on her forehead and was about to get up to carry her to bed when my phone vibrated. Yinka stirred but she didn't wake. I would have ignored it, but I'd been waiting for the call. I answered the Facetime on the third ring.

"What you do to my sis? Why is she sleeping already?" Xan asked.

"Man, you worrying about the wrong thing. Did sis have mercy on your crying behind?"

"Black, whatchu take me for? She wasn't leaving this house if she didn't come correct."

Just at that moment, Abi nudged Xan from the frame, waving her left hand displaying the stunning, diamond-cut engagement ring I'd gone with Xan to pick out.

"Don't tell that lie, Xan." Abi chuckled. "But yeah, I said yes."

Something in that phrase got my girl's attention because she instantly woke up and shifted to face the screen.

"Yes! Congratulations...we got a wedding to plan," Yinka said.

Over the next few minutes, we talked to our friends congratulating them on their engagement. No dates were on the table, but according to Xan, the big stuff was out of the way. I knew Abi would say yes, but he was still so nervous. Xan and Abi were staying one more day in Luxe Noir while Yinka and I were heading out in the morning. Soon after, we said our goodbyes. Now I could turn the phone off.

In one quick motion, I stood and adjusted Yinka in my arms bridal style. She yawned and nuzzled closer.

"Babe, I can walk. I don't want you putting pressure on your leg," she said.

"I got it. But I love you for always looking out." I kissed her lips.

"And I love you too."

"Besides, I'm tryin' to practice this carrying over the threshold thing. You do not know the time or the hour when you'll be Mrs.

Chijuka." I entered the room she was staying in and put her on the bed.

"I love the sound of that."

I leaned over her, caging her in with my arms. "I'm glad you do because if you didn't, you'd be straight out of luck, cos I'm never letting you go."

"Hmmm... and I also like the sound of that." She cupped my face and gave me a passionate kiss.

In our exchange, I felt our love, our strength, and our future together. And rested in my belief in God that the best was yet to come.

THE END

glossary

<u>Pidgin/Enuani/Yoruba Translations</u>

Nonso is from Anioma tribe (My tribe). We speak a slightly different dialect of the Igbo language called Enuani. Yinka is Yoruba. Both of them are children of immigrants who grew up in America but were immersed in Nigerian culture at home. Below are translations (done to the best of my ability) to the languages I used in the story. I have this in the order in which they appear.

Chukwu Daalu: Thank God (Enuani)

Mba o: No o (Enuani)

Maṣe gbiyanju rẹ: Don't Try it (Yoruba)

How Far?: What's good (Pidgin)

I dey: I'm good (Pidgin)

See me see wahala: Look at trouble in a joking way (Pidgin)

I carry betta eye go market: I made a great choice (Pidgin)

Oya, o ṣe ileri, dide: Get up, you promised. (Yoruba)

O re mi. O kan nitori iresi kekere: I'm tired. Just because of the little rice. (Yoruba)

Se diedie o: Slow down (Yoruba)

Omo mi: My Child (Yoruba)

Glossary

Ẹ káàsán: Good Afternoon. (Yoruba) When the elder person replies, the *E* is taken off. *káàsán*

Kú àbọ̀: Welcome (Yoruba)

Kilode: Why (Yoruba)

adupe lowo Olorun: Thank God (Yoruba)

Isi ki?: What did you say? (Enuani)

Asim mba: I said no (Enuani)

Ezi okwu: True talk. In this context however it means Really? (Enuani)

final note

Wow! Aren't you just happy for Xander & Abi? They are engaged! Read their journey to love, in Holiday Hideaway. Who knows, we just might be invited to the wedding.

Thank you for reading Nonso and Yinka's story. Please consider leaving a review/rating on the platform you bought the book from. I greatly appreciate your honest feedback. They really go a long way. The number of reviews a book receives greatly improves its visibility.

If you liked this story, I trust you might like some of my other titles. But before we get to those, I'd love to stay connected. Never miss a sale, short stories, new release announcements, or freebies. You can ensure you're in the know by joining my mailing list.

We're headed to Tweede Kans Cove next, the home of the DuBois-Arazis. Get your tickets here to ensure you're all caught up!

also by unoma nwankwor

Stand Alone Books

An Unexpected Blessing

He Changed My Name

When You Let Go

Full Circle

Holiday Hideaway

The Ultimatum Series

The Christmas Ultimatum

The Final Ultimatum

Sons of Ishmael Series

A Scoop of Love

Anchored by Love

Mended with Love

Redeemed Through Love

Mixed Tidings

The Invisible Shackles Series

To Live Again,

To Breathe Again

Home for the Holidays

The DuBois-Arazi Family Novels

A Promise Fulfilled

Destiny Fulfilled

Vows Fulfilled

The Billionaire Pact

Vegas Nights

Second Shot

Pretend Bae

Away To Africa

New Year's Kiss (Prequel)

Rent-A-Bae

His Makeshift Fiancée

A Suitable Wife

Elevate My Soul

www.ingramcontent.com/pod-product-compliance
Lightning Source LLC
Chambersburg PA
CBHW031444200726
48289CB00007BB/2210